THE BRIDE
OF A MOMENT

THE BRIDE
OF A MOMENT

CAROLYN WELLS

WILDSIDE PRESS

Originally published in 1916.
Published by Wildside Press, LLC.
Visit us online at wildsidepress.com.

INTRODUCTION
BY KARL WURF

Carolyn Wells (1862–1942) was one of the most prolific and beloved mystery writers of the early twentieth century, producing over 170 books during her remarkable career. While she wrote across multiple genres—including poetry, children's books, and humor—Wells is best remembered for her contributions to the Golden Age of detective fiction. Her mysteries captivated readers with their clever plotting, impossible crimes, and engaging amateur sleuths who approached each puzzle with wit and determination.

Wells created several memorable series detectives throughout her career, most notably Fleming Stone, the brilliant consulting detective who appeared in more than sixty novels. Stone, with his methodical approach and penetrating insight, became one of American mystery fiction's most enduring characters. Wells also wrote mysteries featuring detective Pennington Wise and his psychic assistant Ziza. However, before these famous sleuths came Alan Ford, the detective introduced in *The Bride of a Moment* (1916).

The Bride of a Moment represents Wells at the height of her powers, crafting a seemingly impossible mystery that begins with one of detective fiction's most dramatic opening scenes: a bride shot dead at the altar moments after saying "I do." The novel showcases Wells's talent for the "locked room" style mystery that would become her trademark—crimes committed under seemingly impossible circumstances, with no apparent means of execution. Detective Alan Ford must untangle a web of cryptograms, missing diamonds, and multiple suspects, each wsith compelling motives.

In the pantheon of classic mystery fiction, Carolyn Wells occupies an important position as one of the few women writing detective novels during the genre's formative years. She helped establish many conventions that would become staples of the mystery field, and her influence extended beyond her own writing—she was also an anthologist and critic who compiled *The Technique of the Mystery Story* (1913), one of the earliest analytical works on detective fiction. While Fleming Stone would eventually overshadow her other detectives in popularity, the Alan Ford series demonstrates Wells's early mastery of the intricate plotting and clever misdirection that made her a household name among mystery enthusiasts of her era.

CHAPTER 1

A JUNE WEDDING

A big limousine came to a standstill beneath the porte-cochère of the church, and with much watchful protection of their frocks from possible damage, two girls got out of the car and hurried into the church.

Their elaborate gowns, exactly alike, their twin flower-decked hats, and their enormous bouquets proclaimed them bridesmaids. Smilingly they separated themselves from the crowd pouring in at the church doors, and then stood waiting in that end of the vestibule reserved for the purpose.

"I'm glad we're here first," exclaimed Betty Stratton, in a stage whisper; "and oh, goody! somebody has put a long mirror here. Aren't our frocks wonderful? I'm just crazy over them!" She smiled and preened before the glass in a very ecstasy of delightful excitement. "It'll be the greatest wedding ever! Ethel is the most beautiful girl I know."

"Yes, in her way," agreed the other bridesmaid, as she elbowed Betty away from the mirror, and carefully touched her pink cheek with a powder-puff; "she's stunning—like a statuesque goddess—"

"No, she's more like those wax angels we used to have at the top of a Christmas tree. How do you like him?" and Betty gazed in absorbed admiration at her own fascinating reflection.

"Mr. Bingham? I don't know him very well, but I think he's just the man for a bridegroom. He's so perfectly polished—if you know what I mean."

"Yes, isn't he! They'll look wonderful coming down the other aisle, afterward. The presents are beyond words! My *dear!* she has forty-eight silver candlesticks! Forty-eight! And the silver bowls and dishes! M—m—!"

"What did he give her?"

"A solitaire diamond pendant. The biggest one I ever saw, and more than flawless! No setting, you know, just a thread of a silver chain. Oh, Molly, *do* you s'pose I'll ever get married to a rich man—"

"Hush; here comes the bride, and the other girls—oh, *Ethel!*"

With the aid of several assistants and advisers, the bride and her regalia were safely piloted from the motor car to the church, and in the vestibule the lovely vision was disclosed to the adoring eyes of her satellites.

The bridal gown was the last word of fashion, and the cap, for a wonder becoming, crowned the soft golden hair and exquisite face of the most haughty beauty of Boscombe Fells. But the face was as white as the encircling lace. The pale lips trembled and the violet eyes now stared with a frightened look, and now were hidden by the white, golden-fringed lids that drooped over them.

For once the cool, calm poise of Ethel Moulton was shaken. For once the proud, imperious beauty looked humble and even afraid. She stood passively while attendants adjusted her train and veil. She watched with unseeing eyes as the rest of the bridal party gathered and formed in line. She glanced in the mirror, and, seeing the white, scared face, she smiled and flushed scarlet, only to turn ashy pale again the next moment.

"Now, Ethel," said Betty Stratton for the twentieth time, "you *must* control yourself! Smile and look happy or I'll shake you! Look as pensive as you like, but don't spoil this whole show by acting as if you were a lamb dragged to the altar—or whatever it is. Get your mind off of it, if it affects you that way. Think of the last vaudeville show you saw—think of chicken hash with green peppers—think of anything pleasant and gay!"

"Stop it, Betty," said Eileen Randall, the maid of honour, "let her alone! She shan't be bused! It's quite all right for a bride to look nervous—it's much more interesting. Isn't it time to start?"

The whole bridal cortège was now crowded into the vestibule of the church, nervously awaiting the stroke of twelve. The bridesmaids stood demurely, if restlessly, in their appointed places, but the maid of honour still darted about here and there, adjusting, supervising, reminding.

"Cheer up, Mr. Swift," she said to the soldierly-looking grey-haired man who stood beside the bride; "you'll never have to give Ethel away again, so do it prettily this time. Keep your eyes straight ahead, don't look either up or down, and everybody will say, 'How beautifully he behaves!' Ethel, dear, now do brace up! Bridal shyness is all very well—but you mustn't look like a wilted lily. What time is it, Mr. Farrish? Oh, you men do look sweet in your clean white kimonos."

Guy Farrish, one of the vested choir who were waiting to lead the bridal procession down the aisle, answered: "Only four minutes more, Miss Randall! Better get your place."

The bride looked up, startled. Only four minutes more! "I can't—" she said; "I can't go—oh, I *can't* go!"

"There, there, Ethel," said her uncle, "don't talk like that, my girl. Brace up; come, now, is your bouquet all right? It's about time to start."

"Yes, it's all right," said the maid of honour, giving the mass of white orchids and valley lilies a final pat and then, after a swift glance in the long mirror at her own pink-streamered bunch of roses, she slipped into her place, and said, "Ready, girls! Watch your step!"

Eileen Randall was a born commander. As maid of honour at her friend's wedding, she had organized and directed all the elaborate details of the affair. It was she who had insisted on the full choral service, who had designed the wonderful floral decorations, and who had even chosen the costumes, the bridesmaids' frocks of pale pink taffeta brocaded with blue and silver roses, her own pink tulle over blue, and even the bridal gown of white and silver brocade. She had planned the procession and conducted its rehearsal, and now at the last moment she glanced around, well satisfied with her results.

The first two choristers stood in the doorway that led into the church, their eyes on the organ at the farther end. The ushers came, importantly, and took their places. Through a tiny opening of the door beside the pulpit, the best man watched, and reported progress in whispers to the determinedly composed bridegroom.

The church, a complacent, comfortable affair, of Congregational denomination, was usually of a dim unresponsiveness, but today it seemed to shine and sing in epithalamium. The June sunshine crowded in at the open windows, and the stained-glass panes above threw riotous colour-effects on the already gaily clad audience.

For Boscombe Fells was as pretentious as its name indicates. A small settlement of exclusive people, not far from New York City, it prided itself on being a worth-while place to live, and in such matters as wedding pageants and the like its taste was correct and exacting.

The first note of noon pealed from the church clock. The organ sounded, the eight members of the vested choir started singing, down the aisle toward the flower-banked pulpit. Followed the ushers, the dainty bridesmaids, the maid of honour, and then the bride, beautiful Ethel Moulton, on the arm of her uncle, Everson Swift. White as her own orange-blossoms, the girl trembled until her uncle, alarmed, so far forgot the instructions of the maid of honour as to steal a side glance at his charge. An instant's flash of her blue eyes reassured him, and he thought no more of the bride's most natural agitation. Her trembling ceased and she was calm save for the quick rise and fall of the great diamond, the gift of the bridegroom, which hung on her breast, held only by an invisible silver chain.

On they went to the music of the processional; slowly, and still singing, the choir ascended into the organ loft, behind the pulpit, the bridesmaids took their places indicated by faint chalk marks on the carpet, and the maid of honour, seeing that the bridegroom and best man were conducting themselves correctly, took her own place at the left of the bride.

The music grew fainter. The whispered harmonies of "The Voice That Breathed O'er Eden" did not drown the sonorous tones of the minister, who asked the vital questions of the pair kneeling before him.

Mr. Swift gave his niece away, with a heart full of gladness. He loved the girl, his dead sister's child, and he knew he was giving her to a man of fine, sterling character. Stanford Bingham, a man of nearly thirty, was well-born, rich, and talented. What more could he ask for Ethel? And Mrs. Swift, in her place in the front pew, looked on complacently, as she awaited her husband's return to her side. His part done, Everson Swift turned, smiling, and went to his seat in the front pew, and Ethel was left, her hand in that of the man who in another moment would be her husband.

Parrot-like, the vows were repeated after the minister. The ring was placed carefully on the white finger in its ripped glove, and Doctor Van Sutton pronounced Stanford Bingham and Ethel Moulton man and wife.

The benediction was spoken, and then, as the minister smilingly took the bride's hand, the organ pealed, the choir sounded forth glorious notes, and the hush that had been upon the assemblage gave way to a sudden hubbub of gay laughter and chatter.

And then, without a word, without a sound, the bride dropped to the floor.

The maid of honour who was adjusting the white and silver brocaded train, preparatory to the march down the other aisle, gazed, stunned, at a crimson stain that spread slowly over the bridal veil and bodice. She saw the beautiful terrified face, and the wide, frightened eyes, and then the lovely head fell, and veil, silver brocade, and white orchids were crushed in a terrible crumpled heap.

What had happened? The bridegroom stood as if turned to stone. The bridesmaids screamed. The maid of honour clenched her hands and gritted her teeth in a determination not to faint, and Mrs. Everson Swift turned uncomprehending eyes to her husband, saying, "What is the matter, dear?"

It was the best man who made the first move. Warren Swift, Ethel's cousin, tried to raise the fallen figure.

"My God! She's shot!" he exclaimed, without thought of decorum or caution. He lifted his head, wild-eyed, and looked around.

Others crowded up then. The ushers, the people from the front pews, the bridesmaids, all glanced at the bride, and then turned, white-faced, to gaze at each other. The choristers and organist came down from their places and stood aside, aghast.

Everson Swift went to his niece, as the others fell back to let him pass. "Has she fainted?" he said, tremblingly, not willing to believe or imply what he feared.

"She is shot, father," said his son, Warren; "shot."

"But I heard no sound, no shot—" and the older man looked dazed and helpless.

"Lift her up," said Eileen Randall, imperatively; "don't leave her there on the floor! She *isn't* dead."

Hesitatingly, Warren Swift leaned toward the ghastly heap of bridal finery, and then drew back, unable to obey the dictatorial maid of honour.

Two of the ushers stepped forward. "We will take her," said one of them; "where to, Miss Randall?"

"Into the church parlour—I'll show you the way."

Eileen crossed to the right of the pulpit and opened a door, the one through which the bridegroom and his best man had come so short a time before. It opened into a quaint old-fashioned room, known as the church parlour, which was used for meetings of the Sewing Society and other church organizations. The two men followed, gently bearing their pathetic burden.

"Lay her here," directed Eileen, as she smoothed a pillow on a wide old-fashioned sofa.

And there they laid the beautiful, still form of the white-robed bride.

Unable to keep away, others came. The uncle and aunt, the cousin, and then the bridegroom—looking like a man in a dream. He stood staring at his bride, at the masses of white satin and lace and tulle that seemed to billow over the old sofa and lie in foamy waves on the floor, at the terrible, hideous wound that changed the beautiful face to a horror.

Doctor Endicott, the family physician of the Swifts, came hurrying in. Pushing the others away, he examined the wound in the right temple; he felt the pulse; he listened for heart-beats. Eagerly he strove to find some sign of life—some ground for hope. But at last, with a sigh of despair, he shook his head.

"Death was instantaneous," he said, straightforwardly. "Who fired that bullet?"

Not only did no one answer, but almost none present grasped the significance of his words. A bride, shot and killed at the altar! It was too unbelievable! Such a thing *could* not happen. Mrs. Swift clung to her husband in dumb terror. The bridesmaids huddled together in shuddering fear. Even the capable and brave Eileen succumbed and dropping into a chair hid her face and sobbed. The men stood baffled and helpless. Warren Swift looked dazed and terror-stricken, as he edged over toward his father and mother in an impulse of family feeling.

The bridegroom stood alone. At the head of the couch where lay his new-made bride, Stanford Bingham stood, with folded arms and set face, looking down at the awful sight.

Into the hushed room came the minister.

"I must dismiss the congregation," he said, addressing himself to Mrs. Swift.

"Yes," replied her husband, for she could not speak, nor, indeed, understand what was said.

Then Everson Swift pulled himself together. Many things must be attended to, and he, of course, must take the helm.

"Yes, Doctor Van Sutton," he went on; "ask the people to go away, and then we must—we must notify the—the police, I suppose."

"Yes, it is necessary. Perhaps Mrs. Swift will go home now?"

"It would be better. Go, my dear; Warren, go with your mother."

Submissively, Warren Swift took his mother by the arm and led her away. Her gorgeous gown of pearl-embroidered mauve satin trailed far behind her, and accented the awfulness of the occasion. "Oh," she cried suddenly, "I *can't* go home—to that house!"

And all suddenly had a mental vision of the spacious home, decorated in gala mood, for the home-coming of the bride; the floral bower in the drawing-room, the laden tables in the dining-room, the going-away gown and hat in Ethel's own room—how *could* she go back there?

"Don't go there now, Mrs. Swift," said Eileen Randall, raising her head; "oh, *don't*! Go to my home; Charlotte is there, she'll look after you. Take your mother there, Warry."

And still Stanford Bingham stood, immovable, looking down on his murdered bride.

The minister returned to the church. The tumultuous throng of wedding guests hushed their excited talk to listen to him. He told them the bride had died suddenly, he did not say by what means. He asked them to go home, and he pronounced a broken-voiced benediction. In many strange positions the Reverend Doctor Van Sutton had found himself, but never before in one so terrible as this.

The congregation moved out slowly. The better-minded ones went at once, but others, curious and questioning, could not tear themselves from the scene of mystery and tragedy.

Twice, at intervals, the minister repeated his request that the church be vacated. The second time he was obliged to make it an order, and even then, it was not until the blue-coated officers of the law appeared that the last intrusive lingerers were induced to go.

Seeing a great heap of white flowers in front of him, half unconsciously the minister picked up the bride's bouquet. Helplessly he gathered up its trailing, ribbon-tied sprays, and returning to the church parlour, he laid it, with a vague idea of the fitness of things, on the breast of the still white form on the sofa.

It was too dreadful. That touch completed the horrible mockery of the wedding array, and with an hysterical scream Betty Stratton ran out of the room and went home. The other three bridesmaids followed her, but Eileen Randall stayed, shaken to her very soul, but ready to do her part, whatever it might be.

CHAPTER 2

THE SILENT SHOT

Inspector Kinney entered the church parlour with an expression of profound bewilderment on his big, homely face. Accustomed as he was to all manner of dreadful and horrible crimes, the murder of a bride at the altar was startling even to him. Baring his head, he advanced reverently to the beautiful still figure on the sofa.

"Who done it?" he said, clenching his fists and glancing from one to another of the silent people gathered about.

"We have no idea," said Mr. Swift, who was naturally spokesman; "she was, of course, shot, but no one seems to have heard the report of a pistol."

"One of them newfangled kind; they don't make no noise, hardly," and Kinney nodded his head, sagaciously. "Better get the detectives on the case, right off. And there's too many people in here. Everybody must clear out, exceptin' the nearest kin."

"I must stay," said Eileen Randall, assertively, "I'm the maid of honour, and I want to stay near Ethel, whatever happens."

"All right, miss, you can stay."

Kinney was also willing that the bridegroom should stay, and the uncle of the dead girl, but others he put out.

"You three choir men, now," he went on, glancing at the group in cassocks and cottas, "you ain't got no call here, 'ceptin' curiosity, and you'd better go."

The three, who were all friends of the dead bride, started, on being thus spoken to, and rather reluctantly moved away. Guy Farrish cast a last glance at the fair white face, and left the room. Hal Kennedy paused a moment for a longer look, and then followed. But Eugene Hall, the third of the singers, asked permission to stay until the coroner came.

"Oh, well, stay if you want to," said the Inspector, "you can, of course, only I don't want a lot of unnecessary folks around."

"You're right, Kinney," said a voice, and a young man came in from the church. "There's a crowd outside getting bigger every minute. Don't let any more in here."

The newcomer was Bob Keene, a reporter, who had expected to write up a graphic account of the wedding, and who now found it his dreadful duty to report the tragedy.

"I tried to keep out of this," he said to Eileen, whom he knew, "but my boss insisted I should come. Who could have done it? Have you any idea?"

"No," returned the girl, in low tones like his own. "I can't see any light on the mystery or any way to look for light. The whole thing is so—so unbelievable! I can't realize yet that Ethel is—is gone!"

"Old Bingham can't either! Look at him! He seems absolutely dazed."

"Of course he is! Think of the shock. Poor man—"

"It's fierce! I was in the church, and I didn't hear anything that sounded like a shot."

"Neither did I. Mr. Kinney says there are pistols that don't make any noise—it must have been one of those."

"I've heard of them, but I didn't know they were really soundless. However, I suppose the music drowned what sound there was. Hello, here's the Coroner. Hartt's a good fellow, he'll find out something, I've no doubt."

Coroner Hartt came in, followed by a detective of the Police Bureau. Hartt was a capable-looking man, more intelligent in appearance than the average coroner, and of alert and energetic manners. He spoke to Doctor Van Sutton and the bridegroom, and then addressed himself mainly to the uncle of the bride.

"Have you any knowledge of who could possibly have done this thing?" he asked of Mr. Swift.

"Not the slightest. My niece hadn't an enemy in the world, that I am aware of. And yet, I can't think it could have been an accident."

"Accident! No! But there's a devilish crime to be discovered and punished. Who saw the lady fall?"

"Everybody in the front part of the church, I suppose," answered Mr. Swift. "That is, everybody who could see her at all. Of course, as there was such a crowd, the ones behind could not see clearly."

"Who was nearest to her?" went on Mr. Hartt.

"I was," said Eileen Randall, quickly; "I was stooping down to arrange her train, for her to walk down the aisle, when she just sank down in a heap."

"You heard no sound, as of a pistol?"

"No; but that was not strange, if it was one of those silent ones, for the music had just burst forth and the choir was singing, and besides that, the audience had begun to laugh and chatter as they always do after a wedding ceremony is completed."

"And Miss Moulton—er—Mrs. Bingham made no sound?"

"No scream or anything like that. There was a little queer, gurgling sound in her throat—but it was involuntary, I'm sure."

"Do you think she had any idea of who shot her?"

"I have no means of judging that. It was all over in an instant. The fall, I mean. She fell all in a heap—she didn't sink down slowly."

"Death was instantaneous," said Doctor Endicott, who had been away and returned. "The shot went straight through the temple to the brain."

"Did you see her fall?" said the Coroner, turning suddenly to Stanford Bingham.

"Eh, what?" said the bridegroom, looking up from the attitude of dejection he had shown ever since the tragedy.

"Did you see your wife fall?" repeated Hartt, looking at him steadily.

"I saw her fall, yes," replied Bingham, "but at that moment Dr. Van Sutton was speaking to me, congratulating me, in fact, and I was paying attention to him. I felt, rather than saw Ethel fall, and I turned, to see her on the floor. I can't remember clearly after that—for the shock unnerved me."

"Small wonder!" said Eileen, sympathetically, and she looked at Bingham with infinite compassion.

Bob Keene noted the two. As many reporters grow to be, he was almost clairvoyant in his perceptions, and he seemed to sense a sort of telepathic communication between Bingham and the maid of honour.

"And you have no suspicion of the criminal?" went on Mr. Hartt.

"Not the slightest," returned Bingham. "Indeed, I can scarcely believe there could have been such a crime. Could it have been an accident? Could the shot have been intended for some one else? Myself, for instance. Or any other of the bridal party? How could any one want to kill Ethel?"

Bingham's face was ghastly. He looked like death, himself. His fingers twisted nervously round each other, and great beads of perspiration formed on his brow. Occasionally he darted a sudden quick glance at the dead form near him and as quickly glanced away again.

"We can't judge of that," said the Coroner, "until we know where the shot came from. The bride, of course, stood at your left, Mr. Bingham?"

"Yes," assented Bingham, but he spoke almost doubtfully, and glanced uncertainly at his left arm.

"Of course she did," broke in Eileen. "Brides always stand the same way. Ethel was on Mr. Bingham's left side. As she fell I was practically between them, as I stooped down to arrange her train."

"Then as the shot is in her right temple, we know it must have been fired by some one on the same side of her as Mr. Bingham was," declared the Coroner. "That is, it was fired by some one on that side of the church, the east side. Now, to discover how far away the assailant stood. I should judge some several feet; but there are practically no powder marks to be seen, as the bullet entered the brain through a thick roll or puff of hair."

Doctor Endicott agreed with this conclusion, and the Coroner went on.

"Assuming, then, that the criminal was in the church, it must have been one of the audience, or one of the bridal group."

"Oh, Mr. Hartt," cried Eileen, "it *couldn't* have been one of the bridal party! How can you suggest such a thing?"

"It is not for any one to say what could or could not have been except as it is proved to us by evidence. Granting this horrible crime there must be a criminal, and we must seek him wherever the evidence points. It is difficult to see how a member of the audience could have fired the shot unseen, but we must believe that it was done, for there is no alternative. What we must get at first, is the distance and direction of the hand that held the revolver."

"And the motive," put in Mr. Swift. "What could be the motive for the shooting of a young and lovely girl at her wedding altar?"

"There are not many motives for murder," began the Coroner, thoughtfully. "Could it have been robbery? Is anything missing?"

Eileen gave a sudden exclamation. "There is!" she said; "Ethel's pendant is gone! Her great diamond!"

Bingham started out of his reverie. He gave a quick glance at the fair white throat of his bride, and said, "So it is! Her diamond is gone!"

"Was it a valuable gem?" asked Hartt.

"Very," said Eileen, as Bingham did not make any reply. "It was a priceless stone, worthy of a princess. It hung by the slenderest chain of fine platinum links, and now it is gone!"

"Absurd!" said Mr. Swift. "If the jewel is gone, it is because it slipped off when she fell. No sane human being would or could shoot a bride to steal her jewels! Such a theory is untenable."

"I think so, too," agreed Bingham. "The slight chain probably broke when she fell, and the stone either slipped down into her clothing or it has dropped to the floor. It is of no consequence in view of the greater crime."

"Not comparatively, of course," said the Coroner, "but this matter should be looked into. The theft of the jewel may be a clue."

"If it was a theft," repeated Bingham. "I don't believe the gem is stolen. It must have fallen off accidentally."

"Let us go and look in the church," said Eileen, rising.

Whereupon several of them went back into the church, deserted now, save for the sexton, who was sitting in the end of one of the forward pews.

Questioned, he said he had not swept up or in any way disturbed the space about the pulpit where the bridal party had stood.

But careful search showed no trace of the diamond or the little chain. It might be found on the bride's person, or it might never be found. Stanford Bingham showed not the slightest interest in the matter, but both Mr. Swift and Eileen were greatly worried about it.

"I'm sure Ethel was shot for that reason," said the girl; "some horrible criminal was clever enough to kill her, and then afterward, in the flurry and excitement, he could get near enough to steal the diamond unobserved. That must be the solution of the mystery, for what other is there? Nobody could have any other reason for killing Ethel."

The Coroner pondered. It was far-fetched and well-nigh impossible that it should be as Eileen assumed, and yet, as she said, what other theory could be advanced?

"It's a most baffling case," he said at last. "There are no clues, there is no one to suspect, there are no witnesses—that is, no one who knows anything definite—and yet there were hundreds of witnesses!"

Then the detective who had come with the Coroner spoke. "It seems to me," he said, slowly, "that we are getting nowhere."

"Because there's nowhere to get," grumbled the Coroner.

"But let us think it out," went on Mr. Ferrall, the detective; "we know the shot was fired from the east side of the church; that is, from some one who stood on the right side of the bride, but we do *not* know that that some one was in the church. The windows are all open, might not the murderer have stood outside and fired through the window?"

"Good work!" said Inspector Kinney; "that's the first glimmer of light I've seen. It's much more likely that's the truth, than that one of the audience could do it, unobserved by his near neighbours."

Coroner Hartt looked dubious and a little sulky. He was angry that he hadn't thought of it himself.

"In that case," he said, "we've got to look for a regular crook. Some of the well-known professionals. Only such a one would dare anything so dangerous to pull off."

"I don't believe the shot was fired through the window," said Mr. Swift. "It's too far away and, too, the windows are too high. No one could fire through them without standing up on something, and then he would have been seen."

"The windows are high," agreed the detective, "but they are banked up on the outside where vines are planted. I'm not sure, it must be investigated, but I think a man could easily shoot through that front window on the east side."

"It was that window, if any," said Mr. Swift, thoughtfully. "If so, wouldn't there be footprints, or some evidence?"

"Ought to be," said Ferrall; "I'll go and have a look."

He left the group and went out of the church by its front door and made his way around to the window in question.

"A fool's errand," said the Coroner; "that shot was fired at closer range than the window. It was the work of some clever crook who was in the audience, dressed like a gentleman, and who, with an automatic pistol, committed the deed, while everybody was looking at the bride, and he was unnoticed. Then, later, in the excitement, he mingled with the crowd around the body, and managed to get the diamond—also unobserved."

"There wasn't any crowd around the body except our own people," said Mr. Swift. "If any stranger had come near Ethel, I should have noticed him. You didn't see any one, Eileen?"

"No; no one but our own crowd. However, I was so overcome and almost crazy, I doubt if I should have noticed any one."

"But I know there were no strangers near Ethel," went on Mr. Swift. "I tried to go to her when she fell, but I seemed paralyzed with shock and fright. Then Warren went to her, and he cried out, 'She's shot!' and then the others closed in around her, but they were only the bridesmaids, and ushers, I am sure. You saw no one, did you, Doctor Van Sutton?"

"No one but the ones who were there all through the ceremony," replied the minister. "Then the organist and several of the choir came down. If any stranger was about, they would know it, for they saw it all from the choir loft, and could tell better than we, who were down on the floor."

"I'm sure we shall find the jewel on the body," said Bingham. "When can we take it away, Mr. Hartt?"

"I think you can take it any time now, sir. So far as this inquiry is concerned, I think we can find out no more at present. If you desire, Mr. Bingham—or, Mr. Swift—you may remove the body at once."

"It must be taken to my home, of course," said Everson Swift, with a deep sigh.

Stanford Bingham seemed about to speak, and then thought better of it, for he said nothing, but he looked unutterably agonized and helpless.

"Shall I telephone for an undertaker, Mr. Swift?" suggested Bob Keene, moved to do anything he could to help.

"Yes, if you will," and Mr. Swift showed relief at being released from that sad duty.

And then Doctor Van Sutton returned to the room where lay all that was mortal of the beautiful bride, and the others prepared to go home.

CHAPTER 3

A FEW BARS OF MUSIC

Keene ran across the street to telephone, and returned just as Detective Ferrall was going back into the church.

The group near the pulpit, not yet dispersed, asked Ferrall of his search.

"Footprints by dozens," he replied. "All over the ground, under every window. The windows are too high to look in at, but there are old boxes and benches beneath them. You see, there were any number of curiosity-seekers who couldn't get into the church, but who wanted to see the show. There must have been several peepers at each window."

"Perhaps some of them could tell of the shooting," suggested Keene; "they would have a better view than those inside."

"There was nothing to see," said Ferrall, decidedly; "I haven't a doubt the deed was done with one of those new automatics. They're hammerless, and the pocket model, as they call it, is tiny. Why, the whole affair is only about four inches long. A man can hold it in his hand, absolutely unseen. And he can discharge it from his pocket, or from under a handkerchief or any concealing material. They're dead easy to aim, and they make almost no sound and practically no smoke."

"That must have been the way of it," said Stanford Bingham, "yet, even granting all that you say, how *could* any one hit Ethel from a distance, with other people in between?"

"He watched his chance," said the detective, "and shot when the opportunity presented itself. And I'm not sure he was so far away as we think. The appearance of the wound is not an infallible indication of the distance from which the pistol was fired, since her thick hair allowed no trace of powder marks."

Just then Warren Swift returned. "I think you'd better go home, father," he said to the elder Swift. "Mother is pretty well broken up, the house all decorated, you know, and those caterers all about—oh, it's awful!"

"Yes, yes, Warry; I'll go. I suppose I can't do anything here?"

"No, Mr. Swift," said Inspector Kinney. "The undertaker will attend to the removal of the body, and bring it to your home. You had better go there to receive it."

With bowed head, Everson Swift turned to leave the church. To walk back along the aisle up which he had so short a time before led his beautiful niece, in all the panoply of her wedding array! All were silent at the tragedy of it, and Eileen bowed her head in her hands and wept.

The bridegroom touched her arm, lightly. "You'd better go home, dear," he said, in a low tone.

Eileen looked up with frightened eyes. "Don't," she whispered; "oh, Stanford, *don't!*"

Bingham stepped hastily back from the girl, but not before the quick eye of the detective had caught his expression of solicitude and the tender note in his voice.

"Is Mr. Swift here?" said the undertaker's assistant, coming in from the parlour.

"No," said Warren, "he's gone home. What is it?"

"Why, here's a paper that we found in the lady's glove. We thought you ought to have it."

"In her glove?" said Warren, as he took the paper.

"Yes, sir, it was folded small and stuffed into her right-hand glove."

"Let me see it," said Bingham, and the man handed it over to him.

The detective watched closely, and saw a small slip of paper containing a few bars of instrumental music, with no accompanying words.

"A memorandum for the organist?" asked Ferrall, looking at the music.

"I hardly think so," returned Bingham, studying the paper. "I'm not very musical, but I'm sure this is no music for the organ or choir."

"Let me see," said Eugene Hall, the one of the choristers who had asked to remain. "No, that's no music for to-day's use. Maybe it's a talisman, or something. You know brides often have superstitions about carrying good-luck omens."

Remembering the fate that had overtaken the bride, a shudder passed over all who heard.

"Give it to me," said Eileen; "it is no doubt something of that sort. I'll keep it."

She put it away in her own glove, when the sexton volunteered information.

"I gave that to Miss Moulton," he said.

"You did!" exclaimed the detective. "When?"

"In the vestibule, just before she was married. Doctor Van Sutton gave it to me, before that, and told me to be sure to hand it to the bride before she started to march down the aisle."

"How extraordinary!" said the bridegroom. "Why did he do that?"

"I don't know, sir, I'm sure."

"I'll ask him," said Ferrall; "it may be an important clue!"

In response to a summons, Doctor Van Sutton came in from the parlour. "Yes," he said, "I gave that to John, just as he says."

"Where did it come from?" asked Bingham.

"It came to me in the morning's mail," replied the minister; "it was enclosed in a letter asking me to see that the bride received it just before she started to walk up the aisle. Of course, I did as requested, and I told John to give it to Miss Moulton in the vestibule. I assumed it was a message of good luck, or something like that from a friend."

"Doubtless that is what it is," said Eileen; "I shall keep it as a souvenir."

But Ferrall was not quite satisfied. "Was the letter signed, Doctor Van Sutton?" he asked.

"No, it was not. I don't usually take notice of anonymous notes, but this seemed different. Surely there can be no harm in it?"

"No; I don't see how there can be, and yet it was a queer circumstance." The detective shook his head, uncertainly.

"I think the fact of the tragedy leads you to attach undue importance to it," said the minister. "But I can never understand how that shot was fired. I know all you say about the pistol being soundless and smokeless, but there were so many of us all about, how could it have happened? I stood here," and Doctor Van Sutton took the place he had occupied during the ceremony; "Ethel was in front of me, a little at my right. You see, I had spoken to her, and was just shaking hands with Mr. Bingham, so he and I were practically between the bride and the crowd on the east side, from which direction you say the shot came."

"I can't see either how it was," said Eugene Hall. "We fellows up in the choir had a chance to see all that was going on, and if any one in the church had looked suspicious we should have noticed it."

"I doubt if you would, Hall," said Warren Swift. "Of course, you were looking at the bride, or at the general show, and not thinking of any wrong-doing. And, too, with all that forest of flowers and palms in front of you, you couldn't see very well what was going on."

The rail that separated the low organ loft from the pulpit was banked with palms and ferns mingled with Ascension lilies. These decorations formed a screen between the choir and the audience, which, while it did not entirely hide one from the other, yet made it difficult to see clearly.

"Oh, we pushed the flowers more or less aside," said Hall; "we wanted to see, of course; and, too, we had to lay our music out on the greenery, and then we could pretty much see over. I can't help thinking we must have seen any man shoot."

"Nonsense!" cried Inspector Kinney. "You *didn't* see him shoot, and yet he *did* shoot. So there's no use blinking the question. The lady was shot, and somebody must have done it. I incline to the belief that the murderer was inside the church, but he may not have been. But the matter must be ferreted out, and it shall be. Such a strange crime cannot long remain a secret. What are these chalk marks on the floor?"

"They were put there to show the bridesmaids and ushers where to stand," said Eileen. "This mark is for the bride herself. We rehearsed last night, and we put the marks carefully, so everybody would be just in the right spot."

"Then here is where the bride stood when she fell," said Ferrall, pointing to the mark Eileen had indicated. "This may be of great importance."

"Yes, that is where Ethel was standing. She had stepped forward the least mite, so I could fix her train for the march back. You've no idea what it means to get that mass of heavy satin into place."

"Come, Eileen," said Warren Swift, seeing the girl was about to break down again at the thought of the doomed bride, who had never made that return march down the church aisle; "let us go home. We can do nothing here, and I know mother will be glad to have you with her."

"Yes, Warry, I will go with you. Will you come, Stanford?"

"Yes, if you're going." Bingham gave a last look at the scene of his wedding ceremony, and then turned to Eileen. Only the watchful eyes of Detective Ferrall saw the look which the bridegroom gave to her who had so lately filled the post of maid of honour to the fated bride. Only the abnormally sharp ears of the detective heard Bingham breathe in the faintest whisper, "Oh, Eileen! now we—"

But the girl laid her finger on her lip, and glancing hurriedly around, shook her head warningly at the white-faced bridegroom.

"H'm," said Detective Ferrall to himself.

"No, Mr. Bingham, you'd better not go home," he said, aloud. "I think you ought to stay here till they take Mrs. Bingham away. There's no telling what they might want you for."

Bingham raised startled eyes at the unfamiliar name for Ethel, but said only, "Very well, Mr. Ferrall, I will remain."

"Not necessary at all," said the minister, kindly. "Mr. Bingham is not needed here. I will attend to any emergencies that may arise, and I am sure Mr. Bingham needs rest and quiet for a time."

Stanford Bingham merely looked his gratitude, and with Warren Swift and Eileen Randall he left the church.

"You oughtn't to have let him go, dominie," said Ferrall; "I feel pretty sure that man can tell us more than he has."

"What do you mean, Mr. Ferrall?" asked Doctor Van Sutton. "Do you think Stanford Bingham knows anything about this matter that he hasn't told?"

"I wouldn't go so far as to say that—but I think he ought to be kept in sight."

"Why?"

"Well, you know the reason of this marriage, don't you? It's town talk."

"Explain yourself, Ferrall," said the Coroner. "I don't know what you mean."

"Why, only that it's what the whole town knows. It's that queer will of Stanford Bingham's father. If Stanford didn't get married before he was thirty, he was slated to lose all his father's fortune. It was only left to him on condition that he took a wife before his thirtieth birthday. And that same birthday is due to occur next week. So you see the fortune is O.K. And as it's a little matter of a million or more, I reckon the bridegroom is glad the knot was tied before—before—" but even the stolid detective could not put in words the cold-blooded hint.

"Do you mean to imply, Mr. Ferrall," said Doctor Van Sutton, "that this marriage took place merely for the securing of that fortune?"

"What do you think yourself, dominie?"

"I have no reason to think the young people were not in love with one another, as bridal couples usually are."

There was a silence, and then Eugene Hall said, "I don't know anything about the pair, but I did notice that the bride looked awful scared during the ceremony. Did you notice that, Doctor?"

The minister hesitated.

"Speak up, dominie," said the detective. "If you know anything you've no right to hold it back. Tell all you know."

"I don't know anything at all," and the Reverend Doctor Van Sutton spoke coldly. "I did notice that the bride looked nervous and shaken during the ceremony, but that is not at all unusual. Indeed it would have been the exception had she not done so. I have never married a bride who was entirely calm and cool at the altar."

"Now, wait a minute," and the detective spoke very earnestly, "we've got to get at the truth of this thing; with your experience, Doctor, don't you *know* the difference between the natural nervousness of a girl getting married and a girl who is really frightened of something? Well, I ask you squarely, if you can honestly say that, in your opinion, Miss Moulton was only suffering the usual and natural nervousness common to all brides, or whether she was afraid of something tragic."

Doctor Van Sutton considered a long time and then spoke slowly, as if choosing his words with care. "I am forced to admit, since you put it that way, that Miss Moulton did show an apprehensiveness that seemed more that of a vague fear than the mere nervousness usual to the occasion."

"That's all I want," and the detective showed satisfaction in his face. "That proves that she expected trouble."

"Don't go too fast, Ferrall," said the Inspector, "that's your failing, you always jump at conclusions. Remember your mistake in the Pollard case!"

"I know; and I'm not concluding anything except what the evidence shows. But I want the Reverend Doctor to tell us just what he noticed about this bride's behaviour different from others."

"I can only say," the minister stated, "that she looked up once or twice with an expression of fear on her face. It was not definite; indeed, had this awful affair not happened, I should never have thought of it again. But during the responses, the bride did look up, first at Mr. Bingham, and afterward at me, with a white, yes, an almost deathly white face, as if filled with a real terror."

"Did the bridegroom appear to notice this?"

"I think not. His eyes were downcast, as were the bride's, except on the occasions I mention."

"And she looked at you, did she?"

"She looked up toward me. I cannot say she looked at me definitely—she seemed to gaze affrightedly into space."

"I saw that look!" exclaimed Eugene Hall. "We, up in the choir, could see her clearly, of course. We were singing, very low, merely breathing the words, and as, of course, we know that wedding music by heart, we didn't have to stick to our notes. I was naturally looking at the bride, for she was a beautiful sight. And I saw her glance at Bingham as she took her vows. I thought nothing strange of that, for it's a solemn moment, if you have any sentiment at all, and then when the Doctor pronounced them man and wife, I saw Ethel give that awful terrorized look, right up at the minister. It mightn't have been meant for him, particularly, nor for anybody, but it looked to me like the dying prayer of a doomed woman. If you ask me, I should say that the girl was looking for that shot! And it wasn't a minute later when she fell! The Doctor had spoken to her, as he always does to a bride, and then he turned to Bingham—and the next instant she went down in a heap. I was so dazed I scarcely knew what had happened, but I only thought she had fainted, for I had heard no report. I suppose, as we were so close to the organ, the sound and vibration of that would have deadened the other sound, but as nobody else heard it either, it must have been a silenced pistol. Of course, as the wound is in the right temple, the shot must have come from the east side of the church, and *I* think the villain who fired it stood outside the window."

Detective Ferrall looked at the speaker. "Thank you, Mr. Hall," he said, "for a clear account of what you saw. But excuse me if I disagree with you about the assailant having been outside. It would be much easier to commit such a deed unseen, in the church, where every one's attention was on the bridal party, than outside the window, where all the bystanders, and there were many, must have observed the criminal."

"Perhaps you're right," said Hall, thoughtfully; "just *inside* the window, over there by the wall, would have been a likely place. A man there would be behind the audience, and yet near enough for an easy aim."

"But I hold that the pistol was discharged at closer range," declared the detective, obstinately. "In fact, I hold that it may well have been discharged by a person standing very near to the bride herself."

"You may as well speak out, Ferrall," said the Coroner, gravely; "there's no one here who oughtn't to know anything that's to be known. So say what's on your mind."

"Well, then, it's my opinion that Mr. Stanford Bingham himself is responsible for his wife's death."

A silence greeted this, and then the minister said, slowly: "It seems to me absurd to hold such a theory."

"Not absurd at all!" declared the detective. "Who had motive? Mr. Bingham. What was it? To get his fortune. Did anybody else have any motive whatever? Nobody. Did he have opportunity? He did. Was he likely to be suspected? He was not! My theory may be wrong, but it is *not* absurd!"

The entrance of Stanford Bingham himself put an end to this conversation.

CHAPTER 4

THE PEARL VEIL PIN

If Bingham had appeared to be dazed and stunned before, he was not so now. His eyes blazed, and every muscle of his body was tense and rigid as he said to the detective:

"I overheard your words as I entered the church. Do I understand, Mr. Ferrall, that you are accusing me of the murder of my wife?"

The words, though not loud, were tense and sharp, and the speaker seemed to be holding himself in by main force from flying at Ferrall's throat. His hands clenched as he awaited the reply.

But Ferrall was not the sort to be intimidated by any one's anger, and he said, "I don't accuse anybody, Mr. Bingham. It is my duty as a detective to investigate, not to accuse. What I said, I stand by. Is it true, sir, or is it not, that unless you were married before you were thirty, you would lose your fortune?"

"It is true," replied Bingham, coldly. "But don't make a fool of yourself, Mr. Ferrall. Had I wished to marry in order to inherit my father's estate, and afterward commit a crime to rid myself of my bride, I most certainly should not have chosen the wedding altar as the scene of the tragedy!"

"That's so," said the Inspector, "it would be most unlikely!"

"Not at all," insisted Ferrall. "Whoever chose the church as the place least likely of discovery, did a mighty cute thing. If we grant a murderer—and there sure was one—we must give him credit for great premeditation and foresight. As a detective, I've got to consider these things, and see where they lead me. Likewise, I've got to cast about for a motive. Where, I say, is there any possible motive to be found, except in this inheritance business? Who is going to murder a lovely young lady, with no reason for it? I'm not saying Mr. Bingham is the guilty man, but I *am* saying I haven't seen any other direction to look, as yet. And, what I say, Mr. Bingham, I'm quite willing to say to your face, and give you all chance to defend yourself, if you've got a defence."

"I have no defence, because none is needed," returned Bingham, still in a constrained, nervous voice. "Your suspicion is too absurd even to call forth denial! Wait a minute—I scorn to reply to your insinuations, but I see some men in the back of the church, who can at least tell you how ridiculous your talk is."

Kennedy and Farrish, the two choristers who had gone away earlier, had returned, drawn no doubt by an irresistible anxiety to learn of further developments. Eugene Hall, another chorister, was there, too, and the bridegroom called on these men, all acquaintances of his, to tell anything they knew.

"You fellows all stood up there in the choir," Bingham said; "if I had shot Ethel, would you not have seen me?"

"Of course," said Farrish. "I was looking at you both from the beginning of the ceremony to the end."

"So was I," said Kennedy. "I saw you, Bing, when you put up your hand to fix Ethel's veil—or something like that."

"Eh?" spoke up the detective, "fix the lady's veil? What do you mean?"

"Yes, I did," said Bingham. "Dr. Van Sutton had just spoken to Ethel, and was turning to me, when I saw a pearl pin loosened a little at the side of her head, and—"

"The right side?" asked the detective.

"Of course; that was the side toward me. I'm fussy about such things. The pin would have dropped out in a moment, and so I pushed it in with a light touch. I was surely privileged to do this to my own wife!"

"Of course," said Kennedy; "I just happened to notice it, because naturally I was looking at you both."

"And it was the next instant that the lady fell to the floor," said Ferrall, looking intently at Bingham.

"Good Lord, Mr. Ferrall!" cried the bridegroom, "are you going to say I shot my bride while arranging that veil pin?"

"I am not saying that. I am asking you if there was any perceptible interval between your manœuvring with the pin and the lady's fall?"

"How do I know?" cried Bingham, angrily. "At such a time one cannot remember minute details clearly! I fixed my wife's veil. I admit it. My wife fell to the floor. The two incidents had no bearing on one another."

"That is yet to be seen," said Ferrall, ominously.

"But they couldn't," protested Guy Farrish. "We in the choir could see all clearly, as Bingham says, and while I didn't especially notice the veil incident, I know I should have seen anything that looked like a shooting!"

"That's just the point," observed Inspector Kinney, "it *didn't* look like a shooting! It's a wonderfully mysterious crime and a wonderfully clever criminal we have to deal with, and we must look out for most unusual and unprecedented circumstances."

"That's true enough," assented Farrish, "but you must have a little common sense in the matter."

"That's so, Mr. Farrish," said Kinney. "I'm afraid, Ferrall, you're going too fast. Only further investigation can show who had a motive for desiring the death of the ill-fated bride. You have no idea of any such person, Mr. Bingham?"

"Certainly not. And I must say that I think the mystery will never be solved if left in such incompetent hands as are managing it at present."

"By Jove, that's right!" and Eugene Hall jumped to his feet. "I move we get a first-class detective on the case!"

"You are a little premature, Mr. Hall," said Bingham; "I have no fault to find with Mr. Ferrall's work. As he says, he must investigate; and as his first investigations point in my direction, I am content to let him run that line down and then turn to some more promising suspect."

"Now, that's white of you, Mr. Bingham," said the somewhat crestfallen detective; "I can't rightly say that I suspected you really, but there seemed to be no way to look—"

"There will be ways to look, Ferrall," and the Inspector's voice was grave, "but we can't see things clearly all at once. A crime like this means premeditation and preparation. The criminal was prepared for it before the ceremony began. It was no sudden or spontaneous act."

"It's mysterious enough," said Eugene Hall. "I wish I could be of definite help. But as I've told all I know, I may as well go home. Going my way, Farrish?"

Farrish was, and the two men left the church together, just as a coloured woman entered it by the side door.

"I'm Charlotte," she stated, curtsying to the group of men who still stood by the pulpit.

"Yes, Charlotte, what is it?" and Stanford Bingham turned to greet her with a startled look in his eyes. "Charlotte is Miss Randall's maid," he added, by way of explanation of his own interest.

"Miss Randall she sent me ovah, suhs, to say as how Miss Ethel's dimun ain't been found on her pusson, suhs. An' Miss Eileen, she say won't you-all please look most ca'ful roun' about dis yer chu'ch. De doctahs, dey done had a nawtopsy, an' dey cyan't fine de dimun anyw'eres on Miss Ethel. An' Miss Eileen, she say it mus' be in de chu'ch, summers."

"I don't think so," said Bingham, slowly; "if that diamond is not on Ethel—caught in her clothing or veil—then it has been stolen. Had it been here on the floor, where she stood, some one must have seen it before this. It is too large to escape observation."

"What was its value?" asked Ferrall.

"It cost more than fifty thousand dollars," replied Bingham, "but it has no value now, in my eyes. It was my wedding gift to my wife; as I have now no wife, I have no use for the diamond."

"Oh, I don't know!" said Ferrall, with a distinctly offensive look at Bingham.

"Explain that speech!" cried Bingham, his eyes blazing again, as he turned on the detective.

"I only meant," said Ferrall, slowly, and a little insolently, "that as you are so unconcerned about the loss of a great treasure, perhaps it is not so mysteriously or so irrecoverably missing!"

Stanford Bingham went white. "You mean that I know where it is?" he whispered, hoarsely.

"Something like that," admitted the detective.

"I can't stand any more of this," said Bingham, passing his hand wearily across his forehead. "I think I will go home."

"I think you won't," said Ferrall, but Kinney interrupted. "Yes, he may. Certainly, Mr. Bingham, go. You have stood enough for a man in such trouble as you are in. You will be at home if we want to see you again?"

"Certainly," said Bingham, and with the staggering step of a half-dazed man, he left the church.

"You ought not to have let him go!" cried Ferrall. "He'll light out and we'll never see him again! Of course, he is the guilty man! His very attitude condemns him. He had motive, opportunity, and he is intensely clever, just such a one as could carry out such a crime!"

"But it is absurd, on the face of it!" expostulated Kinney. "For a man to shoot his own bride at his own wedding altar! It is incredible!"

"Lots of murders are incredible. Who else wanted to be rid of that woman? Not her aunt or uncle or any of her relatives or friends. She was a greatly admired young lady, a favourite, a belle, a most popular society girl. But Bingham had to marry her to get his fortune. So—his fortune secured—he rid himself of her, in circumstances so diabolically clever, that he thought he never would be suspected. Nor would he have been, if I did not happen to know that he did not love the lady he made his wife."

"Didn't love her? What do you mean? How do you know?"

"I don't *know*, that is, not positively. That's why I wanted to talk to him, and get him to incriminate himself."

"Nonsense, Ferrall, you're romancing. You have formed a crazy theory and you have let it run away with your common sense. But that is your habit, as I've often had cause to note. Now, then, come back to material things. Where's the big diamond? Or do you think Bingham stole his own property?"

"Of course he stole it! It wasn't his, after he gave it to her. He wanted it back, and he could get it no other way, so he took it. He had plenty of chances during the first immediate excitement."

"But it would have been his. Of course, all the property his wife died possessed of, must necessarily have reverted to him."

"Oh, well, that may be so, but he knew if he were suspected of the crime, he might have difficulty in getting possession of the diamond. So he made sure of it. Why, man, he *must* have done so! If any other person were the assassin, he couldn't get near enough to the body to take the jewel. And you can't for a moment believe that some bystander, one of the wedding party, took it!"

"Why not? I'd just as soon think it of one of the ushers as of the bridegroom himself."

"But the bridegroom had a motive for the murder, and so, for the theft. The ushers had no motive for murder—"

"You don't *know* that!"

"Well, it can be proved, I've no doubt."

"The bride had many admirers."

"Yes, more than any girl in town. She was the reigning belle."

"Then the deed may have been the desperation of a discarded lover."

"That will mean raking the town with a fine-tooth comb. For every young blade in Boscombe Fells was in love with the beautiful Ethel Moulton."

"Then get to work and rake, before you accuse the bridegroom!"

"I'll rake, all right; but there was no other man who had the cleverness or the nerve to plan and carry through this horrible performance."

"Suppose you take a try at finding the diamond first; that may give a clue to the murderer. Indeed, I think it's bound to. Here, you, Charlotte—if that's your name, you run along home. I forgot you were here. You tell Miss Randall that the police are searching for the jewel, and will report progress, when there is any to report."

"Yassah. An' can I tell yo' sumpin, suh?"

"Certainly. What is it?"

"Well, I knows who kilt Miss Ethel."

Charlotte was a very black negro, and as she spoke, she rolled her eyes in a tragic and mysterious manner. Inspector Kinney had heard this sort of fairy-tale evidence before, and he was for putting the woman out without listening further. But Ferrall wanted to hear her story.

"It means nothing, Ferrall," said Kinney; "these darkies are always ready to make up yarns for the excitement of the thing."

"But she may know something. Surely it will do no harm to listen to what she has to tell."

"Go on, then," said the other.

"Well, yo' see, suh," began the dusky servant woman, "I was outside that there window, a-lookin' in."

"That window!" exclaimed Ferrall, for Charlotte had indicated the first window on the east side of the church, the one directly inside range of the bride and groom as they stood at the altar.

"Yes, suh, dat berry window. An' I knows as how nobody outside dat window didn't shoot thoo it, kase ef dey had I'd 'a' seen 'em, dat I would. Well, suh, dere was a man jest inside de chu'ch, an' he was a-watchin' ob de bride-lady, an' he kep' his hank'chif all ober his hand all de time. Now, suh, says I, moughtn't he be de vilyun dat shot Miss Ethel?"

"Rubbish," said the Inspector. "It was simply a man holding his handkerchief carelessly in his hand. It means nothing at all."

"Don't jump at conclusions so!" said Ferrall, getting back; "tell us more, Charlotte. What did the man look like?"

"I dunno, suh. I didn' notice him much, kase I was a-watchin' de bride myself. But I sort o' sensed him all de time, an' he nebber took dat hank'chif offen o' dat hand!"

"Would you know the man if you saw him again?"

The black woman looked uncertain. "I mought an' I moughtn't," she said, at last. "You see, his back was to me. But he had red hair."

"Really red? Very red?" And Ferrall spoke excitedly.

"Well, not fi'ry red. But moh sorta aubuhn, suh."

"You're wasting time, Ferrall; send her home, and let us go home ourselves and think this thing out. We know a lot of facts that need to be straightened out and considered. Run along, Charlotte. Tell Miss Randall you delivered her message, and Mr. Kinney will see her tomorrow."

"Yas, suh. Will yo' come to huh house, suh?"

"I don't know. If I do, I'll telephone first, and make an appointment."

The black woman went away. "You talked too much before her, Ferrall," said Kinney, reprovingly.

"Oh, I didn't say anything that oughtn't to be repeated. And she didn't understand, anyway. She's an ignorant thing."

"Not so awfully ignorant! I saw her watching you out of the corner of her eye, and she's no fool. She made up that story of the 'red-headed man'!"

"Ridiculous! She did nothing of the sort!"

"Well, see if you ever find him, that's all!"

CHAPTER 5

THE EAST SIDE OR THE WEST?

From the church, Detective Ferrall went to the Swift home.

It was ghastly, as he had anticipated, to see the caterer's men taking away the chairs and decorations. The laden tables in the dining-room had already been denuded and the waiters dismissed. Many people were in the house, standing in groups in the various rooms, some of them still in their gala attire.

On a sofa near the front window were Bob Keene and Betty Stratton, who had been one of the bridesmaids; they were talking earnestly in low whispers.

Ferrall joined them, hoping to pick up stray information of some sort.

But neither of the young people was at all cordial and Ferrall went on in search of Mr. Swift.

He found him in the library, and behind closed doors the men sat down for a serious talk over the tragedy.

Ferrall told frankly his suspicions of Stanford Bingham. At first immeasurably shocked, Mr. Swift listened more and more intently to the detective's reasoning, and at last said:

"It's unthinkable, it's well-nigh impossible, and I can't and won't believe it, and yet—and yet, there *was* something between Bingham and Ethel that I never quite understood. We all knew that the man must marry before he was thirty to inherit his father's fortune, but he and Ethel had been engaged a long time, and we were all satisfied that, while he desired, naturally, to be wed before the prescribed time, yet they would have been married had there been no complication about the money."

"How long had they been engaged, Mr. Swift?"

"Let me see; it's June now. Well, they were engaged last Summer, I think, about July or August."

"Why weren't they married sooner?"

"Bless my soul! I don't know. I suppose because they didn't want to be. Probably Ethel wanted a June wedding. I know she wanted every furbelow or gimcrackery there was. That chorus choir, for instance, and an orchestra here at the house. Well, I'm glad now that I denied her nothing. I let her have it all just as she chose. She was the orphan child of my favourite sister, and as I've never had any daughter of my own, I indulged her as I would have my own child."

"Did Mrs. Swift feel the same affection?"

"Almost, I think. Of course, Ethel was my niece, not hers, but she was always kind to the girl, and they never had any differences that I know of."

"And your son. Were he and your niece friendly?"

"Very, indeed. In fact, at one time I thought Warren was in love with her. But I think it was only a cousinly attachment. They were always good chums, though, and as he was best man, I fancy his heart wasn't broken beyond remedy at her marriage. But now, the poor boy is nearly prostrated. Both he and my wife are suffering intensely from the shock and nervous prostration."

"Miss Moulton was a great belle, I'm told."

"Yes, Ethel was always a heart-breaker. I don't know how many men have asked me for her hand, but she never favoured any one as she did Bingham. I sometimes thought it was because he was rich. My niece had most extravagant tastes."

"Had she money of her own?"

"Some. She inherited about twenty-five thousand dollars from her father, but the interest of that was not enough for her to spend. Or, at least, she thought not, and I was glad to give her what more she wanted."

"She was fond of dress, then?"

"Yes, and of jewels, and of running about travelling here and there. I indulged her, as I say, because I had no daughter, and my wife and I have rather simple tastes."

"Was your niece—pardon me—was she what could be called a flirt?"

"She was, indeed! Ethel would flirt with a messenger boy if she chose! It was all harmless flirting, she was as good as gold, but she could no more help flirting than she could help breathing. Every man in town will tell you that— and many out of town. We always joked her about it, but she only laughed and said it was the spice of life to her. Her aunt and I hoped she would get over it and settle down after she married Bingham."

"You've known Mr. Bingham long?"

"Yes, for years."

"You admire him?"

"Indeed, yes. He's a fine man, a splendid man, in every way, and yet— this is confidential, Mr. Ferrall, there seemed to be something of late that made me uneasy about him and Ethel."

"In what way?"

"I don't know how to tell you; it is so intangible. It almost seemed, at times, as if he wanted to back out of the wedding, and yet, I know that couldn't have been so."

"Why couldn't it?"

"Why? Oh, bless my soul! Bingham's not that sort of a man. No, I must have imagined it, I suppose. But there seemed a constraint between him and Ethel that became more and more noticeable as their wedding day neared."

"Did you speak of it to them?"

"To Ethel, yes; never to him. She laughed at me, and said if Stanford were any more devoted to her than he was, she couldn't stand it."

"What did she mean by that?"

"Between you and me, I think she was bluffing. I think he was not so demonstrative as Ethel would have liked, and her proud spirit wouldn't admit it, and even went to the extreme of overdenying it."

"Then you really think, in your heart, that Bingham did not want to marry your niece?"

"Mr. Ferrall, I have never gone so far as to say that to any one, not even my wife; but since I know you ask in the interests of law and justice, I will confess to you that that thought was in my mind as I walked up that church aisle today. And I cannot help thinking it was in Ethel's mind, too. She was nervous and unstrung more than the occasion demanded. I have never seen her so distraught before. My wife didn't notice this as I did, because she was in the pew while I was right with Ethel and beside her all the way. And I tell you, Mr. Ferrall, that girl was afraid of something. Of something not definite, perhaps, but she was conscious of a vague danger of some sort."

"Then, Mr. Swift—I don't wonder you're shocked—but you can not be so greatly surprised when I tell you I have reason to suspect Mr. Bingham of being in some way responsible for his wife's death."

"I wish I could feel more surprised, but I am forced to admit, Mr. Ferrall, that I have been haunted by that suspicion, myself. I can't see how it is possible, I hope and pray that it is *not* true, but I can think of no other living human being who had the least reason to desire Ethel's death. It is absurd to think for a moment that any of the many men who admired her would be so desperate at thought of her marriage to Bingham that one of them could go so far as to murder her in cold blood."

"Who were some of these men, Mr. Swift?"

"Let me see; in fact it would be easier to think of men whom she had not had affairs with. Two of the ushers, Stone and Benson, have both been refused by the dear girl. Eugene Hall is another who was hard hit at the news of her marriage; and Guy Farrish and Chester Morton—but it's too absurd! Not one of these men would have harmed a hair of her head! Nor can I really think Stanford would. But what else is there to think? It is impossible that it could have been an accident. And then, again, how could Bingham have done it? The doctors agree that the assailant probably stood several feet away, and the bridegroom was no more than two or three feet away at the utmost."

"But that sort of thing is uncertain, Mr. Swift, and as the shot entered through her hair, we cannot know—"

"Oh, heavens, man! It isn't possible! I can't, I *won't* believe that any man on earth could be black enough of soul to stand there and shoot the woman he had just married! It is unspeakable!"

"Most murders are unspeakable, Mr. Swift. And think what the man had at stake! To get his million dollars—I understand the fortune is a million or more—he had to be married before next month, when his thirtieth birthday occurs. It would be practically impossible for him to break with Miss Moulton and arrange to marry anyone else in the meantime—this is supposing for the moment that he loved another—so he married Miss Moulton, and then, if, as you fear, he did not want her for a wife, except to secure his fortune, what cleverer way could be devised to rid himself of her? Had they gone away on a wedding tour, his deed must surely have been discovered. How plausible, then, for the villain to think that this way, this fiendish way, was the safest and surest for himself?"

"You sound convincing, Mr. Ferrall, and yet, now that you put it into words, I cannot believe it. It is too incredible!"

"I'm not urging you to believe it, Mr. Swift. It is my duty, as a detective, to try to get at the truth of this dreadful affair. I have my suspicions, I must ascertain if they are true or false. You must help me in any way you can, not to prove my theories, but to learn the truth. But, of course, you must see that what you have told me goes far toward confirming my belief in Mr. Bingham's guilt, though as yet I cannot imagine just how he accomplished his awful purpose."

A tap at the library door interrupted their conversation.

It was Betty Stratton, the pretty little bridesmaid, and Bob Keene, the reporter.

"We've found out something!" Betty announced, as she entered the room, followed by Keene.

"Of importance?" asked Ferrall, frowning slightly, for he had little use for the discoveries of these "youngsters."

"Yes, it is of importance," answered Keene. "It's a distinct point, anyway. You have all decided, haven't you, that the shot was fired from the east side of the church, whether inside or outside?"

"Yes, of course," said Ferrall; "as the bride faced the altar, her right side was toward the east, and as the wound is in her right temple, why, it inevitably—"

"But that's just it!" cried Keene; "she *didn't* face the altar! You see, she had turned, the bride had, for Miss Randall to adjust her long, heavy train, and as she turned, toward the other aisle, the west aisle, her right cheek came around toward the west, and when she was shot she had turned and was really facing the back of the church, ready to walk down that west aisle. She was expecting the bridegroom to join her as soon as he had spoken with the minister—all this was rehearsed, you know—and—well, the point is, that the bride had turned round, and was standing with her right side to the *west* when she was shot!"

"H'm, all very fine, but how do you know it?" demanded Mr. Ferrall.

"I'm the one who knows it," put in Betty Stratton. "You see, it was this way. All us bridesmaids were looking forward to catching Ethel's bouquet when she threw it, later on, of course, as brides always do when they go away. Well, when I went back to the altar after they had taken Ethel away, I saw her bouquet lying where she had dropped it as she fell, and it made me feel so awful! I thought at first I ought to pick it up and carry it into the other room where Ethel was, and then I just couldn't do that! You know what it means to pick up a bride's bouquet! Well, then, I noticed that it lay right on the chalk mark that had been mine! I mean, the place where I had to stand, quite west of the bride. And don't you see, Ethel *couldn't* have dropped it there, unless she had turned round! So doesn't that prove that she had turned, and that the shot came from the west side of the church?"

"I see what you mean," said Mr. Ferrall, slowly. "If you will, I'd like you to go back to the church with me, and show me exactly where you stood."

So Bob Keene and Betty went back to the church with the detective and showed him. It was certainly as Betty had said. The bride, in order to have let her bouquet fall on the mark that designated Betty's place, *must* have turned round, preparatory to leaving the church.

The bridal party had walked up the east aisle to the altar, and expected to go back down the west aisle. The exact mode of procedure had been carefully rehearsed, and each one knew just where he or she was to stand and in what order to proceed.

"You see," explained Betty, "every bride has her attendants stand just as she wants them. Ethel had us placed with two bridesmaids and two ushers on each side of her and Mr. Bingham. Of course, Eileen, the maid of honour, was at Ethel's left hand, and the best man, Mr. Swift, at the bridegroom's right. Well, after the ceremony, we all stepped back a little to let Ethel's train get by, and as I was directly behind her, she must have already turned round, to have dropped her bouquet right on my chalk mark!" And Betty broke into sobs at the recollection of the awful scene.

"That's right!" said the detective, thinking deeply. "The bride must have turned to have dropped the flowers *there* as she fell. Unless, that is, somebody moved them afterward, inadvertently."

"They didn't," said Betty; "I know, because I saw Ethel fall, I was very near her, you know, and I was so paralyzed I couldn't move or speak, but I can see it all as clearly now as if it were photographed on my brain. Ethel sank all in a heap, and the bouquet fell just where I had stood during the ceremony. And I kept my eyes on those flowers, I don't know why, but they seemed to fascinate me, and nobody touched them till some time after, when Doctor Van Sutton picked them up and carried them in—in where Ethel was."

"Get the dominie over here," said Mr. Ferrall, briefly, and Bob Keene ran over to the parsonage for him. The two returned shortly, and Doctor Van Sutton corroborated all Betty had said.

"Yes; it must be so," said the reverend gentleman, "I know the bride had turned away from me, I was then speaking to the bridegroom, and in order to drop the bouquet just there, she must have turned fully around. And it was from that spot that I picked up the flowers—of that I'm certain. I had no definite reason for picking them up, except that it seemed more decorous than leaving them there on the floor. And, being a little uncertain what to do with them, I laid them on the breast of the bride. I thought of handing them to Mrs. Swift, but she was already so overcome, that it seemed inadvisable."

Doctor Van Sutton was a mild-mannered, typical clergyman, and he was bowed with grief not only at the horror of the tragedy, but that it should have occurred in his church. Such things as crime and mystery had never come into his life before, and he was bewildered at the details to be considered.

"Then we must conclude the shot was fired from the west and not the east," said Mr. Ferrall, looking greatly perplexed.

"That opens up again the question of a window," said Bob Keene; "a window on the other side, of course. I'll skip out and look for footprints."

Ferrall smiled as the young man hurried out of the church. "Trust an amateur detective to fly after footprints!" he said; "Keene has a sleuthing instinct, and he's bright enough, but this mystery is not going to be solved by any of the usual means. I tell you, Doctor Van Sutton, it's a big case. I'm not at all sure we'll ever catch the criminal, but if we do, it will mean some clever work. Well, Keene, what luck?"

"There are footprints," said Keene, joining them, "by that first window on the west side, there are footprints in the soft soil that's banked up around the roots of the ivy vines. And they're the prints of only one person. I'm sure but one person stood there."

"Well, and what about it? Are you such a Sherlock Holmes that you can go out in the street and pick out the man?"

"No, I'm not; but I've always understood that if a detective had good clear footprints, he had—"

"Go 'long, Keene; you understand your own work better than ours. Stick to reporting and don't dabble in detecting. It's a hard enough job for the experienced, let alone amateurs."

"Well, you might be grateful for the help we've given you. I think it's pretty good detective work on the part of Miss Stratton to prove to you that the shot came from the west side of the church, whether fired by some one inside or out."

"That's true; and I am indebted to you, Miss Stratton. You have given me a clear and graphic description of the few moments preceding the shot, and it may be of great help to know from which side it was fired."

"Anyway, it lets old Bingham out!" declared Keene, who was a friend of the bridegroom.

"Not at all," said Ferrall, "it may merely prove that he had an accomplice!"

CHAPTER 6

A WOMAN'S WILL

The wedding had been on Thursday. On Friday the whole town of Boscombe Fells was in an uproar. A steady stream of callers assailed the Swift house, and Mrs. Bingham, the mother of the bridegroom, was also intruded upon by friends and neighbours bringing sympathy and offers of aid.

The tragedy was so dreadful, the crime so horrible, that words were all too weak to express the vindictive and revengeful feelings of the towns-people. Moreover, it was so unheard of that such a thing should occur in that rank of social life to which the bride and groom's families belonged. Murder, as they supposed, was confined to the lower classes, and for beauti-ful, haughty Ethel Moulton to be murdered at her wedding altar savoured of indignity and inappropriateness quite aside from the sad horror of the crime itself. Dozens of citizens flocked to the police headquarters to tell them how to conduct the matter. More went to the District Attorney with their advices, and Mr. Ferrall, too, found his office besieged and his mail crammed with would-be purveyors of clues and evidences intended to aid him.

In the office of the District Attorney, whose name was Somers, Detec-tive Ferrall sat, on Friday afternoon, going over the case. It was an endless subject to discuss, for nothing positive had been learned, yet there was scope for suspicion in every direction.

"That's the worst of it," said Ferrall; "some cases have no possibilities, but this one has so many, I don't know which way to turn."

"Seems to me we must look up that diamond first. The murderer must be hunted down, of course, but the murder is done, and can only be avenged. But the theft is a crime also, and to recover the jewel might very easily give us a line on the murderer."

"That's so, right enough; well, there's no use denying that I think the bridegroom responsible for both crimes."

"Look here, Ferrall, you're just bound Mr. Bingham shall be found guilty, and you bend every bit of evidence toward that end. That isn't fair work for any detective."

"I don't, at all. If I see any evidence pointing to anyone else, I'll jump at it. But I haven't so far. Bingham had motive and opportunity, and no one else did. Either he shot the lady himself or he hired some one else to do it. I'm not greatly impressed with that bridesmaid's story, she may be mistaken. But any way you fix it, there's evidence against Stanford Bingham and against no one else. Who else could have taken that diamond from the bride's neck? Who else would?"

"Well, as to that, why should Bingham take it? It was his anyway, as his wife was dead."

"That's where you're 'way off! Ethel Moulton had made a will two years or more ago, leaving everything of which she died possessed to her cousin, Warren Swift. That gave young Swift the sparkler, and as that wouldn't suit Bingham at all, he made sure of it for himself. Why, there's no doubt of it. Miss Randall told me the gem was on the bride's neck during the ceremony, and when the body was carried to the church parlour it was gone. Of course the criminal took it. There couldn't have been two such fiends in the wedding party!"

"You're 'way off, yourself! You may be a good detective, Ferrall, but you don't know much law! That will that you say Miss Moulton made, as Miss Moulton, became null and void when she married. Her property is all her husband's, no matter if she left forty wills."

"Is that right? Do you mean to say a woman can't will her property as she likes?"

"I mean that marriage nullifies a woman's will. The moment Miss Moulton became Mrs. Bingham, young Swift ceased to be her heir, and Stanford Bingham is entitled to everything his wife died possessed of."

"Well, of course you're right, for you know about those things and I don't, but it's news to me. And, another thing, I'll bet you it'll be news to Stanford Bingham! Of course, with his millions he doesn't care for his wife's money, she hadn't very much, but he does care for that fifty thousand dollar diamond, and he stole it because he thought it would go to Warren Swift. You say it wouldn't, but I'll wager Bingham thought it would, or, at least, was uncertain, and so took no chances. He may not have considered it stealing, but merely taking his own. However, if he took the diamond, it is a small thing compared to his greater crime of murder."

"How you do run on, Ferrall! Any one to hear you would think you had Mr. Bingham arrested, tried, and convicted; whereas, except you, I doubt if any one really suspects him."

"Oho, you doubt that, do you? Well, let me tell you, you won't doubt it long. I may jump at conclusions, but when the conclusions are there pray, why shouldn't I?"

* * * *

From Somers' office, Ferrall went to the Swift house, intent on gaining further information about the bride's will.

He found both Everson Swift and his son at home, and quite ready to talk with him.

"I understand, Mr. Swift," began Ferrall, "that your niece left all her property to her cousin, your son?"

"She did," said Warren Swift, not giving his father time to speak. "Ethel made a will long ago, and I am her sole heir. It seems heartless to talk of it, but it is no secret, and there is no reason it should not be known."

"And you inherit all her belongings?" asked Ferrall, looking hard at the young man.

"Yes; that is, all her money and valuables. Of course, her clothes and such personal belongings I shall turn over to my mother to do as she likes with."

Ferrall began to feel sure that neither young Swift nor his father suspected that Warren was not the heir.

"And the great diamond," Ferrall went on; "if that is found, and, of course, it must be, is that yours, too?"

"It is," said Warren, confidently, and he spoke with a sort of braggadocio far from becoming in a relative of the ill-fated bride. "Do you think the stone will be found, Mr. Ferrall?"

"I do, indeed. An attempt to dispose of it would lead at once to discovery. It is too large a stone to offer for sale without full account of ownership."

"That's good. Then I may yet hope to see it returned to me, its rightful owner. Would you advise offering a reward, Mr. Ferrall?"

But Everson Swift spoke in answer to this. "Why, Warren, I think a reward should be offered for the conviction of Ethel's slayer, before we consider the lesser matter of the diamond."

"And, anyway, if the diamond is found, it will be Mr. Bingham's property." Ferrall spoke carelessly, but he watched every expression of Warren Swift's face.

However, if the expectant heir was surprised, he concealed it fairly well, and said only, "What do you mean by that, Mr. Ferrall?"

But the older man showed a definite surprise. "Why will it be Bingham's?" he said. "Why won't it be Warren's, with the rest of Ethel's belongings?"

"Because none of Mrs. Bingham's property will be Mr. Swift's. Don't you know that marriage nullifies a will?"

His two hearers looked up at him with faces of blank amazement, but it was the father who spoke first.

"No, I don't know any such thing! And I don't believe it! Who's your authority?"

"The District Attorney, for one, but I refer you to any reputable lawyer for confirmation."

"A most unjust law! Then is all Ethel's property now her husband's?"

"Every bit. The will is absolutely nullified."

"I don't so much mind in this instance," and Mr. Swift looked a little ashamed of his ebullition, "but it's wrong on general principles. Why in the name of common sense couldn't my niece leave her money to my son, if she wanted to?"

"Don't ask me, Mr. Swift; ask the laws of your country."

"Never mind, father," said Warren; "don't take it so hard. It's a blow to me, for Stan has all he needs, while I have nothing. I was glad to have Ethel's money, for I know she loved me and wanted me to have it. She often told me I was to be her heir. We were good chums."

Ferrall looked from one man to the other. He was surprised that Everson Swift seemed more disappointed than his son. But perhaps Warren was playing a part. Ferrall was not quick at reading expressions, but he concluded that Warren Swift was more upset at the news he had just received than he wished to have known, and that he was more clever in concealing his disappointment than his father.

"And the diamond will be Bingham's if it is found?" Mr. Swift went on.

"Yes, of course," returned Ferrall, looking at Warren as he spoke.

"That doesn't matter, it must be hunted for and found just the same," Warren said. He spoke in a dull, colourless tone, as if he wanted to do and say the right thing, but found it hard.

"Of course, of course," agreed his father, "but if it is really Bingham's property, it is his place to instigate the search for the gem."

Ferrall was getting bewildered. He was firmly of the opinion that Bingham had himself taken the diamond from his wife's neck, or had picked it up from the floor where it had fallen, and to imagine the criminal instigating a search for the jewel was absurd. But again, perhaps Bingham did not know that his wife's property reverted to himself, and supposing the jewel would fall to Warren, he secured it when he had opportunity. This was all conjecture, but Ferrall was given to conjecture, and to his credit it must be said that more often than not his suppositions were true.

"Didn't you know this fact regarding a will?" asked Ferrall, turning to the younger Swift.

Warren looked at him a moment in silence. Then, rising, he said somewhat peevishly, "I do wish, Mr. Ferrall, you'd stop quizzing my father and me. It's all very well for you to do your detective work, but I, for one, think you ought to ask your questions of people outside the family of the victim of the crime. I can't see what possible good it can do you to learn what I know or knew regarding my cousin's will, and I refuse to be persecuted any longer."

Slamming the door behind him, Warren went from the room.

"Don't mind him," said his father, wearily running his hand through his iron-grey hair. "Warry's of a nervous disposition, and this affair is pretty hard on him. He is amazed, as I am myself, to learn that he will not inherit Ethel's property, but he is too proud to show it. The two were always chums and her death has shocked him horribly. He has been trying at my advice to throw off the sorrowful thoughts and turn his mind to other things, but he can't do it. I doubt if he had thought much about the money, until you spoke of it."

"H'm!" thought Detective Ferrall to himself, "I think he was pretty conscious of that will all the way along!" but aloud he only said, "Very natural, I'm sure, Mr. Swift. It's a terrible thing to come into his young life. Well, I'll be going now, and I'll see you again when I've anything to report."

"A queer lot," he thought, as he left the Swift house. "Not an affectionate family, as far as the niece was concerned. I don't know about Mrs. Swift, but the uncle and cousin are by no means overwhelmed with grief."

However, Ferrall did them an injustice. The Swifts, father and son, were men who rarely showed their feelings, and they would never have dreamed of speaking of Ethel in endearing or even in personal terms before a comparative stranger, least of all, a detective!

* * * *

It was Saturday evening before the detective and the District Attorney had another confab on the subject, and then Ferrall told Somers how surprised the Swifts had been to learn the truth about the bride's will.

"Well, don't tell everybody about it, Ferrall," said the District Attorney, a little sharply. "You talk too much! You tell every one of all your discoveries and all your plans. Do learn to keep your mouth shut."

Ferrall, miffed, relapsed into silence, and it was at this juncture that Bob Keene appeared.

"Anything new?" he asked. "Anything that I can print, I mean. I don't want theories. Any facts yet?"

"Nothing for publication," said Ferrall, glancing at Somers with an air of keeping his own counsel.

"Oh, tell him, if you want to," said Somers. "You will, anyway."

Thus encouraged, Ferrall did tell Keene about the surprise of the Swifts on learning that Warren could not inherit under Ethel's will.

"Yes, I knew that," said Keene, carelessly; "I mean I knew that marriage nullifies a woman's will. I thought everybody knew that. But, I say, this gives a new trend to affairs. If Warry Swift didn't know that he wouldn't inherit, why do you think he didn't kill his cousin to get that same little old inheritance?"

"Rubbish!" ejaculated Somers. "That little whipper-snapper wouldn't have the nerve to kill anybody, and it's too preposterous to think of his killing his cousin!"

"Not half so preposterous as to think of the bridegroom's killing her! I tell you, Mr. Somers, if you've got a murderer to find, you've got to look for him among the most unlikely personages. And, you can't think an utter stranger came along and killed a bride, without any motive. No, sir! There are only three motives for murder, love, money, and revenge. Now, Bingham had none of these reasons to kill his bride; we know of no one who had, until we run up against the man who was to inherit."

"But young Swift doesn't inherit."

"But he thought he did, so it's all the same. I tell you we're on a trail! What do you say, Mr. Ferrall?"

"It doesn't sound to me very plausible, but it may be possible. It will do no harm to look into it. Where was young Swift during the ceremony?"

"He was best man," answered Keene, "so, of course, he stood at the right of the bridegroom."

"Then he was on the right side of the bride, as well. We've concluded she was shot from the other, the west side of the church, so that lets Swift out."

"Oh, I don't know. After the ceremony, just before the shot, there was more or less of a mix-up as they got ready for the return trip down the west aisle. I wouldn't say that he couldn't have gotten a chance then, if he had wanted to."

"I can't seem to see it," and the District Attorney looked blank. "I wasn't at the wedding, and I haven't been over to the church since."

"Then you ought to go," said Keene; "let's run over now."

After a moment's thought the others agreed, and the three went to the church. As it was Saturday night, they found the choir there for practice.

"Good work!" said Keene; "do you know, as those men were up in the choir loft, they had the best possible view of the whole affair and ought to be able to tell us everything about it."

"Be careful," warned Somers; "don't let them know what we are thinking about, just ask them of the positions of the principals."

The choristers were quite willing to describe the programme of the wedding party, and after going over all the others, Keene said, apparently carelessly, "and what about Warry Swift? I mean where was he? On the east side?"

Guy Farrish answered. "He was on the east side at first, in fact until after the ceremony. Then he crossed over to be on the other side ready to walk down the aisle with the maid of honour. These things were all planned and rehearsed, you know."

"Were you here at rehearsal, Mr. Farrish?" asked Somers.

"No, the choir was not needed. We merely preceded the wedding party into the church, and then took our usual places in the choir, and, of course, no rehearsal was needed for that."

"From the choir you had ample opportunity to see the wedding ceremony, hadn't you?"

"Yes, indeed; and what followed," and Farrish turned aside as if to shun the dread subject. But Somers was not through. He questioned Eugene Hall as to Warren Swift's movements.

"Why, yes," Hall said; "I saw Warry cross over behind the minister just after the ceremony was finished. You see his work was all done; he had given the ring to the bridegroom and hadn't dropped it or fumbled it, and he had then to look out for his partner in the march, the maid of honour. He crossed over, I suppose to be ready to escort her after she had finished fixing the bride's furbelows. Oh, I know a lot about it, 'cause I stood here with nothing to do but watch 'em."

"Young Swift was over on the west side of the church some minutes, then, before the shooting took place?"

"He was so. He stood just about there," and Hall indicated a spot in front of the cross pews known as the "Amen Corner."

"Thank you, sir, that's all. We won't detain you longer from your music," and Somers stepped away from the group of choristers who returned to their work.

"You see," whispered Keene to the others with him, "if Swift stood here when the bride passed him, he could easily have fired the shot."

"But he would have been seen," objected Ferrall.

"Not at all, a man can fire one of those little automatics, and keep it concealed in his hand. They're very small. Well, any way, take my advice and look into this matter."

* * * *

Late that night a note was left at the Swift home for Warren.
It ran:

> "I have reason to think you are suspected in connection with the shooting of your cousin. If you want to get away, I'll meet you with my car, corner Broad and Myrtle at midnight. Perhaps it would be better for you to go."
>
> "E."

And that night at midnight, Warren Swift was at the appointed tryst.

CHAPTER 7

WARRY'S GETAWAY

"You came!" said Eugene Hall, with surprise in his tone, as Warry Swift climbed into the car.

"Of course," returned the other, with a somewhat unsuccessful attempt at nonchalance. "But that doesn't mean I'm a murderer. I came to ask the meaning of your extraordinary message."

"Now, Warry, don't try bluffing with me, for it won't go! We're old pals, you and I, and when I heard the talk at the church tonight, I just had to warn you that they're on to you."

Young Swift turned pale and his teeth chattered. "What do you mean, Gene?"

"Tonight we were at choir practice, and the District Attorney and Ferrall came there to look over the place. Keene was with 'em—Bob Keene. They confabbed a lot, and then they put us choristers through a bit of questioning. Well, the up-shot was, Warry, that when they learned that you crossed over to the west side of the church, just before Ethel fell, they immediately began to suspect you. I had been their chief source of information about your crossing over, and when I found it meant trouble for you, I concluded to give you a chance to clear out if you want to. I don't ask you if you did it, I don't want to know. I hate all this detective business, and evidence, and everything. And, you know, old chap, how I felt toward Ethel. She refused to marry me two years ago, but I never quit loving her. If you knew what it meant to me to stand up there and watch her marry Bingham! Well, I had to do it, of course; it would have looked queer to refuse. Where shall I take you?"

"I don't know; I'm all upset! Gene, how *can* they think I would shoot Ethel?"

"Oh, I don't know, man! Don't let's talk about it. I got you into this mess—being suspected, I mean, and I'm willing to help you get out, but I won't discuss it with you."

"What do you mean, that I'm suspected because I crossed over to the west side?"

"I don't know all about it myself. But somehow they've concluded Ethel was shot by some one on the west side of the church—"

"How *could* she be? The wound is in her right temple. That was the side toward Bingham, toward the east."

"I know it, but they say she had turned all the way round, to walk out, when she was struck."

"Turned around! Nonsense! She had scarcely finished her responses."

"I don't know about all that, but I'll tell you one thing, Warry, and I haven't told another soul. Clements, the organist, could see in his organ mirror, you know, and he said to me, that he distinctly saw the back of Ethel's head before she fell. Now, that proves she had turned, and though Clem didn't tell the detectives that, they've got the notion that she did turn, and they're looking for some one on the west side of the church, who could have done the shooting, and—as I told you, for some reason they're leaning toward you."

"But why would I kill Ethel? I was more than half in love with her myself."

"Maybe that's the reason they suspect you. I don't know. But, good Lord, for that reason they could suspect half the men in town! Who didn't love Ethel Moulton? If a man is going to shoot the woman he loves because she marries some one else, then they could suspect a whole lot of us! I adored her, but *I'm* not murderously inclined."

"Neither am I!"

"That may be, but the point is, they think you had a chance and, of course, I didn't. I couldn't very well commit a crime when I was up there in the choir, in full view of the whole audience. But you, on the west side, and as Ethel passed you—"

"Stop, Hall! For Heaven's sake, stop! Of course, I didn't do it!"

"Well, that's all right, but can you prove it?"

"Do I have to?"

"Honestly, Warry, I believe you do. I didn't hear all they said—they were jolly careful we shouldn't—but I know when those men left the church, they had you in mind as first suspect. They had been thinking it might have been Bingham, but—oh, well, I suppose they found it hard to suspect the bridegroom himself. Say, Warry, were he and Ethel much in love?"

"No; I don't know all about it, but there was trouble somewhere. It may have been Ethel's fault. She was as queer as could be all the last days before the wedding. And old Bingham seemed to go back on her, somehow. But Ethel was always queer. She fascinated me, because I never knew what she would do next. And she was such a flirt. She would carry on outrageously with somebody else, right before Bingham's eyes, for no reason but to annoy him. Only a week ago, at a dance, she gave all the dances to Fred Benson, just to make Stanford furious, and another night she left the ball-room, and went for a motor ride with Farrish. Why, the very morning of the wedding, she went off somewhere and stayed an hour, and nobody knew where she was!"

"Don't talk about her as if she did wrong; I can't bear it! When I had to sing at her wedding service, I thought I should go right down there and grab her away from that man. Warry, you don't know what it means to sing at the marriage of the woman you love!"

"But I know what it means to stand by as best man!" returned Swift, in such a desolate voice that Hall started.

"Never mind," he said, roughly; "where do you want to go? Back home?"

"No," said Warren Swift, "you have frightened me. I'm innocent of that crime—but I can't face the music! Oh, help me, Hall! How could I bear to be suspected of anything so horrible! Can't I get away on some plausible pretext, and come back when it blows over?"

"That's what I'm here for. I don't want to talk to you about it, Warry, but I will help you to get away. Suppose I drive you straight to New York, and let you lose yourself there?"

"But what word shall I send back home? And how? Shall I write?"

"No; telegraph. But what's your excuse?"

"I don't know! Gene, I'm in a blue funk over the whole matter. Advise me. What could I say?"

"Oh, say you've gone to hunt down a clue that you believe may lead to the criminal."

"Just the thing! I wish I had your brain and your ingenuity."

"Shut up, that's all. Understand, once for all, Warry, that I believe you may be guilty. That I'm helping you to make a getaway because I don't want Ethel's cousin mixed up in such a terrible affair. I'm your friend—that is, I used to be—but it isn't friendship that makes me help you, it's regard for Ethel's memory. I'd rather they'd never find the murderer than to discover it is her own cousin!"

"But I'm not," protested Swift, in a weak voice.

"Do you suppose you can convince me or anyone else of that? If you were guilty, wouldn't you say you're not, just the same?"

"Gene, you've got me scared to death! Couldn't I make them believe me innocent, really?"

"Not unless you are, and the real murderer can be found. Oh, Warry, what a thing you are! If you were innocent, you would have convinced me right now, without trying at all! You couldn't have helped it! They say it isn't always true that 'murder will out,' but you bet it's true that innocence will out! If you had no hand in this crime, you would be so enraged at this false suspicion that you'd fly all to pieces in your protestations. Now, wouldn't you?"

"I don't know, Gene. I'm all nervous and trembling. The whole affair has upset me so—"

"And well it may! Now stop! If you say another word I'll put you out here on the road and you may get to New York as best you can!"

Warry Swift said no more and after a rushing trip, Hall landed him at a small hotel on a side street, in the city.

"There," said Hall; "go in there, register under an assumed name and stay till morning. Then go where you choose and do as you choose. I've done all I can for you!"

"Don't leave me, Gene! Oh, don't leave me!"

"Yes, I will leave you! Be a man, if you can, which you can't! And save your skin, if there's any way to do it."

Hall whizzed away, leaving Warren Swift at the entrance of the hotel. The fast little runabout went back to Boscombe Fells, and it was between three and four o'clock in the morning when Eugene Hall crept wearily to bed. But not to sleep. For hours he pondered as to whether he had himself committed a crime in aiding Warry to get away. But, his thoughts concluded, I'd do more than that to save Ethel's family from disgrace.

* * * *

The next day was Sunday, and the funeral day of the martyred bride.

None of the family or near friends were visible at the services, so the crowd of curious ones that thronged the house had no means of knowing whether they were present or not. The choristers had been asked to sing, but had one and all declined. Nor could they scarcely be expected to do so, after the awful experiences of the wedding ceremony.

Robed in her wedding gown, from which the long court train had been removed, Ethel Bingham lay, as if asleep. The wound in her temple was covered by soft folds of her hair, and her beauty was unimpaired. The wedding ring gleamed tragically on the white hand, and if further impetus or energy had been needed to rouse the indignation and revenge of the residents of Boscombe Fells, that sight would have supplied it.

More than one declared as the assembly dispersed that justice must be done and that young life avenged. More than one was willing to go to work personally to hunt down the scoundrel who could do the diabolical deed. But the majority were so awed and appalled by the unusual awfulness of the tragedy, that they could say nothing but repeated exclamations of horror and grief.

The family and other close friends were gathered in upper rooms of the big Swift house.

The services over and the lovely clay about to be carried to the grave, Stanford Bingham stood, alone, arms folded, in the upper hall, unable to go down to the room where the casket stood. "No," he said, to himself, "I cannot look at her again, I positively cannot!"

And then, for the hall was darkened, Eileen Randall came softly up to him. Silently, she laid her hand on his, and whispered: "Do go down, dear, it will look so much better."

"I can't, Eily," he whispered back; "it would kill me! Poor Ethel, how *could* I treat her so?"

"Do you regret her death?" and Eileen's beautiful, sirenic face came close to his own. The girl's beauty was of the compelling type; her small, dark face was truly that of a siren, and Bingham caught his breath, as he felt her nearness. Silently he grasped her hand and just breathed into her ear, "Eileen, are you mad? Hush!"

But a quick glance showed the girl there was no one in hearing, and she murmured again, "Tell me, you *shall*! Do you regret her death?"

And as if it were fairly torn from him, Bingham made the admission, "No!" and then they moved apart.

"I *had* to hear you say that," said Eileen, looking at him strangely, "for I may never see you again alone." And she went slowly away into a room and was lost to his view.

Stanford Bingham pulled himself together, and went straight downstairs, out of the house, and home.

Eileen went to Mrs. Swift. "Dear lady," she said, "let me be a niece to you now. You will miss Ethel so dreadfully, but mayn't I fill her place in some ways?"

"Oh, Eileen, you do not know what has happened! Ethel's death is enough, too much, to bear, but now—now, Warry is gone!"

"Gone! What do you mean?"

"We had a telegram this morning—his father did—and Warry says he has gone to hunt down a clue to the—the man who killed Ethel."

"Why, Mrs. Swift, are you not glad of that? Don't you want the man to be found?"

"Yes, but, Eileen, I feel so strangely alarmed over it. Why should Warry go off like that? Why go so late and so secretly? He isn't a detective. It isn't his business to hunt a clue! Why didn't he tell Mr. Ferrall what he had discovered, if anything, and let Mr. Ferrall go or send somebody to Chicago?"

"Yes;" and Eileen looked disturbed; "yes, I should think he would have done that. Where is he?"

"He sent the telegram from New York late last night. Everson got it this morning. He wouldn't tell me at first, but I insisted on knowing where Warry was, and he had to tell me."

"Of course; why any secrecy in the matter?"

"Eileen, don't you, *can't* you see? They have begun to suspect Warry of Ethel's death!"

"Warry! How absurd! Why, he was awfully fond of Ethel."

"I know, but that horrid detective has been here asking all sorts of questions—"

"This morning?"

"Yes; Mr. Swift just told me. I made him tell. He is all broken up, for he knows that under their smooth talk they suspect Warry, my Warry."

"Don't cry, dear; I'm sure you are needlessly alarmed. If Warry says he's gone to hunt a clue, he has. You know that, don't you?"

"Oh, I don't know anything! Everything has happened so fast and everything is so horrible, I don't know *what* to believe!"

"Well, keep faith in Warry. You know he wouldn't do anything wrong."

"Oh, Eileen, I *don't* know! I must speak my fears to somebody or I shall die! I can't tell Mr. Swift, poor man, he is distracted now. Shall I tell you?"

"Yes, dear, tell me. What is it?"

"Only this. Ethel went somewhere the morning of her wedding. Somewhere, secretly, and she had a telephone call just before she went, and I'm afraid—afraid—"

"You're afraid she went out to meet Warry?"

"Yes, that's it."

"But, Mrs. Swift, what harm could that do? I doubt very much if Ethel did such a thing, but even if she did, I can't see why it disturbs you so."

"Oh, I don't know. It's a sort of intuition or premonition or something. You know Warry was devoted to Ethel. He didn't want her to marry Mr. Bingham at all."

"Why did she marry him, anyway?"

"Oh, Eileen, she was desperately in love with him. Desperately!"

"But she has been in love with every man in town."

"No, she hasn't. They were in love with her, lots of them, but she never cared for one of them as she did for Mr. Bingham."

"I wasn't sure of that."

"You may be. Ethel was always a flirt. The poor child couldn't help it. Often she has said to me, laughingly, that she would rather flirt than eat. And every new man she met, she never rested until he had proposed to her. And they usually did. Then she would laugh and refuse them."

"But she cared for Stanford Bingham?"

"Oh, my dear, she worshipped the ground he walked on! Some people thought she was marrying him for his money, but it wasn't so. No, indeed, she just adored him."

"Well, then, she certainly never ran away on her wedding morning to meet Warry or anybody else!"

"No, I suppose not. But what did she go for, that she wouldn't tell about?" But the question was unanswerable.

CHAPTER 8

THE FAMILY LAWYER

The District Attorney and Detective Ferrall set to work in desperate earnest. The community was impatient for the discovery of the criminal, and every impulse of law and order clamoured for developments.

The disappearance of Warren Swift was considered by some a sure proof of his guilt. By others, it was deemed an equally sure indication of innocence.

"Why," they said, "would he run away if he had committed crime? That would be most incriminating. Only a fool would do that!"

To which the retort very often was, "But Warren Swift *is* a fool!"

"What we want to get hold of," said Somers to Ferrall, as they consulted over the case, "is facts, and clues, and evidences."

"We do," agreed Ferrall, "but the facts are pretty much before us; the clues are simply *nil*; and the evidences are not forthcoming."

"Let's sum up. Here we have the fairly sure proof that that shot came from the west side of the church, after the bride had turned round. I hold that lets out Mr. Bingham and presupposes Warren Swift, or some party unknown, either outside the church or in it."

"Good as far as it goes, but it doesn't let Mr. Bingham out, because he may have employed an accomplice either inside the church or out. And, too, it's especially bewildering because we've no idea how far away the assailant stood."

"That is most unusual, but it seems as if everything connected with this case is unusual. Who ever before heard of a case with no witnesses to question, and yet there were hundreds of witnesses! No clue to the slayer, and yet he must have stood elbow to elbow with some onlooker. No sound, smoke, or odour to give an idea of the direction the shot came from. By the way, I never knew before that even an automatic could be so literally soundless and smokeless."

"It's true, though," said Ferrall. "I actually went and discussed the matter with the inventor of one of the models. He says a man may stand close to you, and fire the thing from his pocket without your being aware of it in any way."

"From his pocket?"

"Yes; or concealed in a handkerchief or any such thing."

"And he aims it—"

"He says the instinctive aiming of the pistol by placing the index finger along the barrel is surer than the eye aim—that is, that the aiming in this way is practically sure with so short a barrel. You know the whole thing measures only a trifle over four inches. Of course, it would be a different matter with the aiming of a rifle where it is possible to sight from the butt to the muzzle of the barrel. He gave me a demonstration of this instinctive aiming, and the results as shown on the target were surprisingly accurate."

"And could you hear no sound of the discharge?"

"It was almost unnoticeable in the pistol he used. I kept up a conversation in ordinary tones while he discharged the pistol two or three times, and had I not known that he was trying out the game, I would scarcely have noticed the explosion, though he was only a few feet from where I stood. Again, I watched for any sign of smoke from the pistol. While it was slightly visible, I can understand how to one not looking for such a thing it would not be noticed."

"You went into the matter pretty thoroughly."

"Yes; I even did this. I measured the tone value of the shot and as nearly as I could discover, using the pocket, hammerless model, of .25 calibre, the tone is A-sharp minor, which comes pretty near being the note of the first crash of the organ in the exit music."

"As I see it, then, the sound could not be detected, so closely did it harmonize with the given musical note."

"Yes; you know I held from the first, that the organ would drown the sound and that the preoccupation of the people would prevent their noticing the smoke. Also, the heavy odours of flowers and perfumes would go far toward neutralizing what slight smell of powder there might be."

"And joining to all this, the fact that the bullet entering the brain through a thick roll of hair gave no chance for powder marks, we have every avenue of evidence from the weapon closed."

"And yet, we have negative proofs, if that is the right term. Granting that no smoke, sound, or odour was noticed, we know that it must have been a pistol of that sort that was used. Granting that, so far as we know, no one near the slayer was in any way cognizant of the deed, it proved that a larger or ordinary pistol could not have been used."

"Then, to trace the pistol."

"And that is next to an impossibility."

"But buyers of pistols must give their names."

"But they never give their real names. At least, not people of criminal intent. And I have inquired more or less from places where pistols may be bought, but I've had no enlightening results."

"And so we're as much afloat as ever."

"So far as the pistol is concerned, yes."

"But, at least, it gives us a working hypothesis of a man intelligent enough to own a pistol of that sort; the common tramp or rough would not have one. Also, a man cool-headed enough to stand and aim with deadly intent at a most critical moment, and in most thrilling circumstances. Not everybody is so unmoved by the sight of a wedding ceremony that he can be perfectly cool and calm."

"But he *did* do it. You can't get away from that! Whoever shot that girl did it premeditatedly and in cold blood. He came to the wedding prepared for it and he carried out his plan. To be sure, we cannot say that he was resolved to shoot at that identical moment. He may have been obliged to watch his chance. But he mingled with the crowd, got his chance, and used it."

"You're bound to have him inside the church?"

"I think so, for one outside ran so much more chance of discovery. Still, the shot may have come through a window. However, we can't work any further from that end. I think we must turn to the motive next." And here, Detective Ferrall looked uncomfortable. "In the case of a young girl who has always been a belle and a coquette, it may be that we must look for a discarded suitor."

"Ah, you're hedging away from your certainty of the bridegroom's implication in the matter?"

"Since discovering the shot came from the other side, I can't feel so sure of his guilt. I think he may have had an accomplice who fired through the window, or from the west side, but criminals of this sort don't often have accomplices."

"I agree with you. Now, as to young Swift. What about his sudden departure?"

"Might mean one thing or might mean another. I hate to think of his shooting his cousin; but who is there that we wouldn't hate to think of as doing the deed?"

"And Swift's motive?"

"That's the point. He was her heir. But if he knew that her marriage nullified her will, then he might have killed her to steal the diamond, and if he didn't know about the will, he might have killed her to get the money."

"Who drew up the will?"

"Farrish is the Swifts' lawyer. Guy Farrish, the one in the choir."

"Let's go to see him, he may give us information of some sort."

After some inquiries the two men found that Farrish was at his club and went there to see him. They found him in the smoking room, but he asked them into a smaller room where they might talk privately.

The County Club, an enormous and elaborate structure, was the home of the most exclusive club in the vicinity. There were members from many of the smart New York suburbs, and the clientèle was chosen with meticulous care and precision. To belong to the club was in itself a full guarantee of all that a man ought to be.

Guy Farrish was one of the directors, and was on the eve of being made president. His manner toward his two callers was perhaps a trifle patronizing, but it also showed a kindly courtesy. He was in no doubt as to their errand, and gave them immediate, grave attention when Somers said:

"We understand, Mr. Farrish, that you are the lawyer of the Swift family and connections?"

"Yes, Mr. Somers, I have been that for several years, but they are not people who require much of my service."

"We are, at present, interested only in the matter of the will of the late Mrs. Bingham. I believe you drew up that instrument?"

"Yes, about four years ago. Mrs. Bingham, then Miss Moulton, was ill, and fearing she would die, she called me to make her will."

"And its purport?"

"Was to leave all her fortune to her cousin, Warren Swift."

"That will has never been changed?"

"Not by me, or to my knowledge."

"Was the lady's fortune a large one?"

"A matter of twenty-five thousand dollars, or a trifle more."

"And young Swift was her sole and unconditional heir?"

"Yes. The cousins were fond of each other, I believe, and, too, Miss Moulton was an inmate of her uncle's household, she herself being an orphan."

"The lady was of age, of course, when this will was made?"

"Of course. She was twenty-six when she—died."

Guy Farrish was a strong-looking, square-jawed man of about thirty. His manner was calm and his emotions under control, but he faltered over the reference to the death of his late client. As a member of the choir he must have had full view of the tragedy, and it was small wonder it unnerved him to speak of it.

"It is about this will that we want information," said Detective Ferrall, taking up the questioning; "it is true, is it not, that a woman's marriage nullifies her will?"

"Yes, that is true," and Guy Farrish looked straight at the speaker, "but, I hope, gentlemen, that you will not ask my opinions or surmises in this painful matter. As the lawyer of the family, and especially of the victim of the awful crime, I hope I may be excused from grilling or cross-questioning, as I assure you I have no vital knowledge of the matter."

"We have no intention of putting painful questions," said Ferrall, "but some points must be cleared up. Did Warren Swift know that his cousin's marriage nullified her will, and that he would not inherit in case of her marriage, under that will?"

Farrish hesitated before he replied. Then he said, "How could I know that, Mr. Ferrall?"

Instinct told the detective that Farrish did know, and he set to work to get the knowledge out of him.

"I'm sorry, Mr. Farrish, but it is imperative that we discover the truth on this point. I think you do know, and I think you know that you ought to tell, whether young Swift knew this."

Again Farrish hesitated. Then, with a sigh, he said: "If I must tell you, then, yes, he did know it."

"He asked you regarding the matter?"

"He did."

"When?"

"The day before the wedding of Miss Moulton."

"Ah! And, please answer this straightforwardly, is it your opinion that Warren Swift was in love with his cousin?"

"It is my opinion that he was."

"Then, for I need not conceal from you the fact that suspicion of the crime has been directed toward Warren Swift, then, I say, if he was guilty, he might have committed the deed either from the motive of theft of the great diamond or because of unrequited love, or both."

Guy Farrish looked aghast at this plain talk, but he only said: "Your words, of course, are true, but the idea they convey is too preposterous! It cannot be!"

"The whole case is preposterous, Mr. Farrish. I am sure you never heard of such another in your whole career."

"Thank Heaven, I certainly never did!"

"The facts must be faced. If Warren Swift is innocent, investigation cannot harm him. If he had not known that he would not inherit his cousin's fortune in case of her marriage, unless, of course, she later changed her will, he might have been suspected of killing her in order to get that inheritance. But since you tell us he did know, then his motive must have been theft or jealousy."

"Have you any reason to think Warry has the diamond?" asked Farrish, looking thoughtful.

"No real reason, no. But the diamond is gone. Warren Swift is, in a way, under suspicion. He has disappeared. True, he sent a telegram explaining his absence, but we are inclined to take that with a grain of salt."

"You have, then, shifted your suspicion from the bridegroom to the best man. Why?"

"Suspicion is a pretty strong word," broke in Somers. "We have, for the moment, shifted our investigation. And we have done so for the reason that we have proved that the bride had turned round before she was shot. This, it would seem, must place the murderer on the west side of the church. Swift was on the west side, and Bingham was not."

"You, in the choir, could see it all, Mr. Farrish," said Ferrall; "was young Swift in a position to do this deed?"

"In a position, yes, certainly. But so were a hundred other people who were on that side of the church. Why pick him out?"

"Only because he may be said to have had motive. One can't go round and accuse all the wedding guests who were on that side of the church."

"Somehow it seems to me quite as logical as to suspect the bride's cousin."

"You saw nothing to give you the slightest inkling of where the shot came from?" Somers looked closely at Farrish as he said this, for he had a feeling the man was shielding somebody, and who, if not Warren Swift?

"No," returned Farrish, slowly; "I saw absolutely nothing like the smoke of a pistol, nor did I see any movement on the part of anybody as if he were shooting. But this is not at all surprising. Everybody was looking at the bride, no one was looking about for possible assassins."

"Yet you had a clear, uninterrupted view."

"In a general way, yes; but the masses of ferns, palms, and flowers nearly cut off our vision. The choir rail was wound and wreathed, and tall Ascension lilies were between us and the bridal party."

"You seemed surprised that we do not more strongly suspect Mr. Bingham. Have you any cause to think in that direction, Mr. Farrish?" Ferrall shot the question at the lawyer quickly, hoping to take him off guard. But, as he had feared, Guy Farrish looked at him calmly and said, "Certainly not. And if I had, I should not admit it to the public. Mr. Bingham is my friend, and as I am by no means on the witness stand, I most assuredly refuse to discuss his probable, possible, or imaginary connection with this crime."

"But you know, do you not, that unless Mr. Bingham married this month, or next, he must lose his inheritance?"

"That, I think, is a matter of general gossip, and in no way affects my determination not to discuss him with you. And now, gentlemen, may we not consider this interview at an end?"

There was nothing to do but go, and the two callers went.

But as they were about to leave the clubhouse they were addressed by a young man, a member of the club, Fred Benson.

"If I may have a word with you," he began, and both Somers and Ferrall gladly followed him to a secluded corner of the wide veranda.

"I felt I must tell you something," he said, hurriedly, and in a whisper. "If you are trying to get evidence regarding the murder, I can tell you something. I saw you talking to Mr. Farrish. Did he tell you that he met Miss Moulton alone and by appointment on the morning of her wedding day?"

"No," rejoined Somers, looking at the young man, curiously. "Why do you tell us?"

"Only because it was by appointment, and they both seemed to be so secret about it."

CHAPTER 9

THE TURNING POINT

"How do you mean, secret?" and Ferrall pricked up his ears.

"Why, I was walking through the Fells Park, and up near the north end, where it's woodsy, you know, I saw Mr. Farrish waiting round as if expecting somebody. He didn't see me, and as he seemed both disturbed and impatient, I paused a moment, out of sheer curiosity, and then I saw Miss Moulton join him. She glanced around in a frightened way, and then when she saw him she ran to him with a little cry, and they took the path through the wood. It was none of my business, of course, but as the lady was to be married at noon, and as I was to be one of the ushers at the wedding, I felt a sort of right to notice it, at least. But I didn't follow them or intrude in any way. And I'm telling you this only because Mr. Farrish might have learned in that interview some fact that might have a bearing on the mystery of the murder."

"At what hour was this?"

"I don't know exactly, but it couldn't have been much later than nine or so, for after that I had ample time to dress and go to the wedding, and, of course, it took a much longer time for the bride to get arrayed."

"Are you sure it was Miss Moulton?"

"Perfectly sure."

"Thank you, Mr. Benson," said Somers, breaking in on the conversation, "I'll ask Mr. Farrish. It might, as you suggest, lead to some information. But tell me, you were an usher, you say?"

"Yes, Mr. Somers."

"Did you see or hear anything, anything at all, that could give you the slightest clue to the perpetrator of the crime?"

"No, sir; not a thing. Why, it's the greatest mystery in the world! A shot, from nowhere! Invisible, inaudible! No suspect, no motive! I never knew anything like it!"

"You have no suspicions, then, of the criminal?"

"Indeed I haven't! Or I'd soon show him up! I've heard hints of suspicion directed toward the bridegroom, but that's too dreadful to think of!"

"It isn't too dreadful to think of, if it isn't too dreadful to happen, Mr. Benson."

"Come now, what do you mean? That it did happen? But how—how could a man shoot his bride and no one know it?"

"Never mind that for the moment. Granting it were possible, do you know of anything that would make you believe it were probable?"

"Nothing but that speech Stan Bingham made at his bachelor's dinner," and Benson frowned a little.

"Speech? What was it?"

"Oh, we had rather a gay time; you know, bridegrooms' bachelor dinners are not apt to be tame affairs, and we drank toasts to everybody concerned, from the bride down to the chauffeur who would take them away. And at last Warry Swift said 'To the Bridegroom,' and then added, looking at Stan, 'I wish I stood in your shoes,' and Bingham said, 'I wish to Heaven you did!' It wasn't only a horrible thing to say, but the earnest way he said it would make your blood run cold. The whole party shut right up; there was an awful silence, and then somebody began to sing, and the incident passed over. I've never spoken of it to any of the men. Somehow I couldn't."

"And it would seem, then, that Bingham married his bride unwillingly?"

"Well, you must admit, Mr. Somers, it looks that way. Why else would he say that? It wasn't a joke. Bingham has too good taste to make a joke like that; and beside, he said it as if out of the fulness of his heart."

"He wasn't affected by wine?"

"No, sir; Bingham is an abstemious chap. He may have been a little excited, and so, heedless; but that man meant what he said! It was too desperately in earnest not to be true."

"It's a strong point, Mr. Benson, and one that requires cautious investigation. You see the remark might only refer to a man's natural embarrassment on the occasion of an elaborate wedding. There never was a man who didn't dread that ordeal."

"That may be, but I doubt it. I can't think Stan Bingham guilty, of course, but neither can I think that he didn't mean what he said that night."

"It would go far to prove that he only married Miss Moulton in order to inherit his own fortune," said Ferrall. "Even if he married her without loving her, he secured his inheritance, which must have been forfeited had he remained unmarried a month or so longer."

"That is true. Here comes Farrish. I'll disappear, if you want to speak to him."

Fred Benson considerately walked away, and as Guy Farrish approached, the detective spoke to him.

"Just a moment, Mr. Farrish. I must trouble you once again. In the interests of justice will you tell us if you met Miss Moulton, by appointment, or otherwise, on the morning of her wedding day?"

Farrish looked troubled. "I did, Mr. Ferrall, but I had hoped it would not be necessary to tell of that."

"Do you object to telling about it?"

"Not if it is required. I met Miss Moulton at her request to answer a question of hers about her—her property."

"Her will?"

"Yes."

"What was the question?"

"Whether her marriage would nullify her will."

"And why did she want to know?"

"What an absurd inquiry! Presumably, because if it did have that effect she naturally desired to know it."

"Would you mind repeating the conversation?"

"I can't do that literally, but it was to the effect that if such were the case, she wished to make a new will, so that her cousin might still be her heir. I told her she could not do this until after she was married, and then she would better confer with her husband in regard to it."

"Was she annoyed at this?"

"Not annoyed; but she was rather surprised at my information."

"You think then she wanted Warren Swift to inherit her property?"

Farrish stared at his questioner. "Why, man alive, of course I think that! How could one think otherwise, after what I have just told you?"

"One other thing, Mr. Farrish," broke in Somers, quickly, lest the fiery temper of the detective take umbrage at the lawyer's scorn, "do you imagine that she asked you about the will at the instigation of Warren Swift?"

"It may be," returned Farrish. "She did not say so, but it seems unlikely she would start out on such an errand on her wedding morning, unless strongly influenced in some way."

"But you have told us that young Swift asked you this same question the day before the wedding day."

"Did you not?" pursued Ferrall, as Farrish made no response.

"Certainly I did."

"How do you explain that?"

"My dear sir, I don't explain it. Why should I? I have told you these things because you have asked me in the name of justice and law, but I am in no way bound to explain them, even if I could do so. However, it does not seem to me that if Mr. Swift wanted to be informed on this subject it was so very strange to ask his cousin to inquire of me. It may seem peculiar that she chose her wedding morning to take up the matter, but surely I am in no way responsible for my clients' vagaries."

"Of course not, Mr. Farrish," and the District Attorney smiled ingratiatingly; "I thank you for the information you have given us, and trust that if in future we want to ask for more we may have that privilege."

"Of course," and Farrish spoke seriously, "I must tell you anything I can, that will further the ends of justice; but I beg you to remember, gentlemen, that all the parties concerned are my long-time friends, and it is hard for me to give out information that might redound to their being unjustly suspected. Now, you must admit, that if young Warren and his cousin had just learned, or heard, that her will would be made void by her marriage, it was most natural that they should inquire about it. For I know the lady wanted her cousin to be her heir—and that, too, was not surprising, as her husband-to-be is a wealthy man. But all that in no way proves, or even suggests, that the boy murdered his cousin. In fact, it seems to me to point the other way."

"But the diamond—" began Somers.

"I really must ask you to excuse me," said Farrish, courteously, but decidedly. "I am very busy today."

* * * *

"Not a very satisfactory chap," growled Ferrall, as they left the Country Club grounds.

"He doesn't want to chatter," returned Somers; "I think he knows something he's holding back. But if we can get on track of it, he'll tell us. I mean, if we find out the truth, he'll admit it, but he won't tell us first, because he's friends with all those Swift and Bingham people, and he hates to be the one to show them up."

The next day, in the District Attorney's office, the pair summed up what they had learned.

"No, sir," Ferrall declared, "young Swift never did it! He hasn't the force required, he adored his cousin, he knew he wouldn't inherit, and—and, anyway, I'm just *sure* he didn't," he concluded a little lamely.

"Then why did he run away? And, too," went on Somers, eagerly, "remember the scene at the bridegroom's dinner. Swift wished he were in Bingham's shoes. That proves, as you say, he adored his cousin. Well, then, he killed her rather than see her the bride of another."

"That would be motive enough for some men—the dashing, reckless sort, who love passionately, desperately, but not for Warry Swift! Why, man, that dinner episode points far more to Bingham than to Swift. I tell you, Somers, that he did not want that girl for his wife, except that he must secure his fortune. He loves somebody else."

"Who?"

"Miss Randall, the girl who was maid of honour."

"How do you know?"

"I saw some looks that passed between them, and I overheard a few words."

"You're romancing. Have you heard a hint of this from anyone else?"

"Yes. Everson Swift, the bride's uncle, told me that Bingham had acted queer of late, as if he wanted to back out of the wedding."

"Back out of it! Did old man Swift really say that?"

"Yes, and he even agreed with me, in a cautious, tentative way, that Bingham shot the girl."

"Agreed with you? You mean, you forced your opinions down his throat, and he was non-committal!"

"I don't mean that at all! Everson Swift hates to suspect the bridegroom as much as anyone else would, but he can't be blind to facts! He knows no one else would benefit by the girl's death, he knows—"

"Pshaw! He knows his own son will be suspected, if Bingham isn't! *That's* what made him agree to your theories, if he did agree!"

"Nothing of the sort. He knows his son isn't clever or ingenious enough to plan and carry through that crime as it was planned and carried through, and he knows Bingham is. Why, that man is a Machiavelli, you can see it in his very eyes!"

"And just how did he contrive to shoot the lady in the temple that was turned away from him?"

"I'm not sure about that, yet. *If* he had an accomplice, but he's too clever for that. By Jove! Somers, wait a minute, let me think. Seems to me—yes— I'm sure, I've heard that people, after they're shot, keep on for a few seconds with the motions or gestures they were making. Now if he did shoot her, just as she was about to turn, she might have kept on turning, and in the few seconds before she fell dead she might have turned all the way round, or at least far enough to drop her flowers where she did drop them."

Somers stared and thought. "I've heard something of the sort, I admit. Let's go and put it up to Doctor Endicott."

"Yes," said the eminent physician, gravely, after his visitors had put the case to him; "given a determined physical impulse, the muscular body follows this impulse, even though a sudden check is met, as of shock, or even mental determination suddenly applied to change the direction of a movement. That is, if a man turns under an impulse, as hearing his name suddenly called from behind, the mere physical movement would continue as to the turning, even though he were called suddenly from the front at an instant after he had started to turn, and even though the mental idea was to turn to the front again."

The detective and the District Attorney listened attentively as the doctor went on.

"I saw this illustrated once, some years ago, at the time of the killing of Jim Pinney. He was walking toward the back of a long room when a man entered the front door and called out, 'Hello, Jim!' loudly. Pinney turned suddenly, and received the full charge of a Winchester squarely in the front of his throat. However, so suddenly had he turned, that the movement of turning kept up, even after the shot, and when he fell, it was with his face almost exactly toward the back of the room, or practically directly away from the man who shot him."

"That, then, was the case with the bride," declared Ferrall, with a look of satisfaction. "She had just begun to turn, and was so imbued with the idea of turning, that she continued to turn, after being shot by the bridegroom, and consequently fell, having turned all the way round, with her face to the back of the church."

Somers mused. "That would explain a shot in her right temple being fired from the east side of the church," he agreed; "but how could the bridegroom do such a thing unseen?"

"There are two ways," said Ferrall, slowly; "you know Bingham himself admitted having raised his hand to the bride's head, just before she fell—"

"What!" exclaimed Dr. Endicott.

"Yes," Ferrall went on, "Mr. Kennedy in the choir saw him do this, and Mr. Bingham said he did so in order to adjust a pearl pin that was falling from the lady's veil."

"Fishy story!" observed Somers.

"I don't know," returned Ferrall. "I scarcely think the man shot her then. I think he shot from under cover, an instant later. Perhaps the weapon was hidden by the very folds of the bridal veil."

"In that case it was a left-handed shot."

"Bingham is ambidextrous, I found that out. But we have our case clear now. Stanford Bingham is our man! His motive, to rid himself of a wife he did not want, save as a means of securing his fortune. His opportunity, shown by the fact that he stood next her, and that it is not only possible but probable that the victim continued to turn after the shot. Further proof, the disappearance of the great diamond, which we shall doubtless find in Bingham's possession."

"But that was his, anyway," objected Somers.

"We have no reason to assume that he knew that. Both the bride and her cousin thought it was willed to Swift, as a possession of the testator. Why didn't Bingham think the same, and take precaution to secure the gem during the excitement at the time? Otherwise, where is it?"

"We must go to see Bingham," said Somers, abruptly; "and we must not take up your time further, Doctor."

So straight to Stanford Bingham's house the two men went.

A man-servant ushered them at once into the library, where Bingham sat at his desk. He rose, looking a little startled, but asked them in cool, even tones to be seated.

"In a moment," said Ferrall, whose quick eyes had noted a sudden nervous movement on the part of his host. "May I ask if you have yet recovered the diamond that is missing?"

"No, I have not," and Bingham looked straight at the detective.

"Then, pardon me, Mr. Bingham, then may I look into this ash receiver on your desk?"

Without waiting for permission, Ferrall overturned a small Japanese ash-bowl, and in the cloudy heap of cigar ashes that fell on the desk was a small, hard object. Dusting it off with his handkerchief, the detective held up between his thumb and forefinger what was undoubtedly the diamond in question!

"Don't perjure yourself," said Ferrall, sternly, as Bingham began to speak. "I saw you drop the stone in the ashes as I entered the room."

CHAPTER 10

THE WOMAN AT THE WINDOW

Stanford Bingham looked dumfounded. In a confused way he reached for the diamond and Ferrall gave it to him.

"I understood you to say, Mr. Bingham, that you had not recovered the diamond stolen from your bride on her wedding day."

As this was not a direct question Bingham made no answer, and this exasperated the detective beyond endurance. "Did you say that, or did you not?" he thundered.

"I did," returned Bingham, who was recovering his poise.

"And at that moment you were concealing the stone in the ashes of your cigar tray!"

"Assuming that the gem is my own, I have a right to put it where I choose, have I not?"

"Look here, Mr. Bingham," interposed Somers, "we want to ask you some questions, and I, for one, would prefer to approach the matter in a calm, practical way. There is no reason for you to tell any falsehoods about that diamond. It is yours, and—by the way, did you know that it would become your property on the death of your wife, or did you not?"

Bingham stared at him. "I never gave the subject a thought," he replied; "but had I done so, I should have supposed that as my wife's property is all willed to her cousin, her jewels would be included with her other belongings."

"That, then," remarked Ferrall, with a nod of satisfaction, "explains why you secured the gem at the time of your wife's decease."

"What!" and Bingham turned white with anger.

"Spare us your dramatics, Mr. Bingham," and Ferrall smiled unpleasantly, "we are here to investigate the death of your wife, and we admit that our suspicions are turned in your direction. Do you own an automatic pistol?"

"I do not."

"Of course you'd deny it, it was a foolish question," put in Somers. "But, to get at the truth of the matter, did you love the woman you married, Mr. Bingham?"

Again the tortured man paled, but this time he showed fear rather than anger. "I see no reason why I should answer that question," he said, after a moment's pause.

"Then the fact that you don't want to answer it, proves that you did not love her," declared Somers, triumphantly. "If you had, you would have no reason to hesitate."

"Of course I loved her," said Bingham, in a burst of indignation, "otherwise why should I have married her?"

"To get your patrimony," said Ferrall, quickly; "is it not true that unless you were married before next month, you would forfeit your inheritance?"

"It is true."

"And to secure that fortune, you married Miss Moulton."

"You have no right to say that!" Bingham spoke quietly, but his eyes were blazing. He seemed to be holding himself in leash, but with danger of letting himself go at any minute.

"Can you deny it?"

"That I married Miss Moulton to secure my fortune? I certainly do deny it!"

"I'm sorry to say your denial carries little weight. When did you become engaged to the lady?"

"Nearly a year ago. Last August, to be exact."

"And later you endeavoured to break that engagement. Why?"

"Mr. Somers, I deny your right to ask me these questions! If you accuse me of the murder of my bride, say so, and I will know what course to pursue. But these personal inquiries are unwarranted, and I refuse to listen to them, let alone answering them."

"It depends largely on your answering these questions whether we accuse you of the murder or not. We do suspect you, and it is your privilege to decrease or augment our suspicions by your reception and response to these queries. Did you or did you not say at your bachelor dinner, to another man, that you wished he stood in your shoes?"

"I decline to reply."

"Come, come, Mr. Bingham," broke in Ferrall, "you know we are not trying to incriminate you. We are only trying to find out the truth. If you made that remark, merely meaning that you felt the natural embarrassment of a fashionable and elaborate wedding celebration, why not say so?"

Bingham looked at the speaker with a slight smile. "I am not such an inexperienced member of the social world, as to be frightened at the formalities of a fashionable wedding," he retorted. "If I made that remark to a personal friend, I see no reason why I should explain it to a representative of the law, unless I am officially called on to do so."

"Your independence of manner is not an aid in establishing your innocence, Mr. Bingham. We have just come from Doctor Endicott's. He has assured us that the victim of the shot in the church, could have turned entirely around before falling to the floor in her death swoon. This, as you must see, would make it possible for you to have fired that shot."

"My God!" exclaimed Bingham, sitting upright and clenching his hands; "you dare accuse me of that!"

"We dare accuse you, Mr. Bingham, because you had motive and opportunity; indeed, it may almost be said, you had exclusive opportunity. You admit raising your hand to the lady's head to adjust a veil pin. At that moment, you might easily have fired a soundless, smokeless, automatic and—the next moment the bride sank to the floor."

"But—but—" stammered Bingham, "how could—how *could* I? Why, at that moment, I had just shaken hands with the minister who married us. I was speaking to him when—when Ethel fell."

"You are known to be ambidextrous, Mr. Bingham. You could have fired with your left hand, as you adjusted the lady's veil. In the noise and excitement of the organ music and the conclusion of the ceremony, no one was noticing you. All eyes were on the bride. Who else had any cause to wish the lady out of existence? Who else had a motive for wishing her dead?"

"You put very painful questions to me, but since you do ask them, I will go so far as to remind you that the—the lady I married had many admirers. She had refused, to my certain knowledge, several men of this town and elsewhere. Is there no ground for suspecting some disappointed and desperate suitor?"

"All very well, if you can suggest the man, and show that he had opportunity."

"Any one in the church had as much opportunity as I did."

"But not an equal motive. You must admit, that even if a disappointed suitor was so desperate as to want to kill the lady, he would scarcely choose such a spectacular occasion as at her wedding altar."

Bingham shrugged his shoulders. "Such arguments apply equally well to myself. Why should *I* choose the spectacular occasion?"

"Because for you it was a safer chance. Who could believe that a bridegroom could be capable of such an act?"

"Who, indeed!" agreed Bingham; "as you say it is preposterous! Unbelievable! And with no proof of any sort, you have no right to suspect me or to imply my guilt. The Coroner's jury returned an open verdict. What further evidence have you than they possessed?"

"It is that evidence that we are trying to get," answered Somers, gravely. "If you are an innocent man, Mr. Bingham, why are you so little concerned in the discovery of your bride's murderer?"

"I am not unconcerned," and Bingham spoke almost flippantly; "I shall be very glad, indeed, to see the criminal brought to justice, and I regret that I can in no way help you to find him."

But the man's words failed to carry conviction to his hearers. Tall and handsome, Stanford Bingham stood before them, coldly courteous, but unmistakably waiting for them to go. His utter indifference to their mission only strengthened their suspicions of his implication in the tragedy, if not his actual guilt.

"One more question," said Ferrall, speaking sternly; "I ask you if that diamond on the table before you is not the one that hung round the neck of your bride at her wedding?"

Bingham stood silent a moment. He looked at the great gem blazing on the table beneath the electric reading lamp, and then he looked at the detective. "No," said he, after a moment; "no, Mr. Ferrall, it is not."

"Do I then conclude," asked the detective, sarcastically, "that you are the fortunate possessor of two such magnificent stones?"

"You conclude whatever you choose," said Bingham, calmly, and after conventional good-nights, the visitors left him.

"Can't get a thing out of him," said Somers, as they walked away. "But I don't understand that diamond business. Of course, he lied; of course it *is* the wedding diamond, but as it is surely his own, why does he deny it? Why pretend that he has two of them? Of course he hasn't; if he had he would have given both as the wedding gift."

"That isn't necessarily so," objected Ferrall, "but if he had two he would have had no reason to hide that one in the ash tray, when we entered unexpectedly. That diamond business is the most mysterious thing about the case."

"Indeed it isn't; the identity of the murderer is that. The unique and inexplicable circumstances of the murder make it just about impossible to get any definite evidence. If anybody had seen anybody shoot, we would probably have heard of it before this. It will doubtless go down in history as one of the never solved mysteries."

"It shan't do that, if I can prevent," declared Ferrall, vehemently. "I'm not ready to lay down on the case yet. I have a hunch that Bingham is the murderer. I've been fairly sure of it all along, and after seeing him tonight, I'm more convinced than ever."

"Hunches and being convinced don't get you anywhere. Evidence, man, that's what we want. And we haven't a shred, against anybody! No weapon, no witnesses that can tell anything, no accusations, no reason, in fact, to suspect any mortal, human being. If that shot had been fired by a supernatural agency, it couldn't have been more mysterious!"

"But it wasn't fired by a supernatural agency, it was fired by a flesh and blood human hand, and I shall never rest till I find out whose. And I tell you it was Stanford Bingham's! Why, the way he acts proves it. If he were guilty of that murder, to insure himself his patrimony, wouldn't he act exactly as he does? Wouldn't he simply deny in a calm, unconcerned way, and not rouse suspicion by emphatic denials? He's a cute one, Bingham is, and only a mighty cute one could have pulled off the affair. Oh, these thoroughbreds, these aristocrats, have brains, and brains are much needed in the business of a first-class criminal!"

"That's all true," agreed Somers, thoughtfully, "and there *are* points against Bingham. What can we do next?"

"It may be a wild-goose chase, but I'm for going to see that coloured woman who told of seeing a red-headed man with a handkerchief over his hand, in the church. He might have been Bingham's accomplice."

"Rubbish! That Charlotte is not a reliable witness."

"Why isn't she? Anyway, I'm going to question her. Outside of Bingham, there's no one to suspect, unless it might be a rejected suitor of the bride's. There were plenty of those, from all I can gather."

"Yes; Miss Moulton was a heart-breaker. A regular flirt, I'm told."

"More than that. She was engaged consecutively to several men, and she refused Lord knows how many others! Small wonder Bingham didn't want her for a wife, except to insure his fortune!"

"Don't say those things, Ferrall. Even if they're true, have a little respect for the dead."

Ferrall stared. "Got to do my duty," he returned, gruffly. "If the lady's coquettish tendencies brought about her death by some love-crazed swain, and if the discovery of it will liberate the bridegroom from suspicion, surely it ought to be tracked down! Will you go with me to see the black Charlotte?"

"No; I've an engagement. Go on, yourself, and tell me tomorrow what you learn."

That evening Ferrall went on alone to the home of Eileen Randall, where Charlotte was employed. The negress herself opened the door, and as Ferrall told her that he wished to talk to her alone, she led him to the kitchen.

With few preliminary words he asked her concerning the red-headed man she had noticed at the wedding.

"Laws, suh, I done foun' out long ago who dat man was. He was on'y de 'sistant clerk ob Mistah Kaber, de druggist, an' he done cut his hand with a busted bottle de day befoh. I hunted out all dat, an' so I know he hadn't noffin' to do with Miss Ethel's muhduh. Dat he hadn't!"

"Very well, Charlotte. Now, listen. You were outside the church, and might have seen something invisible to those inside. We have concluded now, that the shot was fired from the other side, the west side—"

"Laws-a-goodness, suh, den it *was* dat woman!" Charlotte's eyes rolled fearfully and she rocked back and forth in her excitement.

"What woman? Be careful to tell only the truth, Charlotte."

"Yas, suh; only de troot'! Mr. Ferrall, I seen a woman at de window opp'site de one I was a-lookin' in—"

"You mean you saw her at the first window on the west side?"

"Yes, suh, de front one, nearest de altar, on de west side; an' she jest glared at Miss Ethel all thoo de ce'mony. An' she had a long, capey kind o' garment, like it was a ottermobil cloak, an' she kep' it wrop' 'roun' her, like's if she was cold, w'ich ob co'se she couldn't 'a' been. An' after Miss Ethel done fell ober, dat woman picked up her skirts and ran like de debbil!"

"Where to?"

"Right out towa'd de front gate, an' she jumped into a big motor cah, an' dey scooted off like de wind!"

The recital was dramatic, so much so that Ferrall had doubts of its entire truth. But questioning failed to shake Charlotte's story in any detail. She avowed that it all happened exactly as she had related, and said she had not told of it before because she had been told that the shot was fired from the east side and she knew that in that case the woman she saw could not have fired it.

"How did you happen to pay so much attention to this strange woman when there was so much going on inside the church?"

"Well, suh, I'd been a-noticin' ob huh all along; an' den when dey all began to crowd 'roun' Miss Ethel, and hollah an' cry, I couldn't see nothin' much inside, an' I ran 'roun' to de front do' to try to get in de chu'ch, an' den was w'en I seen de woman gettin' in de cah in such a hurry."

"Who was in the car?"

"Dere was a chuffer an' anudder man. Dey was all strangers to me, suh, an' I don't believe dat cah b'longed in town, 'cause I knows most ob de swell cahs, suh. I'se mighty observin', I allus was, suh, an' I most gen'ally notices all what's goin' on."

"What did this woman look like?"

"Well, suh," and Charlotte's eyes rolled in satisfaction at being allowed to launch into description, "she was a lady what has been a ravin' beauty, suh. An' she's some beautiful still, but she's been too gay, suh, too gay, dat's what she's been!"

"Describe her briefly," and Ferrall frowned at Charlotte's verbosity.

"Yes, suh. She had big black eyes dat shet up most to slits w'en she looked at Miss Ethel; she had black hair, but all I could see ob dat was what was plastered down ober her years. Den she had a peart, bright little face with rosy cheeks and 'ceedingly red lips, too red altogether for a decent woman.

'Pon my soul, Mr. Ferrall, I t'ink dat woman was a chorus girl! I've seen dat sort on de stage an' off, an' she jest looked like dat was what she was!"

"You didn't see her shoot?"

"Laws, no, suh; if I had I'd 'a' told you long ago! But bein' a stranger an' a sinner—oh, yas, suh, she *was* a sinner!—why ain't she de li'l piece ob wickedness what shot our Miss Ethel?"

"We'll look into the matter, Charlotte, and meanwhile, don't say a word about it to any one. Did you have full view of Mr. Bingham during the ceremony?"

"Yas, suh, I sho' did. Mighty han'some he looked, po' man!"

"Yes, Mr. Bingham is a fine man. Everybody likes him, don't they?"

"Yes, suh." Charlotte had become suddenly laconic.

"Even your young mistress admires him, eh?"

"I dunno 'bout Miss Eileen, but laws' sakes! How Mr. Bingham does admire huh!"

"They're old friends?" Ferrall was quietly insinuating, and chose his words with infinite care.

"Not so berry old friends. Lessee, de Randalls on'y came here to lib last September, w'en de school year begun in de 'cademy; an' Mr. Bingham, he nebber saw Miss Eileen till after dat."

"Love at first sight?"

"Mighty near it! I thought for sure Miss Eileen was goin' to cut Miss Ethel out wid dat man, but she didn't. Miss Ethel, she wouldn't let him go. Yo' see, suh—"

"Charlotte! What are you talking about? Mr. Ferrall, what are you doing here?"

Eileen Randall appeared in the doorway, with a face like a thundercloud.

"What does this mean?" she went on; "Charlotte, go to your room; Mr. Ferrall, come with me!"

CHAPTER 11

THE WOMAN THE BRIDEGROOM LOVED

Still frowning, Eileen led the way to the library, where her father sat at his desk. He rose, as his daughter and the detective entered, and bowed courteously to the visitor.

"I found Mr. Ferrall in the kitchen, quizzing Charlotte!" exclaimed Eileen. "What do you think of that?"

Doctor Randall smiled. "There, there, my dear, don't excite yourself. Detectives must use every possible means of getting the information they seek."

"Good for you, Doctor Randall!" said Ferrall; "I felt sure you would understand. Miss Randall took umbrage at my unconventional call on her servant, but I am sure she will forgive me in the interests of justice."

Eileen said nothing, but continued to look coldly disapproving.

"Be seated, Mr. Ferrall," went on the Professor, "and tell me what you have done in the matter of the crime."

"We have done very little," confessed Ferrall, ruefully; "it seems impossible to get any clues or evidence of any sort. Your black servant has told me of a mysterious woman, whom she observed on the day of the wedding, but I scarcely dare hope for any great developments from the information."

Doctor Randall's eyes twinkled. "But if you are a detective, Mr. Ferrall, ought you not to take this or any other hint, and go straight to the heart of the mystery?"

"Oh, I'm not one of those story-book detectives, who look at a victim's wound and immediately say, 'The criminal is a dark-haired man with a cast in his left eye, and a tendency to asthma!' I can read a clue with the next one, but I must have the clue. In this case we have no clues, absolutely none."

"And yet," said Doctor Randall, musingly, "these deductive feats, that you satirize, are merely the result of using common sense and common observation. The more you study them, the less marvelous they seem. Indeed, to me, the wonder is, that a detective can fail to deduce the dark-haired and asthmatic criminal."

"You are pleased to belittle my powers, sir," said Ferrall, trying to hide his anger; "could you suggest, perhaps, a direction in which to look for these illuminating clues?"

"I am not a detective, but I am a scientist, a professor of psychology, and as such, I have learned to realize what an exact science criminal investigation has come to be. It all rests on facts. There is no room for unsupported theories or imaginative solutions. Here, for instance, in this case, you have the fact of the murder of Ethel Bingham. You have the fact that she was shot. You have the fact that she was shot in her right temple. You have yet to find the fact of the criminal's identity. But with a systematized study of these known facts, you should be able to find the unknown one."

"Could you do this, sir?" and Ferrall tried hard to keep the sarcastic note out of his voice.

"No; certainly not. I am not a detective. A detective, worthy of the name, must have a comprehensive, exhaustive knowledge of everything pertaining to crime. Not only must he have complete familiarity with every sort of fire-arm or burglar's tool, but he must have an infinite knowledge of the psychology of the criminal mind, and be able to follow its working as accurately as if reading a printed book. You're a professional detective, Mr. Ferrall, and a good one, but you're not a scientific one."

"No, sir, I don't lay claim to psychological hocus-pocus, and—"

"Wait a minute, my dear sir. Only those ignorant of psychology apply to it such terms as 'hocus-pocus.' It merely shows their unfamiliarity with the science, and in no way redounds to their credit. Now, as you yourself say there are no clues in the case we speak of, I will assert that there *are* clues, but they are all psychological ones, and so have been invisible to you."

"Will you, then, kindly show them to me, Doctor Randall?"

Again Ferrall choked down his wrath at his host's attitude, in the hope of learning something of use to himself.

"Don't, father," broke in Eileen, laying her hand on her father's arm. "You are not a detective, and all your visionary reasoning will only hamper Mr. Ferrall, without in any way helping him."

"Don't be alarmed, my dear. Though I would gladly help Mr. Ferrall, I cannot do so, for, as I have said, I am not a detective. No one can be, without giving years to the profound study of one of the greatest of all sciences, psychology of criminalistics."

"You incline to long words, Doctor Randall," said Ferrall, smiling.

"They are necessary if there are no shorter ones for the purpose," returned the Professor testily. "Most so-called detectives have no technique, no system. They know nothing of the impulses that urge or force the criminal to his deeds. They know nothing of the established facts of applied psychology, and what little they hear of them they scorn, thinking thereby to show superiority when really they only expose their ignorance. Had I not shaped my career along other lines, I would have been a detective, for the work fascinates me. But other departments of psychology have claimed my attention, and I have merely noted in passing the wonderful connection between mental processes and criminal impulse."

Now Ferrall took very little stock in this sort of talk, but he determined to get some help from the Professor, if possible, and he turned to definite propositions and repeated what the coloured woman had told him.

Doctor Randall listened attentively, and then said, "But there you are again, Mr. Ferrall. The true detective knows the truth when he hears it. This is not a supernatural faculty, nor is it intuition or clairvoyance, it is merely experience and study. He must know thoroughly how prone human beings are to lie unconsciously. He must realize the impossibility of exact truth telling. Distorted perceptions, lack of a sense of values, uncontrollable emotions, all of these and scores of other influences preclude truth telling, even from those most eager to be veracious. And trained appraisal of these influences is absolutely necessary to a scientific detective."

"Then you make out my case hopeless, Doctor," and Ferrall spoke with a forced jocularity.

But the older man took his speech seriously. "I fear so, Mr. Ferrall. The case of Ethel Bingham can never be solved without the application of the highest type of scientific and psychologic knowledge brought to bear on its mysteries."

"And as that can't be done," said Eileen, "we must be content to let the mystery remain unsolved and the name of the criminal unrevealed. I hope, however, Mr. Ferrall, you will pay no attention to our Charlotte's story. Like all her race, she is imaginative and fanciful. She is inclined often to invent dramatic incidents for the sake of creating a sensation, and I feel sure she has done so in this case. I am convinced, myself, that it would be better to drop the whole matter, for a suspicion directed toward an innocent person would be worse than no suspicion at all."

"Eileen," said her father, looking at her in mild surprise, "why are you taking this attitude? To me it sounds as if you had some hidden reason for wanting the investigations discontinued."

Eileen Randall was accustomed, and had been accustomed all her life to having her father make embarrassing remarks, based on his reading of her thoughts, but in this instance she showed plainly her chagrin and dismay.

Ferrall seized the opportunity. "Yes, Miss Randall," he said, "one would think you were afraid of suspicion resting on some one dear to you."

"How absurd," began Eileen, her cheeks flaming, but Ferrall went relentlessly on: "I feel it my duty to tell you, in this connection, that very grave suspicions are directed toward Mr. Stanford Bingham."

It was one of Ferrall's favourite methods to come out suddenly with a disconcerting statement, and watch for its effects. He was not disappointed.

Eileen Randall turned ghastly white and giving a sharp cry of pain, covered her face with her hands.

"Bingham!" exclaimed Doctor Randall. "Nonsense! I know that man too well to consider such a thing for a moment. Why, he's a fine man! It doesn't require much psychological instinct to know that any suspicion in that direction is rubbish! Absolute rubbish, Mr. Ferrall!"

"Then why is your daughter so unnerved over the mere suggestion?"

"Eh? Unnerved? Are you, Eileen? But that is only natural. Bingham is a great friend of both my daughter and myself. We have known him ever since we came to this town. Last fall, I came here to take the chair of Psychology in the Hillside School, and Bingham was one of the first friends we made, and has proved one of the best. Stanford Bingham a criminal? Never!"

"I'm afraid your friendship influences your judgment, Doctor Randall;" and Ferrall rose to go. "And I'm afraid, too, that we can't secure the services of the sort of transcendent detective you talk about. We'll just have to get along with our own tried and trusty force. But I thank you for this interview. I have learned quite a deal from it, I assure you."

Eileen followed the detective to the door.

"Mr. Ferrall," she said, "have you any definite evidence against Stanford Bingham?"

Ferrall looked at her, searchingly. "Have you?" he said.

"Wha—what do you mean?" and the haughty head drooped and the slight form shivered as Eileen Randall glanced up at the detective with fear in her dark eyes.

"I mean that you have answered my question," said the detective, in a low, exultant tone, as he went down the steps.

Eileen went back to the library. Her father had returned to his interrupted reading, and from his absorbed attitude had apparently forgotten his late visitor. Eileen looked at him and was about to speak, then, changing her mind, she went out into the hall and walked slowly toward a back alcove where a telephone stood. Hesitating at first, and then with an air of decision, she called a number and soon Stanford Bingham answered her.

"I must see you at once," said Eileen. "Can you come here?"

"Certainly. At once. Good-bye."

Eileen hung up the receiver, and paced up and down the hall, waiting.

When she heard Bingham's step on the porch she opened the door herself.

"Come in," she said. "Come into the reception-room. Father is reading in the library, he cannot hear us, and I—I must talk to you."

"What is it, Eileen? What is it—*darling!*"

"Oh, don't! Don't call me that!"

"Why not, sweetheart? You are mine, now. There is no reason any more why you can't be! After this dreadful affair blows over everybody shall know that you belong to me."

In the dim light of the small reception-room, Bingham took the trembling girl in his arms, and held her close. "Dear heart," he whispered, "what is it? What is troubling you?"

"I can't tell you, it seems too wicked to put into words! But they—"

"They suspect me of Ethel's murder? Is that it?"

"Yes! That horrid detective has been here and he says—"

"Well, what does he say?"

"He doesn't say anything definite, but he insinuates, and hints, and implies—that you—that we—"

"Eileen! Does he say that I love you!"

"That's what I mean. He acts as if I—I were trying to shield you from—from suspicion because—I love you."

"And aren't you?" Bingham spoke very softly and his arms tightened round the quivering shoulders of the girl.

"Yes, of course I am! But it's such an unjust suspicion! You didn't do it, how can they charge you with it?"

"How do you know I didn't do it?"

"What a question! I know because I love you. I couldn't love you if you were wicked!"

"*Couldn't* you?" and the low whisper was intense and persuasive.

"Yes!" and Eileen flung her arms round his neck in a mad embrace. "Yes, I should love you if you were the worst criminal on earth! Now, are you satisfied! But I know you only said that to test me! Stan, who did kill Ethel?"

"I don't know, darling, and since I have you, nothing else matters. Don't think me a brute, Eileen, but you know, oh, darling, *you know*, how I hated to marry her!"

"Yet you *would* go through with it."

"How could I help it? She wouldn't let me off; I tried every means to persuade her. I couldn't be such a cad as to *refuse* to marry her after our long engagement. I didn't deceive her. She knew I cared for you, but she wouldn't give me up."

"I know. She was bound to marry you, but she didn't love you, Stan. Not as I do."

"No, dearest, she didn't. Oh, Eileen, be patient with me! I am in a fearful position. Everybody knows I love you, and that I didn't love Ethel, and so—"

"And so they think you killed her. You didn't, did you, Stan?"

"Don't ask me, Eileen! Promise me you will never ask me that question!"

Startled at the vehemence in his voice, Eileen raised her head from Bingham's shoulder to look in his face. He was deathly pale, and his dark eyes were blazing. The girl felt as if a cold hand clutched at her heart. But she looked straight into his eyes. "No," she said, "no, I will never ask you. I know you didn't—but, if you did—it was for me."

"Yes—if I did, it was for you." Bingham spoke almost solemnly, and Eileen shuddered in his arms. "Oh, Stan," she moaned, "don't! I can't bear it! Tell me the truth, whatever it may be!"

"Hush, dear; you promised not to ask that. Keep your faith in me, though no one else in all the world does. Won't you?"

"Yes, I will," said Eileen, and she raised her beautiful face to Bingham's with a look of uttermost faith and trust.

CHAPTER 12

TWO TELEGRAMS

A couple of days later, Guy Farrish was surprised to receive a call from Eileen Randall at his office.

Courteously he greeted her, gave her a chair, and then waited for her to announce her errand.

She hesitated before speaking, but the lawyer felt no impatience as he sat watching the girl before him. In a dainty summer costume of pale buff linen, with a hat to match, Eileen's dark beauty was further enhanced by a cluster of scarlet geranium at her belt and a duplicate cluster in artificial flowers on her hat. A little nervously she played with her buff parasol, and then, in a sudden burst of determination, she said: "Mr. Farrish, will you please tell me anything you know about the murder of Ethel Moulton?"

Farrish looked at her in astonishment.

"What can I tell you, Miss Randall," he said, "that you do not know already? Have you not talked with the District Attorney?"

"Yes, and with Mr. Ferrall. But they know very little, positively. As Ethel's lawyer, I hoped you could tell me something about her personally, that would help me in this matter. For I am trying to do a little detective work myself," Eileen smiled winsomely, "and I so hoped you could help me."

"I wish I might," said Farrish, gazing at her admiringly, "but though you call me Miss Moulton's lawyer, I really did very little for her in a legal way. Of course, she had but few occasions to use my services. I am the lawyer of the Swift family, but even the men of the house rarely have any work for me. In what way did you think I could give you information?"

"In no definite way, I'm afraid. But I thought often lawyers knew secrets about their clients that other people didn't know—"

"And that they were willing to divulge such secrets!"

"Why, yes, if it were in the interests of justice." Eileen's big, dark eyes shone, and her beautiful eager face came a trifle nearer to the lawyer's own. The girl was well aware of her powers of fascination, and voluntarily endeavoured to charm Guy Farrish into a confidence. "I don't know exactly what I want you to tell me, but I do want to know if you know anything of Ethel's private affairs?"

"You probably know, Miss Randall," Farrish said, slowly, "that at one time Ethel Moulton and I were very good friends."

"Of course I know that! Why, I have been told that two years ago everybody said you were engaged to her. But, we all know what Ethel was. A born flirt, an insatiable coquette, a girl who was engaged to one man one week, and another the next."

"Don't speak too lightly of her, please. She was of a butterfly nature, and so fond of admiration that she drifted into affairs—and out of them with equal ease. However, Miss Randall, if in my own acquaintance with her I learned anything of a confidential nature, you can't expect me to tell of it now, can you?"

"Yes, if it will cast any light on the mystery of her death."

"Is that a mystery?"

"Of course it is! Whom do you suspect as the criminal?"

"I don't care to say. But who had reason for desiring her death? Who was near enough to her at the fatal moment to commit the deed unobserved? Who—"

"Stop, Mr. Farrish! I know to whom you refer, and I tell you that Stanford Bingham is as innocent of that crime as you or I. He couldn't do it! He is too fine, too noble a nature! Too clean of heart, and—"

"Stop, Miss Randall! Try to realize that to my experienced ear your assertions are too emphatic to be sincere. They sound rather like the protestations of one who is trying to convince another of what she does not believe herself!"

Eileen's face went white. Her fingers tensely strained themselves round her parasol handle, and her breath came quickly.

"You are a keen observer, Mr. Farrish," she said, controlling herself with an effort. "I will tell you frankly what I have learned myself. I have just come from the Swifts' house, and while there I looked through some of Ethel's papers and letters. I found these two telegrams that arrived the morning of her wedding."

"Brides usually receive a lot of telegrams, do they not?"

"Yes; but read these."

Farrish took the two papers and looked them over with a perplexed glance. One read: "Word my will wedding with go if I remember."

And the other: "Sworn keep I this through you vowed what."

"Some sort of a joke?" he asked, looking inquiringly at Eileen.

"I thought so at first. But I showed them to my father, and he solved the mysterious messages."

"Oh, is it a puzzle? A cryptogram?" and Farrish again pondered over the ambiguous words.

"Not exactly that, but it conveys a concealed warning. I have brought it to you because I hate to give it to the police. I hoped you could help me find out where it came from."

"If you know what it means, tell me, please. I am not always quick at deciphering enigmas."

"Nor I. But my father is very clever at it, and he had looked at these but a moment when he read them intelligibly. See, you must read the words alternately and backward. Begin at 'Remember,' and going backward, take first one paper, then the other."

Slowly, Farrish read as she directed. His eyes stared in horror as he enunciated the message: "Remember what I vowed. If you go through with this wedding I will keep my sworn word."

"Do you believe," he said, slowly, "that this message was sent to Ethel by the—by the man who killed her?"

"Yes, by the man or woman who killed her."

"What do you mean by that?"

And then Eileen told of Charlotte's story of the woman looking in at the west window of the church.

Farrish listened attentively. "Describe the woman again," he said, briefly.

"Dark and beautiful, but from Charlotte's account, 'fast'-looking. Intensely black eyes and hair, and a wicked expression."

"There is a possibility, Miss Randall, that such a woman was there, that she sent these extraordinary telegrams and that she committed the murder. But how could one go about it to find her? Your servant says she was no resident of this town. If she came up from New York—I see the telegrams are from that city—we surely have no clue to her identity."

"That's what I came to ask you. I hoped you might know of some such person who was an enemy of Ethel's. I hate to put this matter in the hands of the police, they bungle everything so. Do you think I ought to, Mr. Farrish?"

"If you look at me so persuasively, Miss Randall, I shall not be able to give you an unbiased answer. If you choose to destroy those telegrams, you may rest assured I shall never disclose their existence."

"But I don't want to do that! I want their sender hunted down and convicted! I'm sure the murderer sent them, and they must be traced."

"But, pardon me if I pain you, Miss Randall, what if they were sent by— by the one who—"

"Oh!" Eileen gave a low moan. "You don't, you *can't* mean Stanford! *Say* you didn't mean that!"

"I mean nothing that you don't want me to mean. But, you *must* see that others—the police, for instance—*might* take it to be his work."

"But it is absurd!"

"Not to an unprejudiced mind." Farrish looked again at the telegrams. "Be frank, please. Don't you *know* that Bingham went to that altar unwillingly?"

Eileen flushed, but she bowed a slow assent.

"Don't you *know* that Miss Moulton practically forced him to keep his part of their marriage compact?"

"How do you know this?" and Eileen's eyes dilated wide with fear at this disclosure of her own secrets.

"You came here to ask me if I knew any secrets of Ethel Moulton's. I know that she wouldn't free the man she married from his promise, although he wished her to, in order that he might marry——"

"Don't! Oh, don't, Mr. Farrish! I don't know how you know these things!"

"Lawyers know many secrets. Now, Miss Randall, don't be alarmed; you may trust me not to reveal the state of things between Bingham and yourself. But you must see that these telegrams could just as plausibly be ascribed to the bridegroom of that unfortunate wedding, as to anyone else. Just for a moment lay aside your own sympathies and look at the case. Indeed, if you are going to do anything in the matter, you *must* look at it impersonally. Here we have an unwilling bridegroom. We have these telegrams anonymously sent. Then we have the tragedy. Is it not obvious that Bingham might have married the lady to secure the fortune that could be his in no other way, and then have her put out of his life by a desperate means, only possible because of his great desire not to have her for his wife, when——he——loved another?"

Across Eileen's mind flashed Bingham's words, "If I did it, I did it for you."

With an agonized face she gazed at Farrish. "I cannot believe it," she murmured. "I shall never believe it."

"Of course not. We cannot believe ill of those we love. But do you not agree with me that it would be better to suppress those telegrams and say nothing that might direct further suspicion Bingham's way?"

"It may be so."

"If you let it alone, the suspicion may die down. After the open verdict of the Coroner's jury, and the entire lack of definite evidence, the police have so little to work on they will be obliged to drop the case."

"But if it should have been that woman Charlotte saw! She calls her 'a little piece of wickedness.' Perhaps the shot was intended for Stanford himself."

"Then that only opens up unpleasant chapters in Bingham's life. Do you want to do that? And, too, I am sure you can never trace that vague, semi-mythical woman, probably existing only in your servant's imagination."

"Did it ever occur to you, Mr. Farrish, that it might have been Warry Swift, after all? I hate to say this, but Warry is a queer sort of nature, and I could believe it of him far easier than of a man like Stanford Bingham."

"So could I. And Swift's sudden disappearance is against him."

"But he's home again, now."

"Is he? When did he return, and what does he say?"

"He came back on Tuesday. He says he went to track down a clue, but it amounted to nothing. The police don't suspect him any more, because they've proved that Ethel could have turned after she was shot, and so they're bound to prove it was Mr. Bingham."

"That is why I advise you, as a friend, if you're anxious to protect Bingham, don't show those telegrams. They're dangerous weapons in the hands of the District Attorney."

"Do you know, Mr. Farrish, what I've just about determined to do? I'm going to send for a friend of my father's, who is a wonderful scientific detective. He can get at the truth of any case."

"And you want the truth revealed?"

"Yes, I do! I am so sure of Stanford's innocence that I am willing to have the matter probed to the utmost. I am going to try to get Alan Ford."

"Alan Ford! Don't do it! Miss Randall, you are sounding the death knell of Stanford Bingham if you get Ford!"

Eileen, who had risen to go, clutched at her chair back. "You mean—" she faltered.

"I mean that Alan Ford is the greatest detective I know of. I mean he will go straight to the heart of this mystery and solve it. And I mean that he will prove beyond all shadow of doubt that Stanford Bingham shot the woman he had just married, in order to secure a fortune!"

Eileen dropped back into the chair. "Please, Mr. Farrish," she begged, "don't say that! You don't really believe—"

"I prefer not to say what I believe. But I tell you if Alan Ford takes up this case, the truth will come out, and if you have any reason to fear the truth, don't put it in that man's hands! I haven't voiced my suspicions definitely, because I don't want to hurt you, but I beg of you, Eileen—Miss Randall, don't, as you value your peace of mind, don't send for Ford."

"Is he so clever, then?"

"He's more than clever. He's a magician! He learns truths where others see no hint, no clue. Why not let the matter rest?"

"Perhaps I will. I cannot say now. I am too unstrung. You have frightened me, Mr. Farrish. I will go now, but may I come and see you again about these matters?"

"Surely! Come whenever you like. I will always see you. I am always glad to see you."

Farrish's tone was a shade too warm to suit Eileen's taste, but she was accustomed to being admired, and rarely met a man who remained unmoved at her beauty and charm.

She hurried home and found Bingham there talking to her father.

"I've been to see Mr. Farrish," she said, as she entered the library where the two men sat.

"Guy Farrish!" exclaimed Bingham; "what for?"

"I wanted to see if he knew anything about Ethel's past."

"Ethel's past! You talk as if she were notorious!"

"No, not that," and Eileen spoke very gently; "but there is much in her life that we don't know about, and as the family lawyer, I thought Mr. Farrish might give me some information."

"And did he?" asked Doctor Randall.

"Not definitely. But he set me thinking. And, father, I've decided that I want you to ask that friend of yours, Alan Ford, to come here for a few days, whether he takes up the case professionally or not."

"Ford, the detective!" exclaimed Bingham. "Oh, don't do that!"

"Do you know him?"

"Not personally; but I know of him. Everybody does. Don't get him, Eileen."

"Why not?" and the girl gazed calmly at Bingham.

"Because, oh, because—I'm afraid to have him come."

"Afraid he'll find out the truth?"

"Yes!" and Bingham's eyes flashed with angry fire. "You know where suspicions are directed. Do you want to bring more trouble on—"

Bingham stopped abruptly. "Do as you like," he said in a hard voice, and turning on his heel he left the house and walked rapidly down the pathway. Eileen ran after him.

"Come in here," she said, gently, urging him toward a small arbour on the lawn. "Now, tell me, Stan, whom are you shielding? I know very well *you* are not afraid of Mr. Ford's investigation, and I know you are fearful for some one else. Who is it? Warry Swift?"

Stanford Bingham took Eileen's face in his two hands. He looked deep into her eyes. For a long moment he gazed hungrily at her, and then with a deep sigh, he said, "Eileen—Sweetheart—don't send for that man. If you do, I will be convicted of Ethel's murder as sure as there is a heaven above us! Don't do it, I beg of you."

With a convulsive movement, Bingham drew her to him, and kissed her passionately on the lips, and then, almost flinging her from him, he left her and walked rapidly away.

After a time Eileen returned to the house and sought her father.

"Do you suppose," she said, "that Mr. Ford could really find out the truth?"

"I am sure of it," returned the Professor, positively. "You see, Eileen, he is of a different calibre from these local detectives."

"You don't think Stan did it, father?"

"Not in a thousand years! Why, Eileen, my entire experience in psychology is all wrong if that man is a criminal! He can't be! It isn't in him!"

"But, sometimes, under great stress of circumstances, mightn't a man who was not of criminal instinct commit a crime—a sort of sporadic instance, you know—"

"Not Bingham! I'd stake my reputation on that!"

"Then, father, let's send for Mr. Ford."

"I'll be glad to, Eileen. It will be most interesting to see him at work."

"Do you think he will come?"

"If he possibly can, he will. We are old friends and he would do for me what he would do for few others."

"But, father, if he should prove Stanford guilty—if he should mistakenly think him so—"

"Alan Ford has no mistaken thoughts. If he proves Stanford Bingham killed his bride, it will be the truth. But, Eileen, he won't prove that."

"And will he find out who did do it?"

"He will. Or, if not, it will be his first failure. I'll write him tonight. I'll ask him to come for a friendly visit, and then we'll await developments."

"And, father, if he does—if he should think Stanford is—is implicated, can we ask him to drop the case?"

"That depends. He won't drop it if he thinks he's on track of the criminal! But don't be alarmed, Puss; there's no danger of his suspecting Bingham, for Bingham is innocent. Mark my word for that!"

But Eileen went away with an agonizing fear at her heart. What if her father should be mistaken in his opinion of Bingham? It was only the opinion of a somewhat erratic psychologist, who was often over sure of himself. And both Bingham and Farrish had urged her not to let Alan Ford come. She pondered long, and then, with sudden decision, she resolved to intercept the letter her father should write and never allow it to be sent.

CHAPTER 13

ALAN FORD

But Professor Randall himself posted his letter to Alan Ford, and Eileen had not her expected chance to intercept it.

And Ford came. An old friend of the Professor's, he was glad to oblige him, and too, the case, as he had heard of it, presented unusual characteristics, and he was not averse to investigating it.

Entering the little library where Eileen and her father awaited him, Ford's presence seemed to fill the whole room. He was a tall man, about six feet three, but with such broad shoulders and such perfect proportions throughout, that one never noticed his height except when he loomed up beside ordinary men. Lean, but as a race horse is lean—strong-featured, with a forceful jaw, but of which one never thought because of his gentle smile; keen grey eyes that looked one through and through, yet so kindly that one never considered himself being scrutinized; in short, a magnetic, winsome personality that inspired confidence and friendliness even in a criminal. Though little over fifty, Alan Ford's hair was silver-grey, the grey of the outside of a clean oyster shell, with fine lines of black in the shadows and white high lights. His eyes, deep-set under dark lashes, were tranquil and a trifle sad, but when his anger was aroused, he seemed to throw off as a garment his pacific air, his eyes flashed fire, his jaw hardened and showed its power, his muscles became visible under his clothing, his whole manner was alert and he looked like a tiger ready to spring. Woe to any one who ever caused him to look like that!

In dress, Ford was a connoisseur, and his carefully built clothes were always correct and never conspicuous. In manner he was a gentleman in the best and finest sense of the much misused word.

Eileen had dreaded his coming, but she could not resist the subtle fascination of his manner as he greeted his hosts. And before she had talked with him ten minutes she was glad to put all her troubles in his capable hands.

"Tell me everything," he said, as, over the tea-cups, they discussed the tragedy.

Supplementing each other Eileen and her father told all the tragic details, and as Ford listened he said little except, "Tell me more."

Briefly, yet graphically, Eileen described the wedding ceremony, and the mysterious death of the bride and subsequent events. Listening intently, Ford nodded his head as he mastered each new point.

"A marvelous criminal!" he said, at last, as if the expression of admiration were wrung from him. "Most murderers are fools as well as villains. They leave clues, more or less obvious; they forget or overlook conditions that fairly shriek incrimination to one who can understand their language; they underdo or overdo their subsequent interest in the case; and their work lacks harmony and plausibility. Now, here, we have a criminal who boldly dared an original plan, a plan so daring and so cold-blooded that we know at once we must look for a genius in crime. No ordinary nature would conceive of a murder at a wedding altar! The very conjunction of terms is unique, hitherto unknown! We need not waste time suspecting a man of low caste or of small education. The criminal is a man of brains, of culture, of poise."

"*Was* it a man?" said Eileen, musingly, and then she told Ford of Charlotte's tale of the beautiful woman looking in at the window of the church.

"It could well have been the work of a jealous woman," Ford agreed; "the human being who can love intensely, is also usually capable of crime. And, man or woman, whoever carries in the heart that deadly, burning acid of jealousy, may, on occasion, give way to the impulse of murder. But the coloured woman's story needs much further evidence and corroboration before it can take shape as a definite suspicion. On the face of it, it seems too daring, too careless of consequences for her to come to the church, openly, and fire through the window, no matter how cleverly she concealed her act. Of course, whoever did it, the act was cleverly concealed, but that would not be difficult, in a crowded church, and with a pocket pistol. It is the master idea, of choosing the circumstances of the deed so cleverly, that makes me know the criminal is a genius. I have long wondered if a crime might not be committed which would be absolutely undiscoverable. This seems to me to present no loophole of discovery by ordinary or by physical means. The only clues must be psychological, not material. We have none of the commonplace evidences of footprints, broken cuff-links, or cigarette stubs. We can only hope to trace the criminal through mental procedure. And that is not an easy task."

"It seems hopeless," said Eileen, slowly; "can you get no idea from the actual facts? Do you care to go to look at the church?"

"I will go, of course, Miss Randall, but I cannot expect much help from that sort of observation. Were there anything to be learned that way, it would have been discovered by your local detectives. For instance, the testimony of the doctor that the bride could have turned round after being struck by the bullet, leaves us no reason to assume the shot came from the left side or from the right. The fact that the bullet entered through her hair and thus left no visible powder mark is another accidental difficulty in placing the distance of the assailant. No, so far as I can see, now, there is no definite, material clue of any sort, though of course, some may yet turn up. Now, for further information about people. To begin with the bride. Was she a lady of varied interests, socially?"

Eileen realized the trend of this inquiry, and replied, "Yes, Mr. Ford, there is no use begging the question; Ethel *was* a flirt, always. She couldn't seem to help it, and she told me often, that she would lead a man on to propose to her, for the fun of refusing him. This is hard to say of the dead, but if you want the truth, that is it."

"But she was in love with Mr. Bingham?"

"Yes—in so far as it was in her nature to love. She had promised to marry him, and even though he—he—"

"My daughter finds it difficult to tell the exact state of things," interrupted Doctor Randall, in his calm, direct way, "but it was this. Stanford Bingham was engaged to Miss Moulton when we came here to live last fall. The pair were not in love with each other—I know that. But Bingham must marry before his birthday of this year, or lose a large fortune. However, when he and my daughter met, it was—"

"Don't, father!" cried Eileen, but the Professor went calmly on, and Eileen ran out of the room.

"Just as well," said her father, "for I want you to understand this, Alan. It was love at first sight with Bingham and Eileen. They tried to conquer it, but they couldn't. Eileen told me only part, but I read the poor child like a book. At last, it was about February, I think, he asked Ethel to set him free, because he loved Eileen. He was frank and manly about it, but Ethel refused to give him up. Many times he asked it, but Ethel held him to his contract, though she knew he loved another. It may be she wanted his money, and it may be she didn't want Eileen to have him. At any rate, I'm sure it was not love for Bingham that made her insist on the marriage, for Ethel had no heart. She proved it by carrying out all her plans, and asking Eileen to be her maid of honour. My daughter's proud spirit caused her to accept the invitation, and what the poor child suffered at that wedding, you may imagine!"

"Do you suspect Bingham of the crime?" asked Ford, abruptly.

"I can't. Like you, I feel the psychology of the case, and every instinct tells me Bingham is not the man to do such a thing. And yet—"

"And yet, was there ever a criminal whose crime was *not* a surprise to his friends? Of course, I'm not speaking now of professional wrong-doers. But this is, in every respect, an exceptional case, and we must look for an exceptional criminal. Not for one whom we would naturally suspect."

"If you talk like that, then I must admit everything points to Bingham. He had motive—not only his love for Eileen, but his natural desire to inherit the money; he had perfect opportunity, he could have done the deed adroitly and unnoticeably; his actions since have been mysterious and a little aggressive; and then, there is the disappearance of the diamond and its subsequent re-appearance in Bingham's possession."

"He said that was not the same one."

"Yes, but it must have been. That diamond business is the worst thing against him to my mind. If he could take and secrete the gem at the moment of his bride's murder, he was cold-blooded enough to commit any crime."

"I'm not sure but that the matter of the diamond is the best thing in Bingham's favour."

"Tell me why. I don't want you running this case with a lot of mysterious theories and deductions that you refuse to share with me. I asked you down here not only to solve the mystery, but to let me work with you, or at least know of your work as you go along."

The Professor spoke peevishly, and Ford smiled. "I'll confide in you, Jim, when I've anything to tell. But I'm not going into this thing as into a game. It's too big, it's too serious. It's the biggest mystery I've ever come across, and I'm going to ferret it out if I can. I don't mind, to you, the apparent conceit of saying that if anybody can do that, I can. It is a case in my own class. I've studied so long and so hard on this class of crime, that I believe I am specially well equipped to work in this instance."

"I know it, Alan, that's why I sent for you. Of course, there's no use in making a secret of our attitude—Eileen's and mine. If Bingham is guilty, I want to know it. If he isn't, I want him to marry Eileen. That's all there is about it. He adores her. He wants to marry her as soon as it's decent. But I will never consent until the veriest shadow of doubt is cleared from his name. I, myself, do not believe he killed Ethel, but lots of people do, and I think he is in a fair way to be openly accused very soon. If you can prevent that, or refute it when it does come, you are a friend indeed. As to fees, I am not rich, but my bank account is yours if you succeed."

"Don't bother about that part of it. I am enough interested in the case to go into it on my own account. What about the uncle and aunt? Are they not anxious to discover the murderer?"

"They profess to be satisfied to leave it all to the local police. But underneath there is the glimmer of fear that their son, Warren, is the criminal. They haven't admitted this, but I know it is true."

"Yes, you told me about young Swift's flight, and he has returned, you say?"

"Yes, came back last Tuesday. Now it is Saturday; just nine days since the wedding. A nine-days' wonder, indeed! But destined to be a longer one, I dare say."

"Not much longer, if I can help it. Now that Miss Randall is absent, tell me more of the victim—the bride. Was she of fine character?"

"It's hard for me to say. The Swifts are among the first families of the town. They move only in the best circles. Ethel was their niece, but she seemed of a different calibre, somehow. She was sly, and well, she was a sort of vampire. Now, my Eileen is fascinating, she can twist any man round her finger, but she is honest and steadfast in her nature. Ethel was engaged half a dozen times before she tied up with Bingham. This is all hearsay, you understand, for I've only lived here since last September, but through Eileen I've heard all the young people's gossip, and Ethel Moulton was never liked by the girls but was always a favourite with the men."

"She was engaged to men of this town? Who were they?"

"I've heard since her death that she has been engaged to young Hall, and to Chester Morton, and to her lawyer, Farrish. Also that she refused Mr. Stone and Fred Benson. These are only reports, but from the people who have long lived here, so I've no doubt they're true."

"Enough to show the girl's fickle nature at any rate. Now I want to meet Mr. Bingham and young Swift without their knowing I'm a detective. Will that be possible?"

"I'll make it so in Swift's case. But Bingham knows of you. By the way wouldn't it be better to keep the fact of your profession a secret from everybody else in town?"

"Yes, except the authorities. I'd rather they'd know. I'll guarantee not to antagonize them or let them resent my connection with the case."

Stanford Bingham came over that evening, unsummoned, so Ford had an opportunity of meeting him casually.

The talk soon turned upon the all-absorbing topic of the murder. It had been noticed by many that Bingham never shunned this subject, but was always willing to talk of it, or to listen to new theories or discuss possibilities. Some argued that this implied his own guilt, others the reverse.

Ford paid deep attention to the two telegrams found in Ethel's room, and which had been received the morning of the wedding. The originals were in the hands of the police, but Eileen had copies.

"This clearly proves," said Ford, "that the bride expected some misfortune or tragedy on her wedding day. This explains why she was so perturbed and nervous both before and during the ceremony. Had she ever mentioned these fears to you, Mr. Bingham?"

"No," said Bingham, fidgeting nervously; "no, of course not. But I couldn't help noticing her extreme pallor and her painfully agitated demeanour when I met her at the altar."

Alan Ford looked at the man curiously. If he were, indeed, the murderer, he was endeavouring, not very successfully, to appear at ease; if not, he was surely excessively embarrassed about something.

The talk became desultory, seeming to get nowhere, and yet, had they but known it, Alan Ford was skilfully leading it, so that at every fresh turn of the conversation he learned something. At last, when the two elder men became involved in a psychological discussion, Bingham and Eileen slipped away for a stroll in the garden.

"Your father's friend is a clever detective," said Bingham, "but he can never fathom this mystery."

"Why do you speak so hopelessly, dear? Mr. Ford has scarcely begun his work yet. He may discover what we have never dreamed of."

"No, Eileen, the secret of Ethel's death can never, *must* never be learned. It is better for us all, that it should not be."

"Stanford, don't have secrets from me! Tell me what you mean by that speech."

"Don't ask me, Eileen. You promised you wouldn't. Just let me forget all these troubles while I am with you. I shall not see you, often, dear. I've decided it's wrong to ask you to link your dear young life with mine. Even though I'm never convicted of this crime, never even openly charged with it, there are scores of people who believe me guilty, and Alan Ford is one of them."

"Mr. Ford! Then, Stanford, show him you're not!"

"I can't, Eileen. I can't prove that."

"But you can tell him so, in a way that he must believe you."

"No, I can't even do that."

"Stanford, dear, you're nervous and worried over it all. Let's not talk of it any more tonight. Let's just be happy together," and in the shadow of an arbour Eileen let one soft, rounded arm steal about his neck and murmured a caressing word.

"Eileen, you drive me crazy!" and Bingham drew her to him in a convulsive clasp. "I *must* have you, dearest, I must have you for my very own. And I can't, while this shadow hangs over me! A shadow I am powerless to remove."

"Tell me one thing, Stan; I promised never to ask you if you *did* do it—but *would* you have done it—for me?"

"Siren! How can you ask such a question as that! But since you ask, I will tell you! Yes, my beauty! My queen! I would have committed, I will yet commit, any crime if necessary, to win you! *You*, you glorious girl! You goddess! You Queen of Hearts!"

Eileen gave a little cry and nestled closer in Bingham's arms. Neither dreamed that Alan Ford was listening to their impassioned words. For a time they were silent, happy in one another's nearness, and then Ford spoke, as if he had just reached the scene. "Ah, are you there, Mr. Bingham? May I speak to you?"

As if in no way intruding, Ford stepped into the old arbour, and the two moved apart, thinking themselves unseen in the gloom.

There was a little chat, and then Alan Ford proposed to walk home with Bingham, and after taking Eileen back to the house, the two men walked away.

CHAPTER 14

A MUSICAL CIPHER

"That boy is scared out of his wits, but he's no murderer," said Alan Ford, as Warren Swift left the Randall house. "I don't altogether understand his extreme fear of my investigation of this case, but I am sure he didn't kill his cousin. He is too inept, too weak-willed to accomplish such a deed. And the motive is insufficient. He knew from Farrish he could not inherit his cousin's money, after she married, and the chance of stealing the diamond was too uncertain for him to take such risks. I don't believe his running away from town that night had anything to do with the matter in hand, unless, indeed, he was actuated by sheer, unreasoning fear. But one thing he said is of decided interest. That his cousin, on the morning of her wedding day, said to him, 'In case anything happens to me—.' She went no further, but that seems to add proof that Miss Moulton anticipated disaster of some sort."

The interview between Ford and Warry Swift had taken place in the library of the Randall home. In accordance with the detective's previous instructions, father and daughter had casually left the room, and Ford had ample opportunity to learn all he wished of the young man's connection with the mystery.

"And so," he went on, "assuming that the bride was fearful of tragedy, we can understand her excessive agitation and her frightened glances, told of by her uncle, by the minister, and by others. So, working on this knowledge, we must search for the man or woman of whom she was afraid."

"And how will you begin?" asked Eileen, her eyes sparkling with interest.

"By looking for the motive. A crime like this one is not committed without a strong motive. It was no impulsive, unpremeditated crime, it was the outcome of a fiendish and carefully contrived plan, which could only have originated in the fertile brain of a desperate, hardened sinner. The casual wedding guest does not carry a pistol in his clothes, unless for a definite purpose. The man, I cannot yet see a woman's hand in it, came to the church and deliberately carried out his premeditated scheme. His success was partly due to his own clever timing of the deed, and partly to the fact that no one looked for or could dream of such a happening. Now, in the absence of material clues we must probe for motive, and that, I feel sure, can best be done by examining the victim's papers or other belongings. We could learn more, I am sure, from a few minutes' work in Miss Moulton's own room, than from a day's examination of the church."

Eileen went with Ford to the Swifts' home. When the detective assured Mrs. Swift that he had no shadow of suspicion of Warren, that lady was entirely willing that he should go to Ethel's room. She herself begged to be excused from participation in the ordeal, and Eileen and the detective went there alone.

"It seems a sacrilege to open Ethel's private papers," said Eileen, "yet it is in the effort to avenge her death, so it must be done."

Alan Ford stood, looking about the ornate room, with eyes that seemed to miss no detail of its furnishings.

His fine face was tense and a trifle stern. Apparently he was forming judgments, not lightly, but with a merciless justice and a keen sense of values.

"The lady was vain of her good looks," he said, at last.

"Why do you think so?" asked Eileen, who was looking a little in dismay at the bundles of notes and papers with which the desk was stuffed.

"Her toilet implements and aids are practical, and have been much used. Some women have these contraptions merely as conventional belongings, but these were her daily servants. How old was she?"

"Twenty-six, but she looked older. I do not say this in a catty spirit, but Ethel, though a very handsome girl, was of the type that ages young, and she never took care of herself in a sane way, but would disregard all laws of health or beauty, and then try to make up for it with creams and cosmetics."

"Yes, that is what I meant. Now, for the secrets of the desk."

"It is a general jumble, Mr. Ford. I doubt if we can find out a thing from it. You know the detective, Mr. Ferrall, has been all through it and found nothing to work on as a clue."

"Well, let us see. Here are diaries, for the last few years. Surely they ought to tell us something."

But a glance through the little books showed nothing of interest. Engagements for parties of all sorts; appointments with dressmakers, photographers, dentists, and beauty parlours filled the pages, but no mention was made of personal thoughts or feelings, as is so often the case with journal confidences.

Here and there among the papers they found bits of music, evidently written with a pen, sometimes on ruled music paper, sometimes with the staff lines also pen drawn.

"Was Miss Moulton musical?" asked Ford, studying these slips.

"Yes, very. And, by the way, Mr. Ford, there was a paper with a few bars of written music found tucked in her glove, after—after they picked her up that day."

"In her glove?"

"Yes; it seems somebody sent it to the minister, Doctor Van Sutton, to be given to Ethel just as she was about to start up the aisle. I saw the sexton give it to her, and she read it and tucked it in her glove."

"Was she affected by it? Did she seem to consider it important?"

"I don't know. She was so nervous, anyway. I suppose it was some sentimental reminder from some of her beaux. You know there were several men pretty much cut up by Ethel's marriage."

"She was a heart-breaker, you say?"

"Yes, indeed! There never was a girl of my acquaintance so attractive to men as Ethel Moulton."

"Yet her beauty was waning?"

"Oh, not really. She was so careless of herself, she resorted to a little artificial help, but it wasn't really necessary. Ethel was a beauty, and more than that, she had a wonderful, an almost magical charm, a fascination no one could resist."

"Yet Mr. Bingham did?"

Eileen blushed. "Mr. Ford," she said, simply, "Stanford Bingham and I were made for each other. By a mere chance of fate he was engaged to Ethel when we met. He acted only the part of an honourable gentleman. He told her the truth and asked her to release him. She refused most positively, so there was nothing for him to do but to marry her. She asked me to be maid of honour, solely to humiliate me and rouse my envy and jealousy. I accepted the post because my pride forbade me to refuse and give her opportunity to gloat over my misery. I practically managed all the wedding details. I was bound she shouldn't think I was wearing the willow!"

"And didn't she think so?"

"I don't know. We never mentioned Stanford after I had agreed to be maid of honour."

"Miss Randall," and Ford gazed deep into her eyes, "*you* had sufficient reason to desire that woman's death."

"I did, Mr. Ford, and I have wondered why no one has voiced suspicion of me. But I did not do it; indeed, the idea is ridiculous; how could I shoot her when I was kneeling at her feet fixing her train, for that's when it happened."

"You didn't do it, Miss Randall, and you will never be suspected. But I feel that you have a motive, and it is motive I am investigating. Now, who had the same motive you did?"

"Stanford Bingham," said Eileen, bravely; "but, Mr. Ford, if your investigation leads you in that direction, I beg you, I *pray* you, to stop it! I agreed to have you come here, in hope that you could find the real criminal! Stanford Bingham never did this thing!"

"Your assertions are of little use. Do you really desire to prove the man's innocence?"

"Do I desire it? I would give my life for it!"

"You needn't do that, but you must agree to help in ways of which you do not yet dream. Could you go through, to use a metaphor, 'fire and water,' to prove the innocence of the man you love?"

"I could," replied Eileen, simply, and her tone was more convincing than any more emphatic protestation could have been.

"Then let us go straight to work. Where is that bit of music that was found in the bride's glove?"

"I took it home with me. It seemed of no value, and then as I thought it *might* mean something, I gave it to Mr. Farrish, Ethel's lawyer. He's musical, you know, he's in the choir, and I asked him if he could see anything in it to suggest any clue."

"And did he?"

"No, he said it was merely a scrap of ordinary music, not an old song or well-known air. I'm not musical myself, and though I could read it well enough to see it was not, 'Thou hast learned to love another,' or anything like that, I didn't know but it might be a bit from the classics."

"Didn't you try it on the piano?"

"No, I didn't think of that. Why, do you consider it important?"

"Can't tell yet. It may be. Suppose you telephone to Mr. Farrish now, and ask him if he can place it?"

Eileen left the room and returned to say that Mr. Farrish considered it a very peculiar matter. He said it was *not* a familiar bit of music, and that he would rather not discuss it over the telephone. If Mr. Ford or Miss Randall would come to his office he would tell them about it, or he would call at the Randall home that evening.

"H'm," said Ford. "I don't want to lose time; suppose we go to his office now."

They started at once, as Alan Ford had examined the papers and letters all he wished to, and had taken a small bundle of them with him. These he sent home by a messenger before they went on their errand.

Guy Farrish received them in his private office, and opened the subject at once.

"It baffles me," he said, with a perplexed expression; "for it seems to me as if it must be a message of some sort. You know what I mean, a cipher or a secret code. For, surely, it is not meant for music."

He handed the little slip of paper to Ford, and awaited his opinion. The detective scrutinized the paper. It was a little soiled and much creased, having been folded into a small wad. It contained several bars of notes, pen-written, and very well done, as if by one accustomed to transcribe music.

Ford whistled the notes as they occurred on the staff. The result was chaotic.

"Rubbish as music," he said, briefly; "I incline to your opinion, Mr. Farrish, it must be a message or memorandum. Unless it is merely a picturesque reminder from some disappointed swain, that the marriage of the lady has turned his life to a hopeless jangle of discord."

"I believe that's it!" exclaimed Farrish. "That would explain it. You see, Mr. Ford, I'm more or less handy at ciphers and cryptograms, and I couldn't even get a start on this in any such direction. You take it, and if you can't detect any hidden meaning I shall believe your view of it correct. It will be a relief to my mind, too, for I hated to think it might be a clue, and yet I couldn't fathom it."

"Very well, I'll take it," and Ford put the paper in his pocket-book. "I, too, am versed in the lore of cipher messages, and if there's a hidden meaning to this music, I fancy I'll read it."

As the detective opened his good-sized wallet, there chanced to be on top of other papers a small photograph of a smiling, girlish face.

"Cap—" exclaimed Farrish, and as Alan Ford glanced quickly up, the lawyer finished the word; "Capital!" he said; "I am glad, Mr. Ford, that you have this case in hand. I want to own up, I opposed your coming, for—well, I'd rather not put it in words, but I had a suspicion of one who may be innocent, and I feared a miscarriage of justice. But since I have met you, I am certain that you will take no steps not entirely in accordance with law and order."

"You may be sure of that, Mr. Farrish," and the interview over, Ford and Eileen went away.

"Clear-headed chap," commented Ford, as they walked along the elm-shaded street.

"Yes; Mr. Farrish is one of our foremost citizens. He will be President of the Country Club this winter, and though it may not mean much to a stranger, that stands for all that is worth while with the people of Boscombe Fells."

Back at the house, Ford devoted the rest of the day to reading Ethel Moulton's diaries and letters which he had procured from her desk.

First of all he devoted some time to solving the musical cryptograms or ciphers, for he soon decided that the bits of musical compositions conveyed hidden messages. None of them was a bit of real music. He took up first the one Farrish had given him, the one that according to Eileen's story had been handed to the bride as she started up the aisle, to her death.

For hours Alan Ford studied it. "It seems as if there must be a key," he said, musingly. "I've no doubt it is the simplest sort of a cipher, if I could but get the key. Usually, I can read these things off like so much print."

But the puzzle continued to baffle his efforts. At last, he took up one of the others. "Why," he exclaimed; "I can read this one!"

Several others were among the papers he had brought from Ethel's desk and he read them all without hesitation.

"Strange!" he said to Doctor Randall, who was working with him, "these old ones I can read, but this latest one is only a jumble of letters without sense."

The messages taken from the desk were all in regard to a proposed journey somewhere. It was evidently the intention of the writer of the cipher notes to keep the matter secret, for only the most guarded allusions were made to dates or places. The papers were much crumpled and timeworn, as if they had been studied carefully.

They gave little information, but it became evident that they were written about a year previous.

"Before we came here to live," said Eileen. "I didn't know Ethel then. Who do you suppose wrote these notes?"

"The man who killed Mrs. Bingham," said Ford, gravely. "They are the work of a strong, determined man who persisted in having his own way, in spite of Miss Moulton's scruples. I am afraid, Miss Randall, that these notes may disclose something questionable in the lady's life. Who is Flora Wood?"

"I don't know, I'm sure; I never heard of any such person. Why?"

"In Miss Moulton's diary, last August, she writes several times of Flora Wood. In one of these ciphers is a reference to Flora Wood. And from the secrecy observed, I can't help thinking there is something wrong. I shall investigate the matter very thoroughly, as it may have a bearing on the mystery. But what I can't understand is reading all the cipher messages easily, except this last one, this one you, too, brought from the church. It may hold the solution of the whole thing, but I can't get at it at all."

"Suppose we get the envelope in which it was sent to Doctor Van Sutton. Could that help any?"

"It might, as a means of tracing the sender. If you will, you might go over to the parsonage and ask for it."

"If it has been kept, but I fear it hasn't. However, I'll go and see."

Eileen went on her errand, and Alan Ford continued to work at the cipher message. But all his efforts to read it were in vain.

"I have the envelope," said Eileen, as she returned later. "The minister had kept it by chance. See, the paper matches it. It was mailed in New York City."

Ford looked eagerly at the type-written address to the minister, and took from the envelope another sheet of the same kind of paper which bore these few words: "Kindly have this music given to the bride just before she starts up the aisle to be married. She will be expecting it."

The words were pen-written, in the style that is called pure Spencerian.

"The hardest kind of a disguised hand to trace!" exclaimed Ford. "Of course, it *is* a disguised hand, no one writes naturally with such careful strokes. It is baffling!"

The letters were formed as carefully as if in a copybook. The slight shading on the down strokes was in accordance with the Spencerian school. In all probability the writer's natural hand-writing was very different. Nor could anything be learned from the typed address. The whole affair was anonymous, and very evidently planned to remain so.

"If I could only get at the message," cried Ford in despair. "Oh!" and a sudden idea struck him, "Oh, Miss Randall, are you sure this is the very same paper that you had at first?"

"The same paper? Why, of course. It's just like the envelope, you see."

"I know. But—who has had this since you received it, beside Mr. Farrish?"

"Several people. Father studied over it, so did Mr. Bingham, so did Warry Swift. And so did Mr. Ferrall. Why?"

"I think the paper has been changed. I think this is not the same message you had at first."

"That may be so," and Eileen looked at the music in perplexity. "But who would do such a thing, and why?"

"I don't know, but I begin to see a little way into the gloom."

And then Ford returned to his reading of the diaries and letters.

CHAPTER 15

FLORA WOOD

Several days passed without much light being thrown on the case, when at last Alan Ford's efforts were rewarded and he discovered Flora Wood. It turned out to be not a person but a place. A sort of inn, or road-house, where motor parties were entertained. While of a rather imposing type and of ornate appointments, the place had a reputation for smartness that was not altogether above criticism. Some men of whom Ford inquired concerning the place, gave a meaning glance and shrugged their shoulders. But it seemed impossible to think of the haughty and exclusive Ethel Moulton having anything to do with such a place.

Ford went there, taking a photograph of Ethel with him.

He learned a great deal. The lady of the house, a Mrs. Ballou, readily recognized the picture. At first she was inclined to be uncommunicative, but Ford persuaded her in the interests of justice to tell all she knew of the matter.

So Mrs. Ballou reluctantly told the story. It seemed that it occurred the summer before, in early August. The young lady, Mrs. Ballou said, came to Flora Wood with a fine-looking gentleman. The pair said they were eloping. They were frank about it; indeed, seemed to look on it as a sort of lark, and showed no seriousness of manner. They planned to be married in the parlour of the hotel, and the man said he would telephone for a minister or a justice to perform the ceremony. The girl was in gay spirits, and asked Mrs. Ballou to stand by her. She assured the landlady that she was doing no harm. Said she was an orphan, and responsible to no one for her actions. They seemed very happy, and Mrs. Ballou contemplated making a little wedding feast for the couple. But before any further steps could be taken, another woman appeared at the house and declared she was the man's wife. There was a terrible scene between the two women, each claiming the man as her own. One strange feature was that no names had been given, and all three refused to give their names. Or rather the man refused to allow them to tell their names. He said his own name was Henry Miller, but Mrs. Ballou knew that was not true. He called for a motor and took away with him the one who said she was his wife. The other lady, the one of the photograph, remained with Mrs. Ballou over night and left the next day. She changed her demeanour and instead of gaiety she showed a sweet, sad side of her character which completely charmed her hostess.

"I was so sorry for her," Mrs. Ballou said, "I was glad to help her in any way I could."

"Do you suppose the whole story was true?" asked Ford, when he had heard this much.

"I'm sure of it. She was a dear, sweet girl. Haughty in her manner at first, but after the trouble she was broken and pathetic. She said she'd rather not tell her name, and I respected her wish and did not ask it. She was utterly crushed at the whole occurrence, and I know she was good and honest. The man was a villain!"

"What did he look like?"

"A fine-looking man, sir. Tall and handsome, with courteous, gentlemanly manners. But a villain! To think of his bringing the lady here with a promise of marriage when he had a wife already! The wretch!"

Ford pondered. It was not a pretty story, even viewed in its best light. If it had no connection with Ethel's murder, and he was very far from sure that it had, what was the use of making it public?

He knew the girl had been impulsive, even rash, and he was not greatly surprised to learn of the escapade. But, except for her own humiliation and chagrin, there had been no real harm done, and why rake up a disagreeable past if it were not necessary? At any rate, he concluded to await further developments of some sort before telling about Flora Wood. And especially, he wanted to learn who the man was, before divulging the secret.

The references in the diary were now explained. There were no definite accounts of the Flora Wood episode, but the veiled allusions could have no other meaning. Also, the musical messages were explained, for many of them referred to the meeting and the journey to Flora Wood, and endearing words about how happy they would be there, and thereafter, being always together.

Ethel had been misled by some man who obviously meant to marry her, although he had a wife at the time. This was villainy enough, but could it be the same man who had killed her on her wedding day?

Ford couldn't make himself think so. In fact, all the details of the matter seemed to him to point to Stanford Bingham as the murderer.

Ford never forgot the strong motive of Bingham for wanting to secure his fortune and not wanting to have Ethel for a life companion. And now, if by any chance Bingham had discovered Ethel's escapade at Flora Wood, that was another reason why he did not want her for a wife. Perhaps he had not known the truth of the story, but had reason to think Ethel was worse than she was. Perhaps he, Ford, had not heard the true story! What if there were more to it, and worse, and, bribed by Miss Moulton, the Ballou woman had not told the truth?

At any rate Ford decided to keep his own counsel until he knew a little more. The police were working vigorously on the case, and though they had not yet reached a conclusion, they were on a widely different track from Ford, and they might be nearer right.

But the detective made an exception in the case of Eileen Randall. Though he did not tell her father, the Professor, he told the girl the whole story of Flora Wood, and asked her if she had any suspicion as to who the man might be.

"No," said Eileen; "it happened before we came here. It was early in August, you say, and we moved here in September. Ethel became engaged to Stanford Bingham in the latter part of August. If she loved this other man, perhaps she took Mr. Bingham in a fit of pique, after the other man treated her so badly."

"You don't think the man in question could have been Bingham himself?"

"Oh, goodness, no! Stanford wasn't married before—before he married Ethel."

"How do you know?"

"Oh, because, I just—*know!* That's all."

"I can't think it was he who took Miss Moulton to Flora Wood, either. But we must find out who it was before we make the matter public."

At that moment Charlotte chanced to come into the library where the discussion was going on. On the table, among other papers, lay a photograph which Ford had brought from Ethel's desk.

"Lawd 'a' massy!" exclaimed Charlotte; "if dat ain't de berry lady now!"

"What lady?" asked Ford.

"Why, suh, de one I seen lookin' in at de winduh ob de chu'ch on de day ob de weddin'."

"Which window?"

"I done tole you 'bout it. De front winduh on de west side."

"Are you sure, Charlotte?" asked Eileen.

"Yas'm, Miss Eily, I'se perf'ly suah. Dat's de one what looked in an' den ran away an' got in de motoh cyar an' scooted off."

"How are you so certain?" asked Ford, interestedly.

"I couldn't mistake huh," returned Charlotte, earnestly. "She was a beautiful lady, right peart an' bright-lookin' as you see in dat picture."

The photograph was indeed that of a bright-looking lady. A beauty, too. Large, dark eyes and black hair, the whole countenance of a Spanish type. The picture had been tucked in Ethel's desk, hidden between some letters. The costume was not strictly up-to-date, but neither was it really old-fashioned.

"We wore gowns like that summer before last," said Eileen, reminiscently. "The picture must have been taken then."

"It would be easy to trace the photograph, if the name of the photographer were on it; but it has been scratched off. Purposely, of course, and very thoroughly. It cannot be traced now."

"Perhaps, after all," observed Eileen, "the picture may have nothing to do with Ethel."

"I am inclined to think, however," Ford returned, "that Charlotte is right in her recognition of the face; and if it is the person who looked in at the church and then went away in a motor, it must be inquired into."

"It sho' is dat same lady," Charlotte insisted, earnestly. "I cyan't be mistooken 'bout dat, no-how!"

The coloured girl went away, and Ford decided to give the picture to the police, as it might be too important a matter to keep back.

As Alan Ford walked over to headquarters, his mind reverted to a half-forgotten impression that lurked in his memory. It seemed to him that when he had called on Farrish, and had accidentally exposed that very photograph, the lawyer had started as if in recognition of it. It was but an uncertain, vague idea, but he determined to go and inquire if it might be so.

Accordingly, he turned and went to the office of Farrish, before taking the picture to the police.

He fortunately found his man in, and asking for a few minutes of his time, Ford drew out the picture and showed it.

"Do you know her?" he asked.

"No," replied Farrish, taking the picture, and looking at it. "But it's a mighty handsome girl! Who is she?"

"I don't know. We found it among Mrs. Bingham's papers. I'm going to take it to the police."

"Why? Has this lady anything to do with the tragedy?"

"That's what I'm trying to find out. I think she is connected in some way, but I've no idea how."

"What do you know? Or don't you care to tell me?"

"Only this; that she is said to have been seen looking in at the church window the day of the murder, and there is a possibility that she might have fired the shot that killed the bride."

"This girl! Why, she looks like a thorough-bred!"

"Oh, I shouldn't say that! To me she looks like a handsome adventuress."

"Yes, in a way, she does; sort of Spanish type. Well, I hope you won't discover that she's a villain, I'm sure. Have you made any real progress, Mr. Ford?"

"I have started several trails, but I haven't run them all down yet. Now, you remember that musical cipher you gave me?"

"Have you proved it to be a musical cipher? It looked to me like rubbish."

"And it is—that is, it seems to mean nothing. But, Mr. Farrish, Miss Moulton had received some several messages that were written in a musical cipher, and in the same general style of bars and notes as that paper shows. How do you explain that?"

"Bless my soul, man! Am I called upon to explain it? And, if so, why?"

"For the very good reason that you changed the papers! The paper you gave to Miss Randall the other day is not the same paper she gave you to decipher. The one that was found in the bride's hand."

"This is strange talk! Explain yourself, Mr. Ford."

"It is for you to explain yourself, Mr. Farrish. Why did you do this thing?"

"How do you know I did do it?"

"Because the other messages in the same cipher all can be easily read, but this one we're talking of is mere gibberish. I believe the message given to the bride before her wedding ceremony to have been a real message. I believe Miss Randall brought it to you, and after you deciphered it, you replaced it by a message written by yourself, which was incapable of sensible interpretation. Did you do this?"

Farrish looked at the detective a moment before he spoke, and then said slowly, "Yes, Mr. Ford, I did."

"Why?"

"Because I wanted to save an innocent man from suspicion."

"Who is the man?"

"Stanford Bingham."

"He didn't do it."

"How do you know?"

"I don't know, except by intuition. I have no proof, as yet."

"Well, I'm sure he didn't do it. But I also felt sure that if that cipher message were made public, it would incriminate him. So I made up one to look similar, but mean nothing. And I'm glad I did it, for you would have read the real one, as easily as I did."

"What did it say?"

"I destroyed it, but it said, word for word, this, 'If you persist in going through with the ceremony, I will surely kill you.' Now, that may have been sent by any one, but with the amount of suspicion already directed toward Bingham, by the police, I feared that the message would strengthen the case against him, and this I did not want to do."

"And, you, a lawyer, did this thing?"

"Yes, and would do it again, if I felt it would save a man from unjust suspicion."

"Why are you so sure Bingham is innocent?"

Farrish looked steadily at Ford. His eyes had a queer expression, and at first Ford did not grasp the man's meaning. At last it dawned on him, and he said, "Mr. Farrish, I understand. You do believe Bingham guilty, and you destroyed that paper lest it really incriminate him!"

"I shall not admit that, Mr. Ford."

"You needn't admit it, I see it myself, now. But I am not so assured of his guilt, and I'm going to clear him, if I can."

"I know you are, and I hope you will. But don't you see that that paper would have been a strong factor to fight against?"

"Why? Could it be proved that Bingham sent it?"

"Would it have to be? You know, as well as I do, that he didn't want to marry Miss Moulton; that he tried every way to get her to release him; that he sent her a telegram the morning of the wedding—"

"What!"

"Haven't you seen that double telegram, sent in two parts; alternate words, to be read backward?"

"Yes, I saw that. How do you know he sent it, or them?"

"Who else? Who else wanted Ethel out of existence?"

"Why are you shielding him? Why don't you want him brought to justice?"

"He is my friend," said Guy Farrish, with a grave look.

CHAPTER 16

HAL KENNEDY

Ford left Farrish with a lot of new ideas. He concluded that the lawyer definitely suspected Bingham of the murder, but out of friendship was willing to suppress what might be incriminating evidence. And yet, it might not. As Ford knew, though he hadn't told Farrish, the musical ciphers were without doubt all written by the same hand, and that hand was surely his who had enticed Ethel to Flora Wood under false promises. There could be little doubt that Ethel did elope to Flora Wood, for the Ballou woman's story was so thoroughly verified by Ethel's diary.

The more Ford thought about it, the more he felt inclined to put the whole matter up to Stanford Bingham. Then, if Bingham were guilty, his manner would probably show it, and if not, he would have a chance to defend himself.

Before doing this, he conferred with Eileen. She thought it over very seriously. "If Stan never knew of Ethel's escapade," she said, "it seems too bad to tell him of it. And yet, it might clear up a lot of the mystery. Yes, Mr. Ford, I say, let's tell him. For, if you don't you say you'll give the picture of that woman to the police, and suppose, just suppose, it should turn out that she is the wife of the man Ethel eloped with!"

Ford smiled. "Why should you jump to that conclusion?"

"Because I am a woman, I suppose, and make my conclusions from my intuitions. That is the only photograph we have found in Ethel's things, of a person absolutely unknown to us. All the others are people I know or her aunt knows, or at least, they are photographs that can be traced through the address of the photographer. This is the only one that has the address carefully scratched out. That makes it peculiar. Add to that, the fact that Charlotte saw this woman looking in at the church, and I believe that story, then why might it not be a picture of the wife who interfered with Ethel's marriage to the man she eloped with?"

"It is possible," agreed Ford; "though a little far-fetched as a conclusion. However, if you are of the same idea, I propose we talk it over with Mr. Bingham."

It required only a telephone message from Eileen to bring Bingham at once to the Randall house.

As succinctly as possible, Ford told him of the revelations of Ethel's diary, and of the facts known of the Flora Wood affair.

To his surprise, Stanford Bingham was furious. His eyes blazed as his listened, and at last he said, "I can scarcely believe it of Ethel! And yet I know it must be true, for it explains some things that were mysterious to me. I asked her, when we became engaged, if she had ever been engaged to anyone else. And she said, 'Yes, twice; to Eugene Hall and to Chester Morton.' But she said these were only boy and girl affairs, one of them occurring while she was still at school, and that she had never really loved before she knew me. Now, as to this elopement, I well know who the man was, must have been. And I could kill him, if it would do any good! But it is all in the past—poor Ethel!"

"You know the man!" exclaimed Ford and Eileen, almost simultaneously.

"Yes; or at least I have the strongest conviction that I do. I won't say his name; you know him, Eileen. But I know that last summer, before Ethel and I were engaged, she went around a great deal with him, and in early August I was away for a week or more, and her aunt and uncle were away, and Ethel, left to her own devices, got into mischief. You know she was a headstrong, impetuous nature, and if she took the notion to elope, she'd fly off like a shot, and with no thought of how sorry she might be afterward! This man is fascinating, young, and of a dare-devil spirit. He is not ostensibly married, that is, no one knows him to be, but if a woman claimed to be his wife, I should not be at all surprised to learn that he had been secretly married. This must be the case, for of course, Ethel would never have gone with a man she knew to be married. Oh, Ethel! How *could* you!"

"And you were betrothed to the lady soon after this?"

"Yes, in the latter part of August. When I returned after my absence, Ethel seemed different, rather quieter and more subdued. Less flirtatious and coquettish. I attribute this change, now, to the experience you tell me about. It would have just that effect on the girl. But the subdued spirit wore away, and during last winter Ethel returned to her teasing, tantalizing ways. I am not the sort of man to be attracted by being piqued, and—well, Mr. Ford, as you already know, I met Miss Randall, and thenceforth Miss Moulton had no charm for me. This may not be a very brave or worthy admission, but it is none the less true. I admit that when I asked Miss Moulton to marry me, it was with the remembrance that I must marry before my birthday in order to inherit a large fortune. But this in no way dishonoured the lady. While I felt no deep love for her, she was at that time the most charming and attractive girl I knew, and her softened, chastened air after her unfortunate 'elopement' made her even more admirable. So it happened, and we were no sooner engaged than I met Miss Randall and knew at once I had made the mistake of my life. I hesitated a few months, and about February I asked my fiancée to release me. This she positively refused to do, and though I frequently requested it, telling her the whole truth, she insisted on my keeping my betrothal vows. I could do nothing but acquiesce. I am not a man who could jilt a woman. But I tell you now, if I had known she eloped in that mad fashion I would never have married her! A woman who would do that is not worthy the name of an honest man!"

Alan Ford looked intently at the speaker.

"Oh, I know what you're thinking, Mr. Ford," said Bingham, bitterly; "you're thinking that with the provocation I had, and with my desire to secure my fortune and my wish to marry Miss Randall, I might have gone through with the ceremony and then rid myself of an unwelcome wife. I admit it does look that way, it does look black against me. But there are reasons why I can't shout my innocence from the house-tops. And yet, if this elopement business is a true bill, there may be another direction in which to look for the criminal. It may be that this man with whom Ethel went off on that mad journey might still be her lover, and might have shot her in a spirit of revenge and disappointed love. He was in the church."

"Who is it?" cried Eileen. "You must tell me, dear! You can't have a secret from me. Who is it, Stan?"

Bingham hesitated, and looked from one to the other. Then, impelled by Eileen's imploring looks, he said, slowly, "Hal Kennedy."

"What!" cried Eileen, "Hal Kennedy! He is a reckless sort, but I didn't know he was ever in love with Ethel!"

"Who wasn't?" said Bingham. "Yes, Kennedy was very much in love with Ethel, but I knew the man well, and I had her promise to drop his acquaintance. When I returned from that trip, I heard some rumours that Ethel had been going around a lot with him, but she denied it, and I believed her. Mark my word, Eileen, if Ethel eloped to Flora Wood last August, it was with Kennedy. But I can't believe he killed her. He is a scamp, a dare-devil, but not a criminal."

"Somebody must be the criminal, Mr. Bingham," put in Ford, "and with a lady of such natural coquetry, I think we may safely assume a man in her own walk of life, with a motive based on love, jealousy, or revenge, or all three. Do you know *this* lady?"

Suddenly Alan Ford showed the photograph of the unknown beauty.

"No," returned Bingham, looking at the picture with little interest.

They told him what they knew of it, and Bingham inclined to Eileen's opinion that it might be the real wife of the man they suspected.

"If Kennedy were secretly married," he said, "at college, say, or after leaving it, that is just the sort of girl he would choose. See how flashy she is, and yet very beautiful. Not of our class, but wonderfully fascinating. Naturally, he tired of her, and either because of real love for Ethel, or just for a lark, he proposed this wild affair of Flora Wood."

"Why not take a photograph of Mr. Kennedy and go out there?" said Eileen. "Then we would know from that landlady if this was the man who went with Ethel."

It was not easy to get a photograph of the young man, secretly, but Ford procured a newspaper picture of him that had been published lately, and the three started in a motor car for the pretty little inn.

It gave Ford great satisfaction that Bingham accompanied them, for though he couldn't believe for a minute it was he who had gone there with Ethel, yet he wanted positive assurance of that.

Mrs. Ballou was not so affable as on the previous occasion, and rather resented further inquiries on the subject.

"I don't know anything about it," she said to Ford, "more than what I've told you. I'm sorry the poor young lady was killed, but I don't want to get mixed up in the matter in any way."

"But, madam," replied Ford, "you're far more likely to get mixed up in it if you *don't* answer our questions. Of course, you will be in no way incriminated. If your story is true, you helped the young lady all you could, and were exceedingly kind to her. Now, I ask you, officially, as a detective, whether this is a picture of the young lady in question?"

"It certainly is," returned the woman as she glanced at Ethel's photograph, "I told you that before."

"I know you did," said Ford, quietly; "now, is this the man who accompanied her?"

Mrs. Ballou took the newspaper cut of Hal Kennedy and scrutinized it. "No," she said at last, "No, it's not."

"Are you sure?"

Again a short hesitation. "Well, I am sure, and yet I don't remember the man so very clearly. You see, he went away, but the lady stayed with me overnight, so I recognize her more easily. And yet, yes, sir, I think I can say I am sure that is not the man."

"Not very satisfactory," began Bingham, when Eileen produced the photograph of the strange girl. "Do you know this?" she asked of Mrs. Ballou.

"Yes, indeed," was the immediate reply. "That is the one who claimed to be the man's wife. He called her Caprice."

"Are you sure?"

"Positive! I couldn't mistake *her*!"

"But," objected Ford, "you tell us that this one went away with the man. Therefore, you saw no more of her than you did of him. But you are not so sure of him."

"It's quite different. She is a most striking-looking lady, a beauty, of a distinct type. I'd know her anywhere. The man was not distinguished, or unusual-looking, and besides that newspaper picture may not look exactly like him. They seldom do."

"That's so," said Bingham. "Yet it seems to me that this is a good likeness of Hal."

"Yes, it is," agreed Eileen. "But we have established the identity of this woman, at any rate. We must get her, somehow, and then we can discover the man easily enough."

"Good reasoning," said Ford, looking at her admiringly. "But how begin that search? Wouldn't it be better to trace Mr. Kennedy's movements last August? Or, even to investigate his past for a secret marriage?"

"I wish the identification of Kennedy with this affair could be more sure before we attack him," said Bingham, looking uncertain. "It's an awful thing to begin to track down a man without positive suspicion. I may have spoken too hastily, when I even mentioned his name."

"You say he was in the church?" asked Ford.

"Why, yes," broke in Eileen, "he was in the choir, you know. There were eight of them who preceded the bridal procession up the aisle, and then they went into the choir loft. It isn't high, you know, it's just up above and behind the minister."

"He couldn't have shot from there," said Ford. "What did he do afterward? After the bride fell?"

"He came into the church parlour, while we were all there," said Eileen, thinking back. "Three or four of the choristers did that, and they stayed till the Coroner or somebody put them out. At least, they all went away then, except Eugene Hall. He stayed longer; I don't know why. It's all like a mixed-up dream, and yet, it all stands out clearly, too."

"It doesn't stand out clearly to me," said Bingham, wearily; "it's like a horrible nightmare. The whole thing is still as unbelievable to me as if it had never happened! I wish we could clear it up."

"We will, Mr. Bingham," said Ford, gently; "there are so many new trails opening up, that some of them must put us on the right track."

After a few more words with Mrs. Ballou, they left, Ford again charging her to say nothing of the matter to anybody, unless it might be the police, should they call. For as Ford and Ferrall were not working in conjunction, the former did not know when the other detective might strike something that would lead him also to Flora Wood.

"Don't use Kennedy's name until you know more," said Bingham, on the way home. "I shall greatly regret having mentioned him, if it is a wrong track."

"Never fear, Mr. Bingham, I shall be very discreet. But I don't place much confidence in Mrs. Ballou's recognition or non-recognition of the picture of him. It is just as she says about newspaper cuts; I've often seen my friends' faces when I couldn't recognize them at all."

"So have I," said Eileen. "And she was sensible, too, in saying that a striking-looking woman was much easier recalled than a usual-looking man."

"The more I think it over, the more I doubt it's being Kennedy, after all," said Bingham. "I believe if it had been she would have remembered his face. And that picture is a good one. Don't say anything about him yet. I think I can get some more light on his connection with it."

"There's one thing, Mr. Bingham," and Ford looked positive, "Mr. Kennedy is musical, and that would point to the fact of his being the author of those musical cipher messages."

"Not necessarily," returned Bingham; "you know if a man is making a cryptogram, he may as well use musical notes as any other characters, whether he is himself a musician or not."

"That is partly true, but the neat way in which these were written seemed to point to one accustomed to writing music, or copying it."

"Are you a musician, Mr. Ford?" said Eileen, impulsively.

"No; that is, not to be able to transcribe notes without great care and difficulty."

"Then you wouldn't notice. But father says that a real musician dashes off his notes like fly tracks, and would never make those very painstakingly correct notes that all the ciphers show."

"That's doubtless true," said Ford. "Doctor Randall is a most acute reasoner. I shall look on those ciphers hereafter as the possible, if not probable, work of one not a musician."

It was characteristic of Alan Ford to accept in all good will a hint from any source that seemed helpful, and it never occurred to him to feel any chagrin that it had not been his own thought. He was too great in his own line of work, to mind taking help from any one in whose reasoning powers he had confidence.

Reaching the Randall house, Ford went off by himself to collate his notes, and the other two were left alone.

In the dim, cool living-room they stood, and Bingham held out his arms. Eileen went into them like a bird to her nest.

For a moment or two he held her close without a word.

Then he whispered: "Oh, Eileen, my own, my darling, if I could only have found you sooner, before I became involved in this awful tangle of horrors."

"Never mind, Stan, dear, it was not to be. Let's be thankful, instead, that we've found each other at all. Oh, Stan, I am awful wicked, I know I am, but I'm glad Ethel is dead. Are you shocked too much at that? Don't be. I can't help it. I love you so, and now I can have you some day for my very own."

CHAPTER 17

THE CIPHER SOLVED

Bingham *was* shocked, but more at the expression of the thing than at the idea itself.

"If you are wicked, I am, too, dear," he said, softly; "I cannot put it into words as you do, and yet, I cannot regret anything that gives me you! Eileen," and he held her from him while he seemed to devour her with his eyes, "you are a siren, a witch! For you I would say anything, admit anything! I shrink in horror from the awful circumstances of Ethel's death, but I welcome the thought that it leaves me free for you. My goddess, my queen! No man ever loved a woman as I love you! Do you believe it, dear heart? You *must* believe it! Tell me you do!"

"Yes, I believe it, dearest, but I want your name cleared before all the world."

"It never can be, Eileen. You must be content, darling, to have me always under the stain of a possible crime."

"But couldn't it have been Hal Kennedy?"

"Of course it was Hal who eloped with Ethel—the cur—the beast! But he didn't shoot her. Hal's too easy-going and good-natured to kill anybody. And why should he?"

"For the best reason in the world. Because he loved her, and couldn't bear to see her marry you!"

"You're imagining, Eileen."

"Yes, but why mayn't it be true? Hal had long been in love with Ethel, and after his plan of wrong-doing was frustrated, he tried, we'll say, to get rid of his wife. Then, if he couldn't do that, perhaps he was bound that if Ethel couldn't be his wife, she shouldn't be anybody's, and so—"

"So he shot her at the altar? No, dearest, Hal couldn't do it."

"But—but his wife—if that woman Charlotte saw *was* his wife—oh, Stan, it's all so mixed up! There's no light anywhere!"

"There's the light of our love, dearest. Let us go away from this town. What do you say to going far away from here to live? Your father could get another professorship, and if he didn't it wouldn't matter. I will always take care of him."

"But it looks like running away. I want you cleared, dear."

"I've told you, Eileen, you can't have that. Be satisfied, my precious girl, with *not* discovering the murderer."

"I don't understand you, Stanford. Ethel was your wife, you can't deny that. Why aren't you desperately anxious to find the criminal and see him punished? Any other man would be."

"There, there, my own girl, you promised not to ask me questions that I can't, I won't answer."

"Not if I beg you to?" and Eileen put her lovely arms round his neck, and looked deep in his eyes with her whole soul of love shining from her own. "Not if I coax you like this?"—and her lips came close to his own, a rare caress, for Eileen as yet had permitted few kisses from him.

Bingham drew his breath sharply. "Stop, Eileen!" he cried. "I can't bear it! If you kiss me, I will tell you everything!"

"Then tell!" and the warm, red lips met his.

The entrance of Ford interrupted the scene.

They heard his step outside, and with a quick movement they fell apart. Eileen, too shaken to speak to Ford, left the room by another door and fled upstairs. Bingham pulled himself together and faced the detective. Ford made no apology, for it was their habit to go about the house at will, and no room was deemed private.

"Why don't you confide in me, Mr. Bingham? Surely, it would be better for all concerned. You must know I will make no wrong use of anything you may tell me, and there are so many bits to this puzzle, that it may well be, a stray hint or two might join them so as to present a perfect whole."

"I'll have to tell you one thing, Mr. Ford, for if I don't, I fear it will come out in some other way, and make even more trouble. What do you think of Warry Swift in connection with the case?"

"Young Swift? I haven't thought much about him. He seems a negligible quantity. Ferrall tells me they talked about him at first, but there is positively nothing to connect him with the crime. He did run away, I believe, but he soon ran back, with some cock-and-bull story about a clue that no one believed."

"Yes, that's all so, but, Mr. Ford, he took the diamond from—that was loosed from my—from Ethel's throat as she fell."

"Young Swift took that diamond! How do you know?"

"I saw him. As I have told you, the whole dreadful scene stunned me, but as I stood there watching them lift Ethel up, I saw the diamond fall to the floor, it hung from a mere thread of a chain, and I distinctly saw Warry pick it up and put it in his pocket. I will say this for him, he did it like a man in a daze, as if he scarce knew what he was doing, or as if he took it for safe-keeping."

"Why haven't you told of this?"

"Because I couldn't bear to bring Ethel's cousin under a possible suspicion."

"More than that! A very obvious suspicion. But Ferrall tells me you have that diamond."

"And I told Ferrall I hadn't. And I told the truth. Warry went away, you know, and when he returned, he came to my house, and gave me a diamond, saying that he had picked it up and kept it for me, and there it was."

"Well?"

"Well, Mr. Ford, that was not my diamond that he gave me, but a paste stone just like it, which he had doubtless had made, or otherwise procured while he was away."

"And Ferrall saw it?"

"Yes, they, Ferrall and Somers, chanced to come in while I was examining it to make sure. Startled, and anxious on Warry's account, I dropped the stone into my ash tray. Ferrall saw me do it, and picked out the stone. Being dusty with ashes, he assumed it was the original. Perhaps he could not have told the difference between the two, anyway, but all over ashes he certainly could not. However he asked me if it was the stone I gave to my bride as a wedding gift, and I said it was not. He didn't believe me, but I didn't care. I only wanted to keep Warry's name out of it all, till I had time to think what to do."

"Are you not over-anxious about young Swift?"

"Mr. Ford, I feel decidedly guilty toward the Swift family for having treated Ethel as I did. Don't think I don't realize what a wrong I did her in turning my heart from her to another. I couldn't control my affections; but none the less I feel sorry and ashamed of it all as it affected Ethel and the Swifts. So, not wanting to get any member of the family into further trouble, and especially Warren, who is the idol of his parents' eyes, I tried not to let his theft of the stone get out. You can see for yourself what the next thought of him would be."

"That he was the murderer, of course!"

"Yes, and I don't believe for a moment that he is. But the least breath of suspicion against him would break his mother's heart."

"Of course it would. I'd like to see young Swift."

"I've been wondering whether to go to see him or not. He knows I saw him take the stone. He knows I accepted the one he returned to me, without a word of objection. And I would be willing to let him keep the real stone rather than have the story get out. But he is not a clever man. He is quite capable of trying to dispose of it in a way to expose himself to discovery. No one could sell that diamond without being asked for its history."

"Is it famous?"

"Not by name, and it is not internationally known. But it is big enough to be familiar by description to many dealers, and it is too valuable to be casually sold. Warry is sure to get into trouble if he tries it, and I feel sure he will try it."

"You don't think he is the murderer?" and Ford looked keenly at Bingham, without appearing to do so.

"He isn't capable of a deed of blood. He is too timid and lacking in courage. Besides, what could be his motive?"

"Disappointed love?"

"No, I'm sure not. He and Ethel were always chums, and though he was more or less in love with her, he knew it was hopeless. No; Warry, I'm sure, took that diamond because he saw it there on the floor and couldn't resist the temptation. That's the whole story."

And it was. The two men went to see Warren Swift, and by tactful questioning and gentle measures they brought him to confess that he had done just what Bingham supposed. He had seen the stone fall from Ethel's neck, and had picked it up for safe-keeping. He had thought Bingham saw him, but was not quite sure of it. So he pocketed the stone, and took it home with him. It was after that that temptation assailed him. He was deeply in debt, and in danger of humiliating exposures. He reasoned with himself, that as Ethel had willed him all her property, and as he had learned that her marriage nullified that will, he had no hope from that source. Bingham might help him, but in the circumstances he hated to ask help, so persuaded himself that the gem, being Ethel's, was, in a way, his.

But this story was not told straightforwardly, or even coherently. The two men only got it out of him by careful and kindly questioning. Warry Swift was a nervous wreck, a ne'er-do-weel, who could never be a man.

"I don't know," was his usual reply to their queries as to his motives or impulses.

"It ought to be mine," he repeated, sullenly, over and over. "Ethel wanted me to have all her stuff, and this was hers when she died."

"Never mind the diamond, Warry," said Bingham. "I mean, never mind who is the legal possessor of it. You have it still, haven't you?"

"Yes; I was afraid to try to sell it."

"And you may well be. Now, give it back to me, and I'll pay off all your debts and let you start with a clean slate."

"You're a good fellow, Bing; you always were good to me. Here it is," and from an inner pocket Warry produced the gem and handed it over to Bingham.

Ford looked at the miserable apology for a man. Swift was pale and haggard; his face was vacuous and weak. Surely he never had the necessary nerve to commit murder. And yet—who could say?

Stanford Bingham, too, looked at him thoughtfully. "You're nothing but a boy, Warry," he said; "and you never will be. But at least, you can be a good boy. Now, don't say a word about this diamond business to any one. I will take care of it. But tell us, if you can, whether you chanced to notice a woman looking in at the church window during the ceremony?"

"A good-looker? A regular beauty? Yes, I saw her, while I stood there with you waiting for Ethel to come. Who was she?"

"What did she look like?"

"Oh, dark, sort of wicked, rather foreign, but a hummer, all right. Who was she?"

"We don't know. Did you see her do anything?"

"Nope; just stood there looking in. She must have been up on something, outside, for her head nearly reached the upper window sash. She rested her hands on the sill. I had just noticed her, when the procession started up the aisle, and I never thought of her again. Why? What about her?"

"Nothing," and Ford looked stern. "Now, see here, Mr. Swift, if you want to be helpful, please answer questions, but don't ask them. First, what do you know of your cousin's acquaintance with the young men of the town, before she became engaged to Mr. Bingham?"

Warry smiled a little. "Only that they were all daffy over her—and she led them all a dance."

"To be definite, then. How did she treat Mr. Kennedy?"

"Hal? Oh, she liked him some. He was dead gone on her about a year ago, just before she was engaged to Stan. But Ethel didn't care specially about him. He had no money and no prospects. Just one of her beaux. She always had forty 'leven."

"Do you know Kennedy well?"

"Yes, pretty well. We went on a fishing trip together last summer, and that's when I found out that he was hopelessly in love with Ethel. We were gone all August, and he poured out his troubles to me like I was his father confessor."

"All August? Last summer?"

"Yes; mother and dad were away, and I had the month's vacation, and so did Hal. We went up to Lake Placid."

"And stayed the whole month? Are you sure?"

"Sure I'm sure. Why?"

"Did Kennedy stay with you the whole time, or was he away a few days?"

"All the time there. Never budged. There were some girls there we liked, and we just loafed around, and fished daytimes, and danced evenings. Why?"

"Nothing," reiterated Ford, and Bingham said, "Warry, I'm going to do all I can for you; I'll say nothing of this diamond affair; I'll help you financially, and any other way I can; all on condition that you repeat no word of what we have said to you, and that you say no word to any one concerning Ethel's death. I mean, of course, in the way of suspicion or evidence. You know nothing, and, if you think you do, consult with me before you tell what you know. I tell you all this, for the police will doubtless try to quiz you. Remember, if you give them any hint of what Mr. Ford and I have talked to you about, you need not look to me for help with your affairs."

The boy promised obedience as humbly as if he were a reprimanded child, and the two men went away.

"A sad example of a mother's spoiled darling," commented Bingham. "Warry Swift will never be a man, because he never was trained to be one."

"He hasn't much material to work on," said Ford; "there must be some natural force before the twig is bent."

"No one who knows him can ever connect him with murder," said Bingham, positively; "and, by the way, his story of the Lake Placid trip seems to let Kennedy out."

"It seems to, but I'm not prepared to say that it does. Going that way? Good-bye, Mr. Bingham; I've an errand across the street."

The men parted, and Ford went to the office of Guy Farrish. The lawyer was out, and a bright-faced boy admitted him.

"When will Mr. Farrish return?" Ford asked.

"Said he'd be back soon, sir. That's all I know."

"I'll wait," and Ford seated himself at Farrish's desk, ignoring the chair the boy indicated for him.

With a deliberate air he began to open the desk drawers. The boy stared. Then he fidgeted. Then he said, "Say, mister, do you think I'd ought to let you do that?"

"Oh, I guess so," returned Ford, carelessly.

But when he had opened several unlocked drawers, and then with a queer-shaped bit of wire began to pick at the lock of one that would not open, the boy interfered.

"Stop! you!" he cried. "If you don't I'll telephone the police."

"Oh, I wouldn't do that, if I were you," said Ford, smiling genially at the boy. "You see—I'm sort of connected with the police myself. Just keep quiet, my young friend, and I'll see that things go all right for *you*."

Something in Ford's eyes or manner convinced the boy, and he said no more.

"Besides, I'm through hunting now," said Ford, pleasantly; "I've found what I want."

What he wanted seemed to be a small, much folded bit of paper. When opened out it showed this:

Absorbedly interested, Ford pored over it, and the boy stared at him, both alarmed and fascinated at the strange procedure.

The door opened, and Guy Farrish came in. The boy, turning scared eyes, saw his master clench his hands and set his jaw as he saw the intruder, but Ford did not at once look up.

"A—hem," said Farrish, with a quizzical smile.

Ford raised his head, and smiled at his host. "Ah, Mr. Farrish, have you come back?"

"I have. Is it asking too much to desire an explanation of this rather unusual scene?"

"Not at all. I wanted to see the bit of music that you said you had destroyed."

"You doubted my word?"

"To be frank, yes, I did. But you certainly have no objection to my seeing this."

Guy Farrish looked thoughtful and a little sad. "I have not, Mr. Ford. None at all. But I am quite willing to admit that I do not like the way you have chosen to get sight of it. I know you are a celebrated detective, and so have rights that ordinary citizens do not possess. But I did not know they included breaking into a man's desk in his absence."

"Perhaps I have overstepped my rights in my eagerness to see this especial bit of paper. But you were not here, and I was in rather a hurry and so—"

"How did you know it was there?"

"Miss Randall remembered seeing you put it in this drawer the day she brought it here to you. Then when you told us you had destroyed it, I thought, perhaps, you might be mistaken."

"I was not mistaken," said Farrish, gravely, after he had sent his boy out of the room and closed the door. "I saved the paper, but I did not want you nor anyone else to see it."

"Why not?"

"You know why not," and the lawyer passed his hand wearily across his brow. "Because it definitely incriminates Stanford Bingham in that murder business."

"Might it not be better, after all, Mr. Farrish, for us to face this incrimination out in the open?"

"I'm not sure but it would, Mr. Ford. If you think so, go ahead."

"As you know, I am working for Mr. Bingham's interests. I do not think he killed his bride, and yet, I cannot find evidence in any other direction. Perhaps if we hunt down this cipher clue, it may turn in his favour instead of against him."

"Then do so, by all means. I am truly glad to cease trying to shield him from suspicion. I did substitute another paper for this, in the hope that the matter would be dropped. But since it isn't, I admit my part in the matter, and now turn the whole affair over to you."

"Thank you, Mr. Farrish, for your co-operation. And, also, for your good-natured acceptance of my intrusion here."

"Oh, that doesn't bother me. I knew as soon as I saw you, what you were after, and that you would disturb nothing else. And as I have no objection to your having the paper, I overlook your method of getting it, and set it down to the love of the detective nature for spectacular performance."

"Yes, we *are* credited with dramatic inclinations. Now let us read this together. You found the key?"

"Yes, without any trouble. But have you?"

"Very well put, Mr. Farrish! I'm not surprised that so keen a man as yourself should suspect me of trying to learn the key from you by pretending to know it myself. Let us each write it down."

Without looking at each other, the two men wrote on bits of paper, and then exchanged the slips.

Both nodded sagaciously.

"To one familiar with ciphers it is an exceedingly easy one," said Farrish. "Merely the two clefs; A being the ledger line below the bass and the alphabet running directly up the lines and spaces."

"Bringing Z on the first ledger line above the treble clef," added Ford.

"Yes. So simple an arrangement could scarcely fail to be seen at once by the expert. But it is admirably obscure to the general reader."

"There is decided artistic ability in the arrangement of the time and measures," went on Ford. "Now, to decipher it."

Ignoring the real letters of the notes on the staff, and counting the alphabet directly from A on the line below the bass, there was no trouble in reading:

"Last warning. If you marry Bingham I will surely kill you."

CHAPTER 18

A DOWNWARD COURSE

"Fancy a bride getting that, and then going right on to the altar!" said Farrish, in a low, awed tone; "yet that is just what she did do."

"And you think Bingham wrote this?"

"Who else?"

"But it speaks of Bingham in the third person. It must have been sent by some one else."

Guy Farrish looked at Ford in astonishment. "I thought you were a detective!" he said. "Can't you see that is just what a man *would* do, to turn suspicion from himself?"

"I thought of that," said Ford, "but I wanted to see if you did. If Bingham sent this, of course he wrote his own name to seem as if some one else did it. At any rate the hand that wrote this, wrote the other cipher messages found in the lady's desk."

"Were there many?"

"Not many. Four or five. It was from them I learned the cipher. How well the notes are made. Bingham is not a musician, they say."

"No, and a musician does not make notes like those. One used to writing music, transcribing music, does it this way."

With a few careless strokes, Farrish dashed off a few bars, thus:

"Yes, I see. By the way, a man's music manuscript is as individual as his chirography, isn't it?"

"Indeed, it is. We do lots of it in the choir work, and I know most of the fellows' notes at a glance."

"And none of them are like these ciphers?"

"Oh, no; they're all more careless. Some of them are almost as illegible as stenography, to a layman."

"When you made the dummy message to give back to Miss Randall, you copied these notes pretty accurately."

"That was no trouble. Those painstaking, colourless signs are far easier to copy than a musician's work. I doubt if any one could copy *my* notes so that I couldn't detect the difference."

"I doubt it, too. Well, I'll jog along. I'm obliged to you for your frankness and courtesy. I'll take this paper, and I think I'll turn the whole cipher matter over to the police. I'm not in any way working against them, though not exactly with them, either. That man, Ferrall, is a bright fellow. He goes slowly, but surely."

"Think so? Somers told me he had the habit of jumping at conclusions."

"He has landed nowhere as yet, but you can't tell; he may have something big up his sleeve."

"If I can help you in any way, Mr. Ford, call on me."

"When you're in or out?" and Ford smiled broadly.

"In for choice. I've been pretty good-natured about your 'burglary' of my desk, but I don't mind telling you, I don't care for that sort of thing as a practice."

"Neither do I, Mr. Farrish, and I promise you, on my honour, never to do it again."

Ford went for a long walk, after leaving Farrish's office. He wanted to straighten out his thoughts and tabulate his facts.

"But," he said to himself, "my facts are so few and so definite, they don't lead anywhere. They just state the case and stop. We have the shot, and no weapon. We have the crime and no suspect. We have clues but no deductions. That cipher business, now, is a picturesque clue—with the Farrish complications almost a bizarre one, and yet where does it lead? Only back to the fact that the victim was warned, more than once, before she was killed."

A long walk, and a long cogitation brought Ford back with a positive hunger for more of the immediate facts of the victim's death. He visited the Coroner, the other doctors, the District Attorney, and the undertaker, and returned to Doctor Randall's a little late for dinner.

As this was an unusual occurrence, he was forgiven by the two who waited for him.

He showed Eileen the cryptogram Farrish had given him, without, however, telling her how he had first obtained it.

"Yes," she said, "this is the one I had first. This is the very one that was in Ethel's glove. I recognize the way the notes run, though I couldn't remember them without the paper. What does it mean?"

Ford told her. The girl refused to believe that the use of Bingham's name was a ruse of his own to direct suspicion away from himself.

But to Doctor Randall it seemed plausible!

"I don't suspect Stanford," he said, "not for a minute! I *know* Stanford isn't guilty. But justice makes me say that I *do* think a man who could conceive and carry out the deep plot that *was* carried out by somebody, would be quite capable of tricky messages of just that sort. I mean, I don't think it strange that Farrish, if he believes Bingham guilty, thought at once that the use of Bingham's own name was a clever ruse."

"I don't know what to think," said Ford, wearily, "but I don't want to talk about it any more tonight. I'm going straight from the dinner table to my room, and I beg to be excused from coming down again this evening. But, tomorrow, I'd like to have a pow-wow with you, Jim, and discuss who's who in Criminalistic Psychology."

Undeterred by the fear of long words and incomprehensible phrases, Eileen insisted on being present at the conference next morning. The three shut themselves in the library, and told Charlotte to admit no one.

"Unless it's Mr. Bingham," the Professor added.

"He isn't in town," said Eileen; "he's gone to New York for the day."

"To begin with," said Ford, frowning, as he stood cutting the end of his cigar, "somebody has been lying. Now, of course, we can't expect criminals to tell incriminating truths, and it is up to the detective to find out who the liars are. Mr. Ferrall thinks that Mr. Bingham and young Swift are both guilty, or have guilty knowledge. Now, wait, Miss Randall," as Eileen began to speak, "Ferrall is a sharp man, and he is undisturbed by personal prejudice or bias, which you and your father cannot say. I've lots of confidence, Jim, in your brain, and mind, but you've got to lay aside your certainty that Mr. Bingham is guiltless, and view this thing squarely for a time."

"All right," agreed the Professor, equably, "I'll hear your points, as you present them, with a calm and impartial judgment. But my belief in Bingham is not because of my friendship for him, it is because I have yet to see anything to point toward his guilt."

"There *isn't* anything!" broke in Eileen.

"This is to be a serious talk, Miss Randall," said Ford, not unkindly, "and unless you are content to listen quietly, I would prefer that you go away."

"I'll be good," promised Eileen, "please let me stay."

"I've learned something new," Ford went on, "that is, it's new to me. I should have inquired about it before, but I had so many other matters to attend to. It seems that when the doctors probed for the bullet, they found that its course into the brain was not quite straight. That is, while there was no evidence as to whether the shot was fired by a right or a left hand, there *was* a slight trend downward as if it had been fired from a point a little higher than the wound itself."

"You don't say!" exclaimed Doctor Randall; "why was this not noticed or commented on before?"

"Nobody seemed to consider it of any importance, as the down grade of the course was very slight, and the fact, though noted in the Coroner's report, made no impression on anybody."

"It seems to me of utmost importance," said the Professor, thinking deeply.

"And to me," said Ford. "Now, remember, Jim; keep your mind unbiased, remember the remarks made about Bingham's having raised his hand to adjust a veil pin, directly before the bride fell. Also of course, before she turned, but it has been shown that she may have turned after being shot. This would, if Bingham shot her then, cause the bullet to go a little downward, as his hand would be higher than her temple, where the shot entered."

"Yes," agreed Randall, "go on."

"Also," Ford continued, "if the shot had been fired by a woman, by any one, outside a window, that too would presuppose a higher point of aim, and the bullet would slant down a little."

"Go on."

"Also, and in spite of Warry Swift's alibi for young Kennedy—he might have been lying—also if Kennedy had fired that shot from the choir, the course would have been downward."

"From the choir! Oh, that's not possible. He would have been seen. But if that woman at the window were Kennedy's accomplice, if she is his wife, and if she acted under his commands, then you have a point there—for to fire in at the window would cause a bullet to go rather downward."

"It *must* have been that woman!" said Eileen. She spoke quietly, but with shining eyes as if greatly rejoiced. "It couldn't have been Stan; even if he did fix Ethel's veil pin, he wouldn't have raised his arm so high. That pin was just behind her ear! And of course, it couldn't have been Hal Kennedy, from the choir loft: everybody would have seen him! The choristers would, any way, and the audience, too. Of course it was that woman! Whether acting for Hal, or on her own account—she did it!"

"By the way," said Ford, looking in his notebook, "it was Mr. Kennedy who told Ferrall of the bridegroom's touching that veil pin just before the bride fell."

"So it was!" cried Eileen. "Of course then it was at Hal's orders, under his compulsion, that the woman fired. If she's Hal's wife, he could make her do it."

"Why?" said Doctor Randall. "I mean, why did he make her do it?"

"Because he was in love with Ethel, and wouldn't let her marry Stan. I know Hal Kennedy! He's a very devil! And since this woman, this Caprice, as he called her, wouldn't let him marry Ethel when he wanted to, he took his revenge this way!"

"Eileen," said her father, "that's a plot worthy of a melodrama, but it's hardly possible in civilized society."

"A murderer isn't civilized society!"

"But he may move in it, and the plan you've laid out is too wildly improbable, my child. Now, I think, Alan—"

The telephone interrupted their talk.

Eileen picked it up from the table and answered the call.

"Some one is asking for you," she said, handing it to Ford. "It's a lady's voice."

Ford took it and informed the speaker of his identity.

"I want to be sure," said the voice, a pleasant, feminine one. "Is this Mr. Alan Ford?"

"Yes."

"The detective?"

"Yes."

"Then I want to tell you that *I* shot the bride in the church, and it is useless for you to pursue the case farther—or—or, to make any arrests."

"Indeed! And who is this speaking?"

"As if I should tell you that! I have safe-guarded this—this conversation, you can never—never trace me—but I feel it my duty to—to prevent the prosecution of—of innocent persons."

"Thank you. And answer one question, will you? Are you Caprice?"

The response to this was a wild shriek, in which dismay, fear, and horror were blended. A shriek so loud and piercing, that Eileen and Doctor Randall heard it clearly, though Ford still held the telephone. And then silence. The call had shut off, no questioning met any further reply, and with that loud scream ringing in their ears, the three looked at each other.

CHAPTER 19

CAPRICE

"I don't like it!" said Ford, as after vain attempts to get further word, he hung up the receiver and set the telephone back on the table. "That woman—you heard her scream?"

"Yes," said the other two.

"That woman was scared to death! She said to me that it was she who shot Ethel Bingham, but she didn't!"

"How do you know?"

"Because she was being forced to send that message! I distinctly heard a man's voice, low, but threatening, prompting her what to say, and muttering at her. She stammered, and her voice trembled. She was in deadly fear of somebody who was with her!"

"You called her Caprice," said Eileen.

"That was a venture. I've been very curious about this Caprice person, and I sung out that name to trap her. She screamed then, but whether because I used that name or not, I do not know. But I am certain that she is not the murderer, whatever her name is. It may be the murderer himself was making her telephone as she did. Perhaps at the pistol's point."

"If it was the woman who looked in at the window," began Doctor Randall, "perhaps she did do the shooting and was forced to tell of it by her conscience. Women are queer that way."

"She was forced to tell of it," agreed Ford, "but not by her conscience! There was a very terrifying man who compelled her to send that message."

"And why did he do it?" asked Doctor Randall, and then answered his own question. "Because he had forced her to shoot that day, and now, fearing detection of his part in the matter, forces her to take the responsibility on herself. Can't we get at this woman?"

"There is nothing so difficult as to trace a telephone call," said Ford, "but I'll try."

However, after a long session with the Central and Information, he succeeded in learning only that the call was from New York City.

Eileen went white. "Don't follow up this thing," she begged. "If this gets to Mr. Ferrall's ears, he'll insist, I know he will, that this woman is mixed up with Stan, somehow! Why, Mr. Farrish said, if we proved a woman to be an accomplice, it would doubtless open up unpleasant chapters in Stan's life! Of course, it has nothing to do with the case, but—but Stan is in New York to-day—and Mr. Ferrall would say—"

"That's so," said her father, "Ferrall is ready to pounce on anything that can be made to point toward Bingham. If some man forced this woman to send that message, we'd better look it up ourselves, or keep the matter quiet for the moment."

"But," objected Ford, "as you both believe in Bingham's innocence, it would be a whole lot better to let these things come out, and be truthfully explained. If we can trace that Caprice woman, it will, of course, go far toward freeing Bingham from suspicion, for it will expose the man with whom she is really connected in the matter."

Ford looked at the other two keenly as he spoke. "You see," he went on, "you are not so sure of Mr. Bingham's innocence as you want to be!"

"I am!" protested Eileen, stoutly; "but I know Mr. Ferrall is not; and I don't want to give him a chance to twist evidence to incriminate Stanford, when it really doesn't."

"I don't like it!" Ford said again, as he walked up and down the room. "This telephone message complicates everything, just as I thought I was getting things straightened out."

"Perhaps it's a trick or hoax of some one's," suggested the Professor.

"No, sir-ee!" declared Ford. "If you had heard that tremulous timid voice, saying words that were commanded—well, that 'Caprice' woman must be found, that's all!"

"Reason it out," said Doctor Randall. "Granting the woman did do the shooting, at the command of the man who forced her to telephone just now, why did she do it? Why did he, how could he make her do it?"

"Too easy," replied Ford. "If that was really Caprice, she's the wife of the man who took Ethel to Flora Wood. She went away from there with him, you remember. He was in love with Ethel. When Ethel married Bingham, or was about to marry him, this man not only resolved to kill her, but sent her warnings to that effect, by telegram and by the cipher message. Unable to make her give up the marriage, he carried out his threat to shoot her; but through this accomplice, who may be his wife and may not. Now, who is this man?"

"Hal Kennedy," said Eileen, promptly.

"But young Swift declares Kennedy was with him all last August, and the Flora Wood date is the seventh of August."

"I don't care what Warry says. Hal may have bribed him to say that. You know what a weak thing Warry is. Hal could easily bribe or threaten him to tell that story and stick to it. You'd better verify it by somebody else."

"It doesn't ring true," and Ford shook his head, dubiously; "I can't see a woman shooting in at the window and not being discovered or suspected."

"Charlotte saw her."

"She didn't see her shoot."

"No, the woman was too clever. And, too, nobody would be looking that way at that time. But directly after, Charlotte saw Caprice run around the church and escape in the waiting motor."

"There's something in it," said Doctor Randall; "but how can we go to work to back up any such theory as that?"

Alan Ford stared at him as if not hearing. Then, *apropos* of nothing, he asked, "What did the choir sing just as the bride fell?"

"They sang Barnby's 'O, Perfect Love,'" Eileen told him. "The first notes of that were to be my signal to fix Ethel's train to go back down the aisle."

"I've got a bee in my bonnet," said Ford, with a certain little smile of his that betokened hopefulness; "and it's buzzing pretty loudly; I'm going out on a few errands. Miss Randall, if any one calls, don't say anything about that telephone message till I return."

Eileen willingly promised this, and as Ford went away, the Professor went back to his study, and Eileen sat alone in the living-room, pondering over her troubles.

She sat there again late in the afternoon. She seemed to have two distinct mentalities. One, actuated by her heart, that knew Bingham to be innocent, the other, ruled by her brain, that saw clearly the dire peril he was in, whether innocent or not.

She thought over the scene of the wedding—the time of the tragedy. She knew Stanford never shot Ethel, yet she knew he could have done so, just as the anthem pealed forth, as the people began to laugh and chat, and she, the maid of honour, stooping to her task, would not have known it. He could not have done it—and yet, he could—he said he could—have done it for the girl he loved. But the idea was too monstrous! How could a man hope for happiness with a girl he loved if he had committed crime to win her? Still, if a man could commit a crime, anything else could be believed of him. She wished she had never let Stanford love her, never let him know she loved him. It was so overwhelming when it came, that great, deep, big love of theirs. Not like any ordinary love. They couldn't ignore it, or stifle it, or prevent its leaping into life and growing daily, hourly, stronger and bigger. Surely a love like that couldn't permit crime—or, couldn't help permitting it!

And as Eileen thought, as it came home to her, that if Stanford Bingham had committed that awful crime to win her, his great love absolved him, to her at least, whatever other people might think.

And even as she forgave him, fully and freely for anything he might have done, the thought haunted her that he did do it. No matter how much she declared to herself her implicit belief in his innocence, she knew that in her soul there was a doubt. This knowledge did not make her love him less; indeed, it rather, she thought, purified and refined her love for him. Nor did she put these thoughts into words. Her belief in his innocence was just a glow of loving faith and her doubt of it was a dim shadow that might or might not have to be reckoned with.

As Eileen mused, the door-bell rang. Half unheeding, the girl heard Charlotte's footsteps in the hall as she went to open the street door.

Brought to alertness by a sharp exclamation from the coloured woman, Eileen stepped out into the hall.

"Miss Eily," and Charlotte's eyes rolled hysterically, "dis yer's de lady what looked in de chu'ch winduh! Yas'm, dat she am!"

A beautiful young woman, in fashionable attire, confronted Eileen.

"Miss Randall?" she asked.

"Yes," said Eileen, too dumfounded to say more.

"May I speak with you a few moments? On a matter of importance."

"Certainly," said Eileen, finding her voice at last. "Come into this room, please."

Leading the way, Eileen preceded the guest into the living-room and closed the door behind them.

The two women looked at each other as if each were taking measure of a foe.

Both were beautiful, both of a dark, alluring type, and not unlike. But Eileen's hair was soft and lustrous, her eyes eloquent of education and culture, and her soft, dainty house gown refined in cut and colour. The visitor, on the other hand, had shining black hair, brushed in exaggerated modishness; her eyes were brilliant and snapping, and showed hardness and worldly knowledge; while her costume was of loud, bizarre hues and flimsy materials.

As she looked, Eileen had a sudden inspiration. She would make this woman serve her own ends; she would find out what she knew, and would use the knowledge as she chose. She would dominate her by force of a superior nature, greater cleverness, and cannier wisdom.

So, to take the guest at a disadvantage, Eileen said, coldly, "You are Caprice. What can you possibly have to say to me?"

Her plan worked well. As always, the lesser nature was cowed by the greater. The stranger looked at Eileen, surprised and abashed. But only for a moment, then she regained her poise, and added a bit of bravado not noticeable before.

"Yes, I am Caprice," she said; "at least that name is all I need tell you now. I am here to tell you what I know of the murder in the church, and to ask you if I shall carry my story to the police."

By a supreme effort, Eileen obeyed her better judgment, though she longed to cry out for the woman's story.

"Why ask me?" she said, evenly; "why not, if you have anything to tell, go straight to the police with it?"

"You're a cool one," and Caprice gave her a look of grudging admiration; "but you'll sing a different song after you've heard me."

"One moment," and Eileen forced herself to speak calmly, though her heart was beating wildly, "did you telephone here this morning that you fired that shot?"

"That *I* did! Are you crazy? Of course I didn't telephone that! Why should I? But I know who did do it, and I saw him."

"Then," and now Eileen had complete mastery over herself, "if you know anything so important as that, I am sure it is your duty to tell the police rather than me."

"And I am sure it isn't! Look here, what's the matter with you? I am here to help you, but if you are so offish, I may go away again."

"I am in no need of assistance, and if I were, I know where to turn for it."

"Yes, to Stanford Bingham. But you make a mistake, my lady. He is the man that fired that shot, and I saw him."

"You are not telling the truth," said Eileen, but she spoke weakly, for though these were the words she had feared, even expected to hear, they came as a shock.

"I am, and what's more, you know it. Now, look here, drop this high and mighty air of yours, and I will give you some really good advice. As Mr. Bingham is the criminal, call off that sleuth-hound of a detective, and so save yourself the pain and ignominy of having the truth made public. For, if Alan Ford keeps on, he will lay bare secrets that will send Stanford Bingham straight to the electric chair!"

Eileen put up her hand as if to ward off a blow, then swiftly calling on all her nerve force to help her, she rose to the occasion, and looking straight into the bold, black eyes of her visitor, she said:

"You have been sent here to say this. You have been commanded—*coerced*, as you were made to telephone here this morning. Now, if you want to keep out of trouble yourself, listen to me, and answer a few questions. Who is the man whom you call husband, who was at Flora Wood last August with Ethel Moulton?"

The question was flung at her so suddenly, that Caprice was caught off guard. "You know that!" she said, with wide eyes.

"Yes, we know all about it, except the name of the man."

"Henry Miller," was the answer, given in a flippant tone.

"His real name, I mean."

"That's all the name you'll ever get from me. But, perhaps, you wouldn't have to go far to learn his real name."

"Was it Kennedy?"

Caprice laughed. It was a short, insolent laugh, showing her white teeth, and displaying a temper which promised to be troublesome if roused.

"I'm not saying. His name may be Kennedy, and it may not. But it is a matter of no moment to us, now. I'm here to ask you if you'll call off your detective or if I shall go to the police with the story of the crime as I saw it."

"As you did *not* see it! As you are making it up! If you saw the shot, why did you run away, in a motor car, and disappear? Why didn't you stay and tell what you had seen?"

"Perhaps *I* don't want Stanford Bingham suspected, either." This, said in a low voice, left no doubt as to the meaning intended to be conveyed. It roused Eileen to fury as nothing else could have done. To have Stanford, her Stanford, spoken of thus by a common, fast-looking woman, was more than Eileen could bear.

"Go!" she cried, "go where you please, and tell whom you please! There is no truth in your story! You *never* saw Stanford Bingham fire that shot, and you know it!"

Eileen's dark eyes were blazing now. Like a lioness at bay defending her young, so bravery, courage, and truth gave her strength, and her voice rang with scorn as she added, "Impostor!"

"No," said Caprice, curiously cool in the face of this outbreak, "no, I am not an impostor. But if you think I am, I do not resent nor wonder at your anger. Perhaps, Miss Randall, it would be better worth your while to make a friend of me rather than an enemy."

Eileen looked at her wonderingly. "How can I, when you are so unfriendly? And, too, why should I?"

"You don't trust me?"

"I most certainly do not. If you wish to please me, you will remove yourself from my presence as soon as you can."

"I have no wish to displease you, so I will go. You are quite willing, then, that I should tell my story to Mr. Somers?"

Eileen wavered. Was she doing wisely to keep up this independent attitude? Oh, if only Alan Ford would come in! An impulse seized her.

"You see," she said, more ingratiatingly, "I have put this matter wholly in Mr. Ford's hands, and I can take no step unadvised by him. Would you dare to state your case to him, if I can arrange for it?"

"Are you crazy? I thought you didn't want Stanford Bingham convicted. Why should I tell Alan Ford the truth? I offer you this; if you will take the case out of Mr. Ford's hands, I will refrain from telling what I know to anybody. If you do not agree to this, I know Ford will run down the crime, and I shall tell Somers first, in revenge for your not doing as I wish. Is that straight?"

"No, I think it decidedly crooked, and also incomprehensible. I decline your offer, and I warn you I shall tell Mr. Ford all you have said to me."

"You will be sorry if you do," and with a strange glance of mingled wistfulness and baffled chagrin, the visitor went away.

CHAPTER 20

THE MUSIC OF THE CHOIR

That same afternoon, Alan Ford met Eugene Hall by appointment at the Country Club. Hall was flattered at the visit of the great detective, and willingly discussed the matter in hand.

"I admit," said Hall, "that I did suspect Warry Swift, but since you tell me he is innocent, I have no idea which way to look."

"I just want to ask a few questions about what you may have seen from the choir," said Ford, in an easy, conversational way; "you have said, I understand, that you saw the bride look up as if frightened, during the ceremony."

"She was frightened all the time," said Hall, decidedly. "On the way up the aisle, and during the ceremony, too, Ethel was in terror of her life. I only dimly sensed it at the time, but now I know she fully expected that shot."

"I'm sure of that, too, from the various warnings she had. You have no suspicion of any one in the choir, Mr. Hall?"

"In the choir! Lord, no! How could that be?"

"And yet the bride glanced up toward the choir, or toward the minister."

"Yes, she did. But who in the choir could be suspected?"

"No one, definitely, perhaps, but you know the shot entered the brain from above, or at least, its course was slightly downward, and as the choir is a few feet higher than the floor of the church—"

"No, Mr. Ford, you're on the wrong tack. If the wretch who fired that shot had been in the choir, the rest of us must have known it. It couldn't be."

"Perhaps not. How were the different choristers affected? Did you stop singing, any of you?"

"I did, I can tell you! Why, when I saw Ethel fall, I knew at once there was something wrong. I didn't think she had merely fainted, as some of the men said."

"Who said that?"

"Let me see: Kennedy, I guess it was. But we were all struck dumb. One or two sang on for a few lines, from sheer force of habit, and then Clements, the organist, stopped playing, and we all went down to the church floor."

"Did Mr. Kennedy drop his music?"

"No, not that I know of. Farrish dropped his, I remember, and as he picked it up he was staring at the bride, and didn't know what he was doing. We all acted demented. You see, Mr. Ford, half that choir were rejected suitors of Miss Moulton, and, of course, we were terribly shocked."

"Of course. Mr. Hall, can I get access to the choir loft at any time?"

"Certainly, Mr. Ford. Come on over there now, if you like. I'll go with you."

The two men stopped at the sexton's for the key of a side door to the church, and went up into the choir loft. Loft is an inappropriate term, as it was merely a small balcony or gallery not more than four feet above the church floor. It was directly behind the pulpit platform, as is usual in Congregational churches.

"Here you are," said Hall, leading the way. "Now, you see, Mr. Ford, it would be practically impossible for one of us to shoot without the knowledge of the others."

"Not with an automatic. In fact, the vines and greenery with which this rail was twined, afforded an excellent screen to shoot through, had one been inclined to do so."

"But who would do it? Not any of us who were fond of her. And as to the others, why?"

"Which of you were 'fond of her'?"

"Kennedy, Farrish, Porter, and I have all been at different times favoured by Miss Moulton's preference. You doubtless know she was a coquette, and always had a love-affair on with somebody. No man could resist her fascinations and she was, in a way, a spoiled beauty. I speak of her thus frankly, for I myself loved her deeply two years ago."

"And you outgrew the affection?"

"Not exactly that, but she threw me over when she had tired of me, and I learned the fickleness of her nature, and naturally lost interest in her."

"And Mr. Kennedy? Did she throw him over, too?"

"Yes, I believe so. And Farrish and Porter. Oh, we are all her cast-offs. But no one of us, I am sure, felt desperate enough about it to want to kill her! Who is in your mind—Kennedy?"

"Yes."

"Put him out, then. Hal Kennedy no more did that thing than I did! Why, he stood next to me, and I was looking at him as Ethel fell. I was looking at Ethel, of course, and as she fell I heard Kennedy exclaim, and turned to glance at him. He was trembling and white, but he held his music firmly, and he couldn't have fired that shot!"

"Where is the music you were using at that time?"

"Here it is," and going to a cupboard, Hall produced a pile of sheet music. Ford looked it over with interest. There were eight copies of "O, Perfect Love."

"I'll take these away with me," said the detective. "Please say nothing of it to any one. I shall keep them but a short time, and return them uninjured. You'll not be wanting them soon?"

"No; I shouldn't think anybody would ever want to be married in this church again."

"Are these copies of the music belonging to you, individually?"

"No, not these. Sometimes we each have our own copy. But these are all alike and we used any of them. Of course, we've sung it before at weddings, but not often. Only about three times since I joined the choir."

"Have you any opinion as to the criminal in this case, Mr. Hall?"

"Indeed I have! I'm sure it was Bingham himself who did it. I thought at first it was Warry Swift, but now I think it must have been Bingham. It's awful to think, I know, but who else could it have been? I'm positive, Mr. Ford, it couldn't have been one of us in the choir, with all due deference to your clever detection. And, own up, now, aren't you straining every nerve to discover somebody beside Bingham to suspect? Would you get up such a far-fetched and unlikely theory as a shot from the choir, if Bingham were not so definitely involved?"

Hall's frank honesty was far removed from impertinence or intrusive curiosity, and Ford answered him with equal straightforwardness:

"You are partly right, Mr. Hall. I do want to find a suspect other than Stanford Bingham, but only because I am convinced that Mr. Bingham is not the criminal. It does look black against him, on account of that peculiar will that gives him his fortune, and because he is said not to have been in love with the lady he married. But I think it was not his hand that fired that shot, and it is my duty to do all I can to prove his innocence."

"Of course, if you feel that way about it. But there is every motive and opportunity for Bingham and none for anybody else. I don't consider that the fact of being a rejected suitor of the bride's is enough to base suspicion on."

"I don't either," returned the detective.

"Then, what else have you got against Kennedy?"

"Nothing definite, I admit. But what I do know must be followed up. I thank you, Mr. Hall, for your help today. And I will detain you no longer. I have your word, have I not, to say nothing of my taking this music?"

"Certainly. And I hold you responsible for its safe return, as it is, of course, the property of the choir."

"Of course, I shall return it safely and promptly."

* * * *

Alan Ford spent the entire evening studying those eight pieces of music.

Before he began, he heard Eileen's story of the woman who called on her that afternoon, and who was, doubtless, Caprice. Ford was interested in the recital, but not so much so as Eileen had expected. He seemed a little preoccupied, and anxious to study the sheets of music. At last he excused himself to Eileen and her father, and taking the music with him, went to his own room.

There with a powerful magnifying-glass, he scrutinized every page of every copy, including the outside covers.

At last his patient work was rewarded by discovering small brownish stains on the covers of two of the copies. One copy showed these stains on its front cover, which bore the title of the song, the other copy had a brown stain on the back cover, which was entirely blank of printing.

Over these stains Ford pored for a long time.

"There is no doubt about it," he said to himself, at last. "But how to prove it! How to bring it home to him! The clever devil! The cold-blooded assassin! And, too, what was his true motive? There's much to be done yet. I never tackled a harder proposition. But it must and shall be proved. Jim will help me with the finger prints, and then we've got him. Only, that thick-headed D. A. will never be convinced!"

* * * *

The next morning, Ford told Doctor Randall and Eileen all he had learned, and all he had concluded from it. He showed them the sheets of music, bidding them handle them carefully, by the margins.

"The assassin was in the choir," the detective announced positively, "but it was not Kennedy. I'm sure of that."

"Who, then?" asked Eileen.

"Have you no idea?"

"Surely not Eugene Hall?"

"No. Now look here. On the back cover of this piece of music is a brown stain that I think is a powder stain, left by the flash of the discharged automatic in the hand of the assassin. He naturally used his right hand, which, shielded by the sheet music, was noticed by no one. The hand rested on the greenery wreathing the choir rail. The music of the organ made the slight sound of the report inaudible, and the heavy scent of flowers overcame any smell of powder. The shot, of course, deflected a little downward, and the victim was hit just as she was turning, in fact, had turned part way, so that her right side was toward the choir. She turned farther before she fell, as the doctors have agreed she would be likely to do. There is, so far, no unexplained condition."

"But who was it?" insisted Eileen.

"Granting that all this happened, the shell would be automatically discharged from the pistol and would fall to the floor. The criminal would doubtless stoop to pick it up, but would drop something also, that his motion might seem natural. I inquired if one had not dropped his sheet of music soon after the shot, and learned that one did."

"Who?"

"Farrish."

"Guy Farrish! Oh, no!" and Eileen looked incredulous.

"Farrish?" Doctor Randall smiled. "Come, come, Ford, you are drawing on your imagination. Or have you any real evidence?"

"It's impossible to tell which men had the various sheets of music as they are not individual property. But, I hold this brown stain to be a powder mark. Smell of it."

Doctor Randall sniffed at the brown mark, and nodded his head. "I can discern it," he said. "But why connect it with Farrish?"

"Partly because he's the only one who stooped to the floor."

"But he dropped his music."

"Purposely, of course. Now, I propose to prove that these are his finger prints on this same sheet of music."

"Pretty difficult," said the Professor. "But it can be done. I mean the prints can be brought out, so that we can compare them. But different men have fingered this music."

"Yes," agreed Ford; "it is a chance, I know, but I'm assuming that a man, necessarily excited and perturbed at such a crisis, would inevitably finger the music nervously, and his hands would perspire from overwrought sensibilities. He would make more definite finger prints than the others, who had no especial nervousness before the shot was fired. At any rate I have discovered such prints on this particular piece of music, and though I have not yet seen Mr. Farrish's finger prints, I think it a chance worth trying."

"But you say there are powder marks on two pieces of music," said Eileen, still incredulous.

"That's part of the evidence. You see these marks are on the back cover, which would naturally be over the holder's right hand. On this other sheet that shows marks, they are on the front cover, which would be held over the left hand of the singer, and would indicate a left-handed man, which none of the choir is."

"Then how did the marks come there?"

"Because the music was piled up by the organist or sexton, and the marks on one sheet are directly over those on the other. See, if the music had been piled up thus, the mark on this back cover would be exactly over the mark on this front cover. They coincide, but the one on the back is much stronger and clearer, showing that the other is merely a smudge from the first one."

"Good work, Ford!" exclaimed Doctor Randall. "You are entirely right, so far. These two powder marks are surely the result of piling up the music, as you say, for they are the same colour and shape, and each has a very faint odour of gunpowder. Moreover, it is clear that the lighter mark is the result of the plainer one. As to these finger marks, I will dust them with black lead and photograph them for you."

"Yes, I thought you'd do that. But I have other reasons for suspecting Farrish. Don't you think he guessed that musical cipher rather quickly, considering he had only that one short sentence to work on? I am an expert at those things, and yet it took me some time to puzzle it out, though I had several examples to work on. And when he made the fake one, which he did make to deceive you, his notation was so nearly like the original as to make me think very strongly that he wrote the originals."

"But," said Eileen, "when he showed you his natural way of writing music it was not at all like that."

"That's just it. He made those ciphers in a different hand so they would not look like his work. When he wanted to make one to look like them, he did so, and when he wanted to show me that he wrote music differently, he did that. I suspect him, principally, because he has not been logical in his connections with the case. He said he replaced that original cipher paper with one of his own making, because he feared the other would incriminate Mr. Bingham. He said it read, 'If you persist in going through the ceremony I will surely kill you,' or words to that effect. Now, as a matter of fact, it read, 'If you marry Bingham, I will surely kill you.' Farrish said that Bingham used his own name that way, to turn suspicion from himself, should the cipher be read by another. But I hold that is absurd on the face of it. Supposing Farrish, being innocent, read that message as it was really sent. Wouldn't he be much more likely to think some one else than Bingham wrote it? Why would he at once jump to the conclusion that Bingham wrote it, and spoke of himself that way as a blind? It isn't logical."

"No, it isn't," said Doctor Randall. "But if you are right, if Farrish shot Ethel, then he was the man who went to Flora Wood with her."

"He must be," said Ford. "Also, he must be the husband of Caprice; also, he must be the man who forced Caprice to telephone here that she killed the lady."

"But she said she didn't do that telephoning," said Eileen.

"I don't believe her," and Ford looked obstinate. "I know I am right. That woman, Caprice, is mixed up in it all, but she didn't do the shooting. There are the powder marks and the finger prints."

"The latter haven't yet been identified," reminded Doctor Randall.

"I know it, but they will surely prove to be Farrish's."

"Also, I doubt if those brown stains will be received as evidence; they may not be powder after all."

"But," said Eileen, "there is one way you can make sure. Take Mr. Farrish's picture to Flora Wood, and ask that landlady there if he is the man who came there with Ethel."

"I have done that," said Ford, looking at her; "I went there yesterday, and took a picture of Guy Farrish and asked her that."

"What did she say?"

"She said no, he was not the man."

"Well?"

"I didn't believe her."

CHAPTER 21

THE CALL OF THE SIREN

"No, Eileen," and Bingham held the girl closely to him, "I don't believe Farrish did it. Why should he?"

"Did you never think, dear, that Mr. Farrish knew Ethel better than you thought he did? Don't you think that it was he who went with her to Flora Wood?"

"But that woman out there swears he is not the man."

"I know, but I don't believe her, and neither does Mr. Ford."

"Do you know, Eily, I don't have much faith in that man Ford's work. What has he done, so far?"

"He's done a lot, Stan, and it's all for you. But that horrid old Mr. Somers—he's so taken up with that 'Caprice' woman, he believes all she says."

"I know. He believes her story of seeing me shoot Ethel. Well, dearest, there's nothing for me to do but stand trial."

"Indeed you sha'n't! Mr. Ford and I have a new plan. I won't tell you about it yet, but I'm going to try it if all else fails."

"Do what you like," said Bingham, wearily; "but, oh, my darling, will it ever be all over and you and I free to go away by ourselves where we shall never hear of this place or these people again? I'd willingly give up my whole fortune to be freed of suspicion, and happy with you."

"Of course, dear, and so would I. Money is as nothing compared to this awful web they have woven around you. Stanford, how *can* people suspect you!"

"It is natural that they should, when you remember the circumstances. That absurd will business, and the fact that I did not love Ethel, is enough to condemn me in the eyes of the public."

"But not in the eyes of those who love you. Father and I know you innocent, and Mr. Ford knows it too. We three will save you yet, or would, if you'd only help a little yourself."

"What can I do? It doesn't help to protest my innocence."

"But at first you wouldn't say that you didn't do it."

"You know that was on account of Warry. After the wrong I had done Ethel, I couldn't turn tale-bearer about her cousin, and I did think him guilty at first."

"I know, on account of the diamond. But, now, there is no suspicion of him. Why not come out and fight for yourself?"

"I would gladly, if I saw any way to fight. I am innocent, I've no idea who is guilty. What can I do?"

The whole affair had unmanned Stanford Bingham. Always reticent, and averse to publicity, this dreadful atmosphere of suspicion had caused him more than ever to retire into himself. He shrank from his fellow-men, he dreaded to go on the streets, he saw no one except the Randalls, if he could possibly avoid it. All this did not militate in his favour with the community; and nine out of ten in the town believed him guilty.

District Attorney Somers was positive of Bingham's guilt, and now that the woman Caprice had told him her story, Somers was working diligently to get further corroboration.

Caprice had given her address and credentials. She asserted that she was a vaudeville actress, living in New York City. That she had been motoring through Boscombe Fells by chance, on the day of the wedding, and, actuated by mere curiosity, had left her car and gone to look in at the window of the church. She said she saw the bridegroom shoot the bride at the altar.

This story was so unsupported by any other evidence than the word of the woman, that Somers hesitated about acting on it without further proof. Charlotte had admitted that she saw the woman looking in at the church, but at Eileen's warning had refused to dilate on the story, and finally said she was not sure it was the same woman, after all.

Somers had not learned of the Flora Wood episode, and as the days went by, Somers and Alan Ford became more and more opposed in their opinions and in their work.

"It's come to an issue between us," declared Ford to Eileen; "Somers is bent on suspecting Bingham, and I know it was Farrish. Why, your father proved that those were Farrish's finger prints on the piece of music that shows the burnt stain, and Somers only pooh-poohs at that."

"How does he explain it?"

"He says there's nothing to explain. Says they're Farrish's prints, all right, but that the brown stain is not a powder stain, and that there is no reason to think of Farrish in connection with it."

"Then there's only one way," and Eileen looked earnestly in the face of the great detective.

"I think there is only one way. It's a very peculiar case. It has no precedent, no parallel. I can't think Somers is personally prejudiced against Bingham; I think the District Attorney is honest in his beliefs. And, too, in a murder case, an eye-witness is invaluable if the statement can be believed. That's why Somers is looking up the Caprice woman so thoroughly. He doesn't want to credit her story unless she is reliable and responsible as a witness, but he hopes to prove that she is."

"What is he doing?"

"He is investigating her past and present history. He has found out little of importance, so far; nothing, in fact, that contradicts her own story. But if he gets hold of the Flora Wood incident, I am afraid there will be trouble. You see, the man that went there with Ethel Moulton was certainly Farrish. But he has bribed that Ballou woman to deny it. Farrish is so deep, so infernally clever, that it is next to impossible to fasten anything on him. But I'll get him yet."

Alan Ford stalked up and down the room in a fury. And Eileen wondered. She had faith in his powers, but he was a queer man, and his theory that Farrish was the criminal had so little to back it up, that she couldn't help doubting. And, too, what was Farrish's motive? He had been in love with Ethel, but of late he had not been very attentive to her; indeed, he had shown a decided preference for Eileen Randall. Surely the thing was a little absurd.

Eileen dressed herself in one of her prettiest costumes, and went to see Farrish in his office.

"Come in," he said, cordially; "this is, indeed, a pleasure?"

"You told me to come when I chose," and Eileen blushed a little, and looked up at him with a timid smile.

"To be sure I did. You are always welcome. What can I do for you?"

"Oh, nothing particular. I just want to talk over the murder case with some one who knows something."

"About it?"

"No; I don't mean about it, exactly; but some one who knows things generally."

Eileen gave him a quick, bright glance from the corner of her eye, and then looked down. It fascinated Farrish, who was susceptible always to woman's beauty, and Eileen had the seductive smile of a siren.

As Farrish didn't speak, she looked up again, to find him smiling back at her, from under half-closed lids. She fluttered, and nervously fingered her pink parasol.

She was looking her prettiest in a thin gown of apple-blossom pink, cut a bit low in the neck, and with transparent sleeves. Her broad-brimmed straw hat was wreathed with pink roses, and round it was draped a filmy white veil. This veil, which had been put back, Eileen now drew over her face with a coquettish gesture, and her dark eyes shone through it with a tantalizing gleam. It was distinctly provocative, and Guy Farrish started from his seat, and stepped forward toward her.

They were alone, in his private office, and as Eileen gave him a startled glance, he gently raised the silken veil and tossed it back over her hat.

"Now I can see you better," he said, smiling down as he stood over her. "Tell me your errand."

"I can't—with you so near—" and Eileen blushed and toyed with her parasol. "I—I—think I'd better go—" and she rose slowly.

"Go!" and Farrish laid a restraining hand on her arm. "Why, you've only just come. What is it you want—Eileen?"

She stood beside him, beautiful, hesitating. Then she put a hand lightly on his shoulder. "No," she said, looking down, and her voice quivered a little, "no, I find I can't tell you, after all—" Her soft voice trailed away to silence, and with eyes cast down and lip trembling, she stood, uncertainly turning toward the door.

The lure of the girl was too much for Farrish. With a quick, uncontrollable movement, he caught her in his arms, and whispered, "Tell me now— *here!* You sweet, *sweet* thing!"

In a fury, Eileen sprang away from him. "Mr. Farrish!" she exclaimed; "how dare you? What do you mean?"

But though the tones expressed deepest indignation, the soft eyes were not altogether chiding.

"What do *you* mean?" he cried, wonderingly; "you tempt me beyond endurance, and then reproach me for yielding to your bewitchment!"

"Hush! You must be mad!" and Eileen looked at him with the stately air of an offended goddess.

"I am! Mad about *you*! Eileen, I didn't know you were so beautiful! What has come to you, girl?"

With no reply in words, Eileen gave him a sweet, shy smile that might mean anything. To Farrish it meant much. Again he clasped her in his arms, with exclamations of endearment. This time she showed no resentment, but said in a whisper, "Please, don't! Please let me go! Oh, what have I done! What am I doing! Oh, Guy, let me go!"

Slowly Farrish released her. "Sit down," he said, commanding himself, "and tell me what you—"

"No, I can't—now—" said Eileen, putting down her veil. "I must go. Don't detain me now! I can't—oh, I can't!"

"Go, then, dear," said Farrish, gently. "Go, and I will come to see you. May I come tonight?"

Eileen gave no sign of assent, except a brief glance, but it seemed enough for Farrish, and he opened the door, and bowed his visitor out with formal courtesy. Eileen went away, and straight home. Going to her room she locked the door, and sat down in her favourite low chair to think.

"It's awful," she said, to herself; "awful! But there *is* something about Guy that is wonderfully fascinating."

* * * *

Farrish came that evening. Bingham called shortly after his arrival, and was told by Charlotte that Miss Eily was not at home.

Uncertain as to the truth of this statement, Bingham went away, dejected and wondering.

Eileen was even more lovely in her evening gown than she had seemed in her morning costume. Her soft, exquisite shoulders were bare, and her dainty arms flashed in and out of the draped lace that served as sleeves. Her laughing eyes were bright, and her cheeks rosy pink, as she smiled at Farrish.

"I don't know what you must have thought of me this morning," she said, glancing up through drooping lashes, "I—I think I—lost my head, a little."

"I know I lost mine, utterly! When did you discover it, Eileen?"

"Discover what?" with a shy, wondering look.

"That you love me! Don't deny it! You can't, for it's true! Gloriously true! Oh, my darling, how beautiful you are!"

"Mr. Farrish! Oh, don't!" for Guy had clasped her wildly to him.

"There, there, my beauty! You know you want me to love you! Why resist, my fluttering bird?"

"Don't kiss me! Don't you dare! No one shall ever kiss me but the man I marry!"

"And you're going to marry me! You are!"

"Mr. Farrish, you must be crazy!" and Eileen disengaged herself from his embrace. "Why, I scarcely know you!"

"You scarcely know me in this rôle, yes. And I scarcely know myself. But it suits me to perfection, and you'll learn rapidly. Eileen, my beauty-girl, say you will marry me—soon—*soon!*"

"I will," breathed Eileen; "and soon, Guy!"

CHAPTER 22

FORD'S THEORY

A few days later, Bingham called again at the Randalls'.

It had been agreed by him and Eileen that they would say nothing of their engagement for a long time; not, at any rate, until the case was cleared up, and the whole affair settled one way or another.

Bingham was in a bad temper. The situation was wearing on him, and the investigations of the Police Detective Bureau were getting annoyingly personal.

"It's plain to be seen," he said, "that Somers is drawing the net closer round me. Unless some other suspect is kind enough to put in an appearance pretty soon, I stand a very strong chance of being arrested."

"Not really, Stan?" said Eileen, looking at him curiously; "how can they arrest you?"

"How can they? Why, because they think they have sufficient evidence, that's all."

"How do you know all about it?"

"I don't know all about it, but I've found out enough to know they're feeling pretty sure."

"Then they're a lot of dunder-heads, and they don't know what they're talking about! Just you have patience a little longer, and you'll see who knows the most about this thing, you or I."

"You are a comfort, Eileen, you're always so hopeful. But you don't realize, dearest, that—"

"Oho! I don't realize, don't I? Well, I just guess I *do*! I realize a heap more than you do, you blessed old stupid."

"I am stupid, I'll admit. This whole business has simply taken away my brain, and I can't see what to do next."

"Don't do anything. Leave it to those who are wiser than you. Here comes one now. Mr. Ford, what do you think? Mr. Bingham says he doesn't know what to do!"

"Neither do I," and Ford looked quizzical. "Those misguided wiseacres in the Police Office are thwarting all my efforts, and I am put to it to keep my plans secret from them, lest they upset them all."

"Do you know, Mr. Ford, I think it would be a good idea if Mr. Bingham went away for a time."

"Run away!" exclaimed Bingham. "I'd be likely to do that!"

"Not exactly run away, but go off for a little rest," and Eileen smiled at him.

Bingham looked at her grimly. "I expect Somers would have something to say about that. No, my dear, I don't think I'll go away for a rest, just at present. In fact, I don't think I'll go until I can take you with me."

"I don't know when that will be, Mr. Bingham," and Ford spoke earnestly; "I advise you to stay here, but I also advise you not to say much. The police are on a new tack, and I don't quite know what they're up to. But I do know if they can twist or convert your speeches to serve their own ends, they are quite ready to do so. They're working on that 'Caprice' story just now, and they're getting a lot out of it. They repudiate the work that I've done; they've no use for my deductions and conclusions, so I'm working on my own; and if I get the truth before they do, and I fully expect to, they will fight hard before they own themselves beaten."

"What is the truth, Mr. Ford?"

"That Guy Farrish shot the bride at the altar."

"I cannot believe it."

"Why not?"

"Principally because I can think of no reason why he should do it. Farrish has not been friendly with Ethel for more than a year, not since Ethel and I—became engaged. Whatever feelings he once entertained for her, must have become more or less effaced in that time. He could hardly have been still so desperately in love with her as to prefer seeing her dead rather than wedded to me."

"Those are the arguments of the police, and they throw suspicion, in their opinion, back on yourself."

"Never mind about me, now; stick to the question of Guy Farrish. Could he have any other motive than jealousy?"

"What makes you ask that question, Mr. Bingham?" and Ford looked at him, keenly.

"Because if he did the deed, it was not through jealousy or envy of me. It was for some other reason, connected with—"

"Yes, connected with—"

"With business matters. But they are subjects I do not feel myself at liberty to mention."

"Not to save yourself from suspicion."

"No. Guy Farrish is not officially suspected of this crime. Unless he were, I should not be justified in telling of these things. I should not have referred to them, but that I thought possibly they might already be in your mind."

"Now, look here, Mr. Bingham," and Ford spoke very seriously; "I am sure of Guy Farrish's guilt. *Sure*, I tell you. But he is a clever and deep scoundrel, and it is going to be very hard, if not impossible, to *prove* his guilt. Therefore, if you can help in any way, it is your duty to do so."

"Why are you so sure of his guilt?"

"First and perhaps, principally, because he tried so hard to turn suspicion toward you."

"Toward me!"

"Yes; that was part of his cleverness. While apparently turning suspicion from you, he really started it in your direction. That cipher business, for instance; he changed it, he *said*, lest it incriminate you; whereas, it was his changed rendition of the thing that made it look like your work."

Bingham listened attentively. Eileen had left the room a short time before and the two men were alone.

"Those two telegrams, too, that came on the morning of the wedding, you remember, they had to be read alternately. They, too, were Farrish's work. All these things were warnings to the girl that if she married you he would kill her. She, I dare say, did not believe he would carry out the threat, but she was in a daze of terror all the time. I have learned from the bridesmaids how agitated and nervous she was even before the ceremony, and the minister and her uncle testify to her extreme panic of fear during the ceremony. When she looked up toward the pastor, as he says, it was really Farrish she was looking at. He held the pistol; he fired it, as she turned toward the other aisle; and this is proved by the powder-burn on the sheet of music that bears his finger prints."

"All very well as a theory, Mr. Ford," and Bingham smiled a little. "And, honestly, I wish I *could* believe it. But it is all so imaginary, so fanciful, that I cannot seem to think it the truth. As I say, I wish I could, for though I should hate to see Farrish found guilty, I should certainly like to have the weight of suspicion removed from my shoulders. Sometimes I think it is a judgment on me, for the wrong I did to Ethel to marry her when I loved another, or, rather, to love another while I was betrothed to her."

"I wouldn't bother about that phase of it. You certainly acted the part of an honourable man."

"That, of course, so far as I could. And it is in pursuance of an honourable course of action that I must refuse to give any hint of any reason Guy Farrish might have had for objecting to my marriage with Ethel, aside from jealousy."

"Very well, Mr. Bingham, but I warn you I shall use every possible means to find that out, and I have not the slightest doubt that I shall succeed."

"Very well, but it won't be by *my* information."

Bingham went away, and Ford chuckled to himself. "Glad he told me that much," he mused; "now I know there *is* a reason. I was sure there must be; but now that I'm certain, I can go to work to ferret it out."

Glancing from the window, just then, he saw Eileen getting into Guy Farrish's smart little runabout car, while that worthy gentleman solicitously looked after her comfort in the matter of robes and cushions. Then he got in himself and they spun away, the girl laughing up in the face of the handsome lawyer.

"Lucky Bingham got off before he saw that," thought Ford. "Great girl, Eileen!"

A great girl, indeed, Eileen Randall looked, in her smart motor garb. A coat of white pongee silk, and a hat that was mostly veil—of shimmering, shaded green. Through the tissue veil her eyes danced as she looked up at Farrish.

"Which way?" he asked, looking admiringly at her, "and do put back that veil! Why do you always tantalize me with a veil?"

"What, spoil my complexion! No, indeed!" and Eileen laughed her gay little laugh, that was provocation itself. "Which way shall we go? How about some nice little wayside inn, where we can get iced tea and iced cakes?"

"To the 'Colonial,' then; that's the best tea place."

"No," and Eileen laid her hand on the steering wheel, "no, let's go to Flora Wood."

"Of all places! Why Flora Wood?"

"Because I say so!" and the red lips pouted saucily. "Do I get my way?"

"Your word is my law, always. But I shall exact a reward. You are to stay there to dinner, too, and we'll come home by moonlight."

"I'm not sure about that, we'll see. And, Mr. Farrish—"

"Mr. Farrish, is it? Don't forget, young lady, you've promised to marry me, and I prefer a less formal address."

"Oh, I didn't promise to marry you, did I?"

"You sure did! And I shall hold you to it."

"But I didn't really mean it, you know. I was—"

"Well, sweetheart, you were what?"

"Oh, I don't know—I was a little infatuated by your—your nearness, I suppose."

"Then that's an infatuation that has come to stay! I shall always be near you, my beloved; I am near you now." Farrish's face was close to Eileen's and his eyes looked deep into her own.

"Don't—Guy—" and Eileen dropped her eyes. "Let's talk of something else," she went on, nervously fingering the dust-robe. But she gave him an oblique glance more eloquent than words could be.

"Siren!" he exclaimed; "that's the only name for you! You are adorable! When will you marry me? *When*, Eileen?"

"Oh, not for a long time. Tell me, Guy, have you ever loved any one before?"

"Not as I love you! I have had love-affairs—who hasn't? But this is the love of my life, my hope for the future—Eileen, you don't *know* what you are to me! I adore you! I can't keep my hands off of you, and yet I worship you and I reverence you. My only love!"

"But you loved Ethel."

"Ethel! That was a momentary infatuation. Ethel was a coquette, and at one time it pleased her to coquet with me. I humoured her, and—but don't let's talk of Ethel."

"Yes, I want to. Do you suppose they'll arrest Stanford Bingham?"

"Probably. But they'll never convict him. There isn't enough evidence."

"But that Caprice woman is an eye-witness, so they say."

"But that isn't enough. Her unsupported testimony won't hang Bingham. Unless he confesses, he'll get off."

"Confesses! Why, he didn't do it!"

"Then who did?"

"Who indeed! Tell me whom you suspect."

"If I do, will you kiss me?"

"What, now?"

"No, not now, it would be too unsatisfactory. But in the garden at Flora Wood. I know a secluded little nook—"

"Just big enough for one kiss? But how do you come to know so much about Flora Wood?"

"Oh, I've been there lots of times. For years it has been the Mecca of afternoon drives."

"Were you ever there with Ethel?"

"H'm, let me see: Yes, I think I have been. Also with Betty Stratton, and several other pretty girls. But never before with you! And, now, never again with any one but you! Tell me, my siren, when can we be married?"

"Don't call me siren. It sounds like those wailing motor horns!"

"Then I'll never call you that again. I'll spend the rest of my life making up names to call you that you do like. 'Queen of my future,'—how's that?"

"Horrid! It seems to imply a Queen of your past!"

"Now you're teasing me. But you may, if you like. Tease me more."

"Who was the 'Queen of your past'? Is there any one, any one at all, who has the slightest claim on you now?"

"Claim on me! How absurd!"

"But is there?"

"No, of course not. Could I ask you to marry me if there were?"

"Well; but—is there any one who thinks she has? Any little actress, or anybody?"

"You little innocent! Do you think every man has some foolish entanglement?"

"Haven't they?" and Eileen's big, dark eyes showed a wistful wonder.

"Some men may have, darling; but don't worry about those. Is there any one in especial you're thinking of?"

"Yes, Caprice."

Eileen flung the words at him and looked straight in his face to see how he took it.

Farrish smiled and then looked grave. "Eileen," he said, gently, "if Caprice is entangled with some one you know, look in another direction; not toward me."

"You mean—Stan—"

"Don't ask me," returned Farrish, but his eyes assented to her half-spoken question.

"How much farther is it?" asked Eileen, after a brief interval of silence.

"Only a few miles. Just beyond the next turn. Shall you be glad to get there? With me?"

A flash of the brown eyes through the gauze veil was his only answer, but Farrish seemed content.

They reached the inn at Flora Wood, and the whole place justified its attractive name. A good-sized grove of waving shade trees made a background for an acre or more of old-fashioned flower gardens. The house, long and rambling of structure, had wide verandas where were tea tables and pleasant lounging-places.

Farrish selected what seemed the most desirable one and Eileen seated herself, and took off her long veil.

"It was worth waiting for," Farrish whispered, as she slowly unswathed the long folds and drew them from her head and neck.

Her motor coat, too, she discarded, and sat, looking fresh and lovely, in a summer gown of soft white lace. The frills fell away from her exquisite throat, which, innocent of beads or necklace, gleamed pearly-white in the dusk of the vine-shaded alcove Farrish had chosen.

"How beautiful you are!" he exclaimed, gazing at her.

"It's rude to stare," she laughed back at him. "Please order me some iced tea, I'm choked with dust."

"You shall have anything you want, to the half of my kingdom, and then, if you want it, you shall have the other half."

"Of course I shall want it. I am not one for half-way measures!"

"Neither am I! And I want you, Eileen, all of you, for my very own. When, dearest, when can I have you?"

"Are we staying here for dinner?" asked Eileen, irrelevantly.

"Indeed we are! I'll order it directly."

"Very well, but I shall not see you again until dinner time. I'm going to freshen up, and then I am going to take a rest in that very tempting-looking cool parlour we passed through when we entered. The landlady looks interesting, I may cultivate her acquaintance. At any rate, I dismiss you till dinner time. Shall we say seven?"

CHAPTER 23

ONLY ONE WAY

Farrish fumed and fretted at the dismissal, but Eileen was obdurate. His only consolation was her gentle though mocking smile and her promise of rejoining him at seven. It was already six, and he killed the time as far as possible in ordering dinner, and strolling round the garden, smoking and selecting the best spot to watch the moon rise later.

Eileen sauntered about the house, and at last encountered the mistress of the place, in a small sitting-room.

With her own tact and charm of manner, Eileen drew her into conversation.

Mrs. Ballou loved to talk, and soon Eileen deftly introduced the subject of the murder. But, then, the older woman became silent, or answered only in monosyllables.

Adroitly, Eileen put forth hints and opened questions, but she learned nothing.

"She's been forbidden to talk," concluded Eileen, thinking to herself—"I must go at it more directly."

"I feel in a confidential mood," she said, with a winning smile at the shrewd-eyed woman; "you can keep a secret, I know. Would you be surprised to know I am going to marry that gentleman who brought me here?"

"No!" and Mrs. Ballou's voice rang out sharply; "oh, no, not that!"

"Why not?" and Eileen's eyes were big and questioning. "He's a fine man."

"Yes, yes;" and the other spoke hurriedly, "but, miss, oh, I mayn't say anything, but, miss, I beg you, *don't!*"

Seizing the chance, Eileen leaned forward and whispered suddenly, "Is he the man who came here last summer with Miss Moulton?"

"Oh!" and Mrs. Ballou gave a slight scream; then, immediately recovering herself, she said, "Oh, mercy, no! How could you ask such a thing as that? Of course not!"

"Why were you so alarmed at the question?" and Eileen eyed her closely.

"I wasn't; but any reference to that murder always gives me a shock. No, miss, he never brought Miss Moulton here, she—she came with—with another man."

"Are you sure?" and Eileen stared, meaningly.

"Yes, yes, of course—of course I'm sure."

"Oh, very well, I've no doubt you are. Now, why is it you advise me not to marry Mr. Farrish?"

"Oh, because—because, he—he seems older than you are."

"He is. But not so very many years. Do you know Caprice?"

Eileen's plan of surprising her hearer attained its object. Mrs. Ballou gasped, and looked at the girl with wild eyes. "What are you?" she cried; "a detective? Another detective?"

"No," said Eileen, soothingly, and fearing she had gone too far. "No, I'm only a tease. I love to tease people, and I said those things for fun. Caprice, as you can read in the papers, is rather a mystery, and as she seems to be mixed up with—"

"With whom?" and the woman's face was white with fear.

"No matter. It's dinner time, isn't it? I promised Mr. Farrish I'd dine at seven. Ah, there you are!"

Farrish appeared in the doorway. He looked annoyed at seeing Eileen's companion. Mrs. Ballou looked helplessly at him.

"It's pleasanter outside," was all he said, as he took Eileen away.

"What were you two hobnobbing about?" he asked, as they seated themselves at dinner.

"That's telling," said Eileen, gaily; "but I'm sure it was nothing that could interest you."

She smiled at him so successfully, that he said, "Nothing interests me but you!"

"Then don't ask irrelevant questions, sir! Let's enjoy the fleeting moment," and Eileen's finger tips lightly touched his hand as it lay on the table.

Willingly enough, Farrish enjoyed the fleeting moments, and dinner over, he bade Eileen hasten, if she would see the moon rise from the glen in the garden.

"No, not tonight," she returned, very decidedly. "I've given you all the fleeting moments I intend to this time."

"But you promised," he said, miserably; "dear, you promised."

"I never keep a promise," she returned, laughing at his long face. "You are going too fast, altogether. I want to go home, and I want to go now."

"And if I refuse to take you?"

"But you won't," and she was wheedlesome. "Why, you promised me half your kingdom! Do you refuse my first request?"

"But such a request!"

"Very well, it is a command, then. Guy, take me home, at once!"

The pretty air of proprietorship and authority over him charmed him into submission, and Farrish ordered his car forthwith.

"But you shall give me the kiss you promised," he told her, as they drove home through the moonlight.

"I didn't promise it," and Eileen laughed daringly at him, "and if I did, I've changed my mind. Anyway, I shall never kiss any man until I am married to him."

"If your promises mean nothing, your assertions are equally worthless," and Farrish spoke as lightly as the girl herself.

"Clever of you to discover that!" and keeping up a tone of banter until they reached her door, Eileen ran into the house with the merest "Goodnight."

* * * *

The next day she sent for Caprice.

Wonderingly, the woman came.

"You want to see me?" she asked, a little pertly, as they met.

"Yes, please," and Eileen eyed her, calmly.

"What for?"

"On various matters. Do you care to answer a few questions truthfully?"

"Depends on the questions."

"Naturally; first, then, are you the wife of Guy Farrish?"

Caprice stared. "What's that to you?" she said, rudely.

"No matter, and don't answer unless you choose."

"All right, I don't choose. What next?"

"Did you go to Flora Wood last summer, to prevent Mr. Farrish's marriage with a lady there?"

"Good heavens! What do you mean?"

"What I say. Did you?"

"I don't choose to answer that, either."

"Very well, then. It only remains for me to tell you I am going to marry Mr. Farrish."

"You! You can't!"

"Why not? Are you his wife?"

"Yes, yes, *yes*! I am! Don't let him deceive you!"

"I can take care of myself. Did Mr. Farrish shoot Ethel Bingham?"

"No!" and the eyes of Caprice grew big with horror.

"Did you see Stanford Bingham do it?"

"Yes," and a hard look settled on Caprice's face. "But I refuse to say any more. I shall prevent it, if you try to marry Guy, as I prevented Ethel Moulton's attempt."

"Very well," and Eileen herself showed her guest out.

On the doorstep Caprice paused. "Are you going to marry him?" she said, a little wistfully.

"How can I, if he is married to you? But I don't believe he is."

"Then make it your business to find out!" and with a gleam of hatred in her dark eyes, Caprice went away.

"She is married to him," said Eileen to Ford, as she told him the story; "I know by her expression she told the truth."

"Then she will never incriminate him."

"No. She never will, anyway. She's desperately in love with him. But why did she come to the church the day of the wedding at all? That's what I can't make out."

"She came, I think, to make sure that it was not Farrish who was to marry Ethel. She is insanely jealous, and if she had just heard of the marriage, by chance, she may have wanted to assure herself that Farrish had not renewed his efforts to marry Miss Moulton."

"I do believe that was it. Then, why does she now swear that she saw Stanford do the shooting?"

"Farrish makes her do it. Farrish has turned everything toward Bingham's guilt. He is canny, clever, powerful. He is even deeper than I thought. We must work hard and quickly to outwit him."

"There is only one way?"

"I fear so."

"I dread it. I loathe it—"

"But, to save Bingham—?"

"Yes, anything to save him."

"Somers considers his guilt a certainty now; I think that he will be arrested within twenty-four hours."

"Mr. Ford! Can you do nothing to prevent it?"

"Nothing more than I have done. Bingham himself is so apathetic that he is no help. Farrish is so diabolically clever there is no escaping his slyness. And Caprice has so bewitched the District Attorney that he thinks every one of her words Gospel truth. So what can we do?"

"There is only one way," repeated Eileen, slowly, and sadly. "Oh, what would Stanford say if he knew!"

"He would never allow the sacrifice. Are you sure yourself you want to make it?"

"To save Stan! Of course, I would make any sacrifice for that."

"Shall you let your father know?"

"No, indeed! Father wouldn't hear of it! He's too fond of me!"

"Hush, here he comes."

The entrance of Doctor Randall put an end to the discussion. Eileen walked away to the window and leaned her throbbing head on her hands.

The telephone rang, and with a sigh Eileen went to answer it.

"Yes," she said to Farrish's call.

"Yes," she said to his invitation to go motoring again that afternoon. And then, to his next suggestion, she laughed, roguishly, and said only, "Oh, you rascal!" speaking softly at him.

She dressed for the ride with especial care. She put on a gown of black chiffon, whose thinness revealed the soft curves of her shoulders, and fell away from her dainty throat and neck. Her dark hair, parted and coiled low, gave her face the seductiveness of the Mona Lisa, and only a black chiffon scarf protected her head. When Farrish called, at six, she threw a long black silk cape round her, and ran down to join him.

"Tell father I've gone out to dinner," she called to Charlotte, and without waiting for a reply, went swiftly on.

Doctor Randall, always absent-minded, took little note of his daughter's goings or comings, and Eileen did as she chose.

To Charlotte her adored mistress' wish was law, and she would as soon have questioned the stars in their courses as Eileen's plans.

And so Farrish, waiting, put her in the little car, and they started.

"Flora Wood again?" he asked, gaily, as they flew along the smooth road.

"If you like," said Eileen, with a quick, soft glance.

"Flora Wood it is, then!" he said, exultingly. "You owe me a trip there to make up for last night. You won't take a whim to return so early tonight, will you, dearest?"

"It depends on how entertaining you are. And, too, the moon doesn't rise until after ten. I can't stay as late as that!"

"With your fiancé, I rather guess you can!"

They drove swiftly through the deepening dusk, and both were somewhat silent.

"Talk to me," said Eileen, at last.

"I'm so happy I can't talk," returned Farrish. "How has it happened, Eileen? Why has this great joy come to me so suddenly? A few weeks ago I scarcely knew you—"

"Why, you've known me nearly a year!"

"Not as I know you now. We were acquaintances, but I didn't realize your sweetness or dream that you cared for me."

"I haven't said that I do," and again the bewildered glance enslaved him afresh.

"You don't have to say so!" and Farrish gave a low laugh of content. "Your presence here proves it!"

"I wonder—" and Eileen spoke vaguely, as if wrapt in happy dreams.

"I'll find out for sure tonight. Dear, let's have our dinner out on the terrace. What do you say?"

"As you like, Guy. It *would* be more to ourselves, wouldn't it?"

"And would you enjoy it for that reason?" There was a light in his eyes which deepened as Eileen whispered, "Try me, and see!"

"What have you been doing all day?" she asked lightly, as later they were at dinner on the terrace.

The terrace tables were each in a secluded arbour, fragrant of honeysuckles and lighted only by shaded candles.

Farrish started. "Why did you ask that?" he cried, almost angrily, and then, recovering his poise, he added, "Forgive me, darling, I lost my head for a moment. What was I doing? I shall tell you, my own, but not until the moon rises."

"I want to know now," and Eileen pouted like a spoiled child.

"Humour me, this once, dear; I'll always obey you else. Just let me wait to tell you, until we are together—watching the rising moon—"

"Aren't you sentimental!" and a rippling laugh showed that Eileen forgave him.

After dinner, Farrish led her to the shady nook among the trees that he had chosen. There was a rustic settee, and across the flower garden an uninterrupted view of the eastern sky.

The moon rose, after a time. In silence Farrish drew Eileen close to him.

"Now I'll tell you what I did to-day," he whispered, exultantly; "I got our marriage license."

"Oh, Guy!" and the veriest school-girl could not have been shyer or more sweetly confused than Eileen Randall. "But we won't be married for a long time."

"It does no harm to have it, and I thought, I hoped you might consent to make it soon. You *said* soon, dearest."

"Did I?" and Eileen looked dreamily thoughtful, as she interlaced her fingers through his clasping ones.

"You did! Darling, I *can't* wait! You have enthralled me! I am mad about you! Crazy! Wild! Don't make me wait, Eileen, sweetest, *don't*!"

"Guy," and the soft fingers caressed his cheek, "suppose we say—now—to-night—"

"Eileen! You don't—you can't mean it! Oh, if you only did! Do you? Dearest, *do* you?"

"I—don't—know—I think I did mean it when I said it, but—it would be too crazy! How could we?"

"It doesn't matter how we could—if you only will, I'll arrange all else! Oh, Eileen!"

Farrish clasped her in a mad embrace, but she put him away, saying, "Wait, let me think."

"No, don't think! I'm afraid to have you think—"

"But if I consent to this mad plan, all must be as I say."

"Of course: what is it you want, sweetheart?"

"Well," and Eileen smiled at him in the moonlight, "first, I don't want to be married by Doctor Van Sutton."

"No," said Farrish.

"Nor by any minister. Could we get a Justice of the Peace, or whatever you call him, as late as this?"

"We will, whether we can or not! And it isn't late, it's only a little after eleven."

"I won't be married before twelve!" the lovely, petulant lips smiled. "A midnight wedding seems so romantic."

"Our wedding is romantic, anyway; but we won't be back to town much before twelve. What else?"

"I want Charlotte with me. She can be a witness, if you like."

"And your father?"

"No, daddy's asleep long before this. Oh, Guy, can we do it?"

"Of course we can, you sweetest thing! Come on, let's start now."

And in a few moments the little car was speeding back to Boscombe Fells.

CHAPTER 24

A MIDNIGHT MARRIAGE

If Mr. Riddell, Justice of the Peace, was surprised by the sudden appearance of two people desirous of being married, he politely concealed his feelings, and asking them to wait until he could array himself more conventionally than in the bath-robe in which he responded to the door-bell, he finally made an appearance in his parlour, properly clothed and accompanied by his wife and a housemaid as witnesses. The hour was shortly after midnight, and Farrish apologized for the disturbance of the Riddells' rest.

"Not at all," responded the jovial Justice, "we're used to it. Mrs. Riddell declares this house is a regular Gretna Green, but as she always pockets the fees, she doesn't mind."

Mrs. Riddell glanced at her husband, reprovingly, for this rather broad hint, but both Farrish and Eileen were so engrossed in their own thoughts they scarcely heard it.

Charlotte was weeping. She could not understand her young mistress, but she had always obeyed her without question, and she said nothing now. Still, it was almost more than she could bear to see her marry this man, when, as Charlotte believed, she loved another.

"Pore lamb," thought the coloured woman, "she's doin' of it to save Mr. Bingham, dat she is! My lubly Miss Eily wouldn't do dis fer no odder puppose, dat she wuddent!"

Meantime, the service took place. Eileen hesitated and stammered as she said the solemn words, but she did say them. Farrish was excited and nervous, but he spoke clearly and firmly. When it was over, Eileen fainted. Farrish caught her in his arms, and Charlotte ran, shrieking, to her side. Mrs. Riddell brought water, and in a moment Eileen was herself again.

"Forgive me," she said, smiling at Guy. "I was foolish to faint. I never do such a thing! But I—I am—nervous."

"Yes, dearest, so you are. Never mind, we're going now, and I'll take care of you."

A substantial douceur found its way to Mrs. Riddell's pocket, and the bride and groom went out to the waiting car.

"You may walk home, Charlotte," said Eileen, "it isn't far. And say nothing to father concerning this. I'll tell him myself, tomorrow."

"Yes, Miss Eily," and Charlotte, mystified and tearful, went home.

"And now for our own home," said Farrish, his voice a little unsteady, as he took the wheel. "To the hotel, dear?"

"No; you—you told me I could have my own way."

"Of course you can, my darling. Where, then?"

"To Colonial Inn, I think. That's pretty and quiet. Not so gay as Flora Wood."

"To the inn it is!" and Farrish turned the car in that direction.

Followed a taxicab, in which were two men, Alan Ford and District Attorney Somers. At a discreet distance they trailed the little car, and as Farrish turned into the drive of the picturesque Colonial Inn, the taxicab waited a moment at the gates and then followed.

Striving to calm his throbbing pulses, Farrish registered, and asked for the best rooms.

The obsequious desk clerk bowed, and smiled, and an attendant showed the guests to an attractive suite on the next floor.

"At last!" cried Farrish, as they were left alone. "Eileen, my darling!"

Eileen stood before the mirror before taking off her hat. She turned and smiled at him. "I expect it's awfully unromantic, but I'm hungry, Guy. Can't we have a little supper?"

"You can have anything under the blue heavens that you want! I'll order something sent up. But, first, Eileen, my love, my wife—one kiss!"

"No, sir," and Eileen pirouetted gaily about, "not till I've eaten. Why, I'm ravenous!"

Farrish looked at her closely, but she only smiled and danced away.

Calling a waiter, he ordered a dainty supper. "Now, my lady," he said, decidedly, "that salad will take a bit of a while to prepare, so you will not keep me waiting—will you—sweetheart?"

Farrish held out his arms, and then Eileen looked serious.

"Wait a moment, Guy; tell me, first, some things that I must know. Who killed Ethel?"

Farrish looked at her with dilated eyes.

"What do you mean?" he said, not so much surprised as puzzled.

"What I say. Who did?"

"I don't know, and it doesn't matter now. You are my wife, don't you let yourself forget that!"

"I am not your wife!" and Eileen faced him bravely. "That woman Caprice is your wife!"

"Eileen, is this a ruse? Did you marry me thinking it was not a marriage because of her?"

"Well, tell me the truth. What is she to you?"

"Nothing," and Farrish looked solemn. "Nothing, Eileen, because she is dead."

"What! Caprice! Dead? What do you mean?"

"Yes, it is true. I heard it tonight, after we reached here. While you went in the house to get Charlotte, I went on an errand or two, and I heard the news. Don't think about her, dearest."

"But, Guy, she was your wife, wasn't she?"

"Don't talk about her, Eileen, I forbid it! You shall talk only of me! Tell me you love me!"

Eileen looked uncertain. She smiled at him a little, but repulsed any attempt of his to touch her.

"Don't, Guy! The waiter will be here in a minute."

"Confound the waiter! Eileen, if you don't let me kiss you, I shall countermand the waiter, and give you no supper."

"Oh, no, you won't! Guy, is that woman really dead? Am I really your wife?"

"Yes, Eileen, she is dead, and you are my wife."

"Then, listen to me. You shall not kiss me, you shall never touch me until you tell me who killed Ethel."

"How do I know?" Farrish spoke almost roughly.

"Tell me the truth," and Eileen came near him and laid her hand on his shoulder. "The truth, Guy. Don't attempt to deceive me, for you can't. And," here her voice faltered, "if I am your wife I can't testify against you. So if it was—you—tell me—dear?"

Eileen's arm slipped round his neck. Her face drew nearer his. But even as he grasped her, she drew away. "No, no," she cried, smiling, "not till you tell me. Was it you? Guy, tell me!"

No one could have resisted that siren face, that seductive smile, the lure of the great half-closed, dark eyes.

"Yes!" cried Farrish; "yes, you temptress, you devil! You heavenly beauty, you! Now kiss me!"

But Eileen sprang away from him. Still smiling, she crossed the room, and spoke calmly: "Well, that's a weight off my mind. Tell me all about it. Don't let's have any secrets between us, ever."

She returned and sat on the arm of his chair. "Why did you do it?"

Like a veritable Delilah, her fingers caressed his hair, and almost delirious with her nearness, Farrish talked. "Don't go away," he murmured, "and I will tell you all. I know you can't repeat it, for I am your husband. It was I who took Ethel to Flora Wood last summer. I bribed the Ballou woman to deny it."

"Yes," said Eileen, with dancing eyes, "go on."

"Keep your hand on my brow, and I will."

Farrish sat with eyes closed, and Eileen gently touched his forehead with her finger tips.

"You see, Ethel and I were pretty intimate, and she knew a lot about me."

"To your discredit?"

"Yes. Enough to keep me from being Club President, and to put me down and out generally. I knew if she married Bingham, she'd tell him all this, and it would be all up with me. So I warned her, repeatedly, that if she persisted in marrying him, I'd kill her. There were plenty of other men she might have married, and it would have done me no harm. But Bingham already suspected what I'd done—"

"What was it, Guy? Anything very bad?"

"Men would think so. I cheated a bit at cards, and a few things like that."

"Go on."

"Well, that's all. I told her I'd do it, and I did do it. I'm sorry—for her, but, why, Eileen, I *had* to, or be ruined myself! I'm ambitious you know, and I foolishly let Ethel know these things, and they had to be hushed up. Bingham would have found them out from her, of course, and he would have put an end to me, so far as my social and business life were concerned. Now, you understand, don't you?"

"Yes," said Eileen, "I understand. But, Guy, suppose they suspect you and accuse you."

"They can't; I've been too careful. I was afraid of that man Ford at first, but I've hoodwinked him. He nearly had me, when he solved the musical cipher, but I wormed out of that."

"That was a clever cipher. Did you make it up?"

"No; somebody showed it to me. I taught it to Ethel, and we used it a lot. I made the notes different from my own transcripts on purpose."

"How clever you are!" and Eileen smiled at him, from the corner of her eye. "And did you send Ethel the telegrams, too?"

"Yes; I gave the girl every chance. She ought not to have defied me. She knew I would keep my word. Poor Ethel!"

"And were you really married to Caprice?"

"Yes, I was. I fell in with her when I was at college, and foolishly married her."

"As you've foolishly married me!" Eileen looked roguish.

"Oh, you angel! Now I *am* going to kiss you! Isn't this grilling nearly over?"

"Just a minute. Sit still, you bad boy! Tell me where has Caprice been all these years?"

"Oh, drifting. She never bothered me unless she thought I was going to get married. That's why she turned up at the church. She was afraid I was the bridegroom instead of Bingham."

"And she is dead? I can't believe it."

"Yes; she committed suicide this afternoon, in her apartment in New York. Now, Eileen, I forbid another word of this sort. You are my wife, this is our wedding night! Stop this unpleasant conversation, and tell me you love me."

Farrish sprang up from his chair and caught her in his arms. Eileen gave a little scream, and the door, left unlocked for the waiter, flew open. Stanford Bingham strode into the room, and as Farrish's arms fell to his side in sheer fright and amazement, Bingham clasped Eileen to himself.

"Oh," she cried, with a glad little cry, "I thought you'd never come!"

Bingham was followed by Alan Ford, Somers, and Ferrall.

"All a plant?" said Farrish, with a sneer, though he was white to the lips.

"All a plant," said Somers, cheerfully. "Dictagraph here," and he showed a receiver behind a picture on the wall. "We in the next room. Stenographer present. All your conversation down in black and white. Good work, eh?"

Alan Ford was looking at Farrish curiously and a little sadly. He was wondering what manner of man this could be, who could tell the story he had just heard by the device of the concealed dictagraph.

But Farrish was beaten.

"I don't understand," he said, weakly; "Eileen, you *are* my wife."

"No!" and Eileen's eyes blazed. "I fooled you! It would have been a despicable thing for any woman to do, with less reason. But I did it for justice—and—for the man I love!"

Encircled by Bingham's arm, Eileen stood triumphant and victorious.

Bingham himself seemed a little dazed. He had heard of the whole scheme only an hour before, and had with difficulty been persuaded to let it go through. Eileen and Ford had planned it in every detail, and even now Bingham seemed to be afraid all was not safe.

"But you *are* my wife!" exulted Farrish. "Nothing can alter that! The marriage by a Justice of the Peace is as binding as if by a clergyman."

Ford looked at Eileen. "You tell him," she said, as she clung to Bingham; "I can't."

"Miss Randall is not your wife," said Ford to Farrish; "for Mr. Riddell is not today a Justice of the Peace. He was appointed, of course, for four years, and his term of office expired at twelve o'clock. As he married you after midnight, the marriage contract is not legal. You have no claim on Miss Randall. Mr. Riddell knew this."

Farrish sat silent. He knew it to be true. With a cry of rage at Ford, and a look of utter agony at Eileen, he buried his face in his hands.

"Also," said Somers, in a low tone, "I accuse you, Mr. Farrish, of the wilful murder of your wife, known as Caprice."

"No!" and Farrish started up, wild-eyed, to deny it.

"There is no use saying anything," said Somers. "You went to New York this afternoon. You went to her apartment and shot her, that you might be free to marry Miss Randall tonight. You cleverly made it appear that she had committed suicide. But she did not die at once, she lingered long enough to call for help, and to tell the truth about you."

"Come, Eileen," said Bingham, in agony; "do not stay here longer. Let me take you home."

"Yes, Stan, let us go." And the two went away, shaken by the cumulative tragedy, but happy in the knowledge of love and freedom.

"How could you, Eileen?" Bingham would repeat over and over. "How *could* you do it?"

"How could I *not* do it?" she corrected. "It was the only way to save you, dearest."

"The price was almost too great."

"Yes; almost, but not quite! It was a dreadful experience, but I went through with it!"

"For me!" and Bingham looked deep in her glorious eyes.

"For us!" and Eileen's lovely face glowed with her happiness.

Few, if any, felt regret or sympathy when Guy Farrish was put behind bars to await a trial that could have only one outcome.

"Strange," mused Alan Ford, talking over the case with Doctor Randall, "we agreed there could be only psychological clues, and yet I traced that criminal by the very material clue of a brown stain of gunpowder on a sheet of music."

"But it was psychology that made us both believe in Bingham's innocence, or we would have been as ready to condemn him as Ferrall was."

"Right. A detective worth his salt must combine psychology and ratiocination in his criminalistic investigations."

"Yes," replied Doctor Randall, who was not afraid of long words. "But even granting those, and also the advantage of modern scientific inventions, only a mere fraction of the murderers are convicted."

"That," said Eileen, who was listening, "is because Alan Ford cannot attend to every case."